Preface

In a multicultural state of the United States, there are activities occurring that are most unheard of by other states in America. This state is known for its overt hospitality, vast farm land, and beautiful acreage. It also shares the initial stand that African Americans made with Martin Luther King's powerful courage and inspiration that commenced in Alabama against racial discrimination, abuse of authority by law enforcement, and lynching and rapes of African-Americans. The increasing criminal activity is least expected of a state that inhabited an abundance of rustic racists in the 1960's; a state that bares a popular image of serene endurance, happy smiles, and innocuous appearing citizens believed to be imitating the lifestyles portrayed through media processes. However, imitated appearances may seem to be projected, the covert criminal activity is real. The capital of this state once ranked among the top 10 most dangerous cities in America.

This book will reflect the reality of this state's street life. The characters and events described in this book are fictional and a product of the author's creativity. The book will provide notions of the reality of street life, but will not use the actual life of anyone to describe it. The actual names of routes or streets will not be used nor will the actual locations or names of businesses, residences, schools, or apartment complexes, and etcetera in order to ensure the protection of the innocent.

Chapter 1

The night air in Jackson, Mississippi was cold, but mildly comfortable if you were wearing the insulated black leather jacket, deep-dark tan sports sweater, black pants, and black sports boots the young man walking down the sidewalk of the low-income apartment complex wore. The young man walked with charisma and yet humbleness illuminated from him. He looked at the exterior of the apartments as he passed them, searching the windows for his nosey neighbors, but disregarding the poor condition of the exterior. The crumbling paint on the exterior walls, the missing window screens, and broken windows seemed to escape his attention. These are conditions he has lived with since birth so the sight is normal to him. As he walked further down the sidewalk, he noticed one of the people he referred to as his partner in crime.

"What's up, nigga?" the young man excitedly said aloud. "I knocked that bitch down," he said, referring to having sex.

The man he was talking to looked about five years older than the young man.

"Who you talkin' 'bout, Soulja?" the man asked the young man, using his nickname.

"Who you say I couldn't fuck?"

"Who? Jen?! Nigga you ain't fuck that bitch."

"Who? C. T. you got me in the mix wit' one of these niggas out here that lie on they dick. You know I don't trip like that," Soulja exclaimed, using the man's name initials.

They began to walk together toward a crowd of about seven people standing directly in front of one of the apartment buildings.

"You must just left from over there or somethin'," C. T. questioned.

"Yeah. You know ol' girl been looking fa' you?"

"Talkin' 'bout, Tammy?"

"Yeah."

"She don't want shit," C. T. said rather flatly.

They both approached the crowd of about seven people and stopped as if they had been there all night.

"Say, check this out. Anybody seen Popeye?" Soulja asked the crowd.

Everyone looked at him shaking their heads to signal that they didn't know where Popeye was except another older looking man. In fact, Soulja was the youngest of them all.

"Yeah. I seen him go over Pattie house earlier," the man said, pointing across the street at another apartment building. His voice had a raspy effect and the five gold teeth in his mouth reflected the light from the night-light pole near them.

"You think he still there?" Soulja asked with the serious expression on his face that they are all so used to.

"I ain't seen him come out. I guess so," the man responded, shrugging his shoulders.

Soulja started walking toward the apartment the man pointed to.

"Where you goin' man?" the man asked.

"Shoot Popeye if he ain't got my money," Soulja responded plainly, stopping momentarily.

"You ain't gone do nothin' but fight, Soulja. Stop frontin'," the man said with a grin, noticing everyone else giggle as Soulja continued to walk toward the apartment.

"You gone make that youngsta try you, Tate," one of the men in the crowd said to the man, using his name.

Soulja was best known for fighting. He grew up fighting in the streets and had beaten up a lot of people. Some of them older than himself. Tate didn't respond to the man. He wanted to avoid conflict of someone telling Soulja that he said something behind his back. Tate knew Soulja's bellicose nature and witnessed a lot of Soulja's battles. Tate was one of the few people Soulja would really listen to; he was one of the few people that could calm Soulja once he became pugnacious, and he wanted to keep it that way.

"Check him out, C.T.," Tate said, tapping C. T. once on the shoulder, looking across the street at the apartment as Soulja knocked on the door. Soulja stood in front of the door, knocking and hollering, "Pattie! Say, Pattie!" Soulja paid no attention to the crowd he just left across the street. A woman opened the door. "Boy, what's wrong wit' you?" she asked stressfully.

"Let me in for a minute, Pattie," Soulja said. "I need to talk to Popeye."

"Unh, uh. You talk to Popeye out here. You know I don't allow no bullshit. Popeye!" the woman screamed, turning her head slightly toward the inside of her apartment, then turning back to face Soulja. She looked at his brown face and dark brown eyes. The smell of incense emanated from Pattie's apartment and she stood at the door in a worn down robe. Soulja could see Popeye walking toward the door. When Popeye saw Soulja at the door, he stopped.

"Come holla at me for a minute, man," Soulja said, waving his hand with an inviting gesture.

Pattie turned to see that Popeye had stopped.

"Unh, uhh muthafucka. You get yo' ass out of here right now," Pattie said with hostility. "I tol' you not to be makin' them ol' fucked up deals with that boy because he don't play that shit. Get yo' ass out of here." Popeye looked to be distraught, but began to walk out of the door. Pattie closed the door with a slam as soon as he walked out.

"What's up, Popeye? You got my little change, man?!" Soulja asked.

"I ain't got nothin' right now, but I'm gon' straighten you."

"Man, you been telling me that shit over a month now," Soulja said with disappointment. Soulja turned as if to walk away calmly, but swiftly turned toward Popeye again, pointing a black snug nose .38 caliber at Popeye's shoulder and pulling the trigger without hesitation. Popeye tried to run away, but Soulja kept shooting. One of the bullets hit Popeye in the leg, causing him to buck and fall to the concrete ground. Soulja didn't notice that the crowd across the street quickly dispersed. He walked over to Popeye in a fast pace. Popeye laid on the cold concrete surrounding the apartment. His blood from the shoulder and leg wound had already formed a puddle underneath him. Soulja began to stomp Popeye viciously. He stomped his head and kicked his upper body, saying nothing, no grunts or hard breathing. Popeye laid there screaming, "Ok, please! I'll get yo' money! I promise!" Pattie ran out of her apartment with her car keys in her hand. She looked at Soulja, still holding the gun, and approached him slowly. She begged, "Please! Let me take 'em to the hospital." Her voice had begun to tremble. Soulja stopped stomping and kicking, then began to look at Pattie. He just stared at her. Her fear and discomfort was obvious. Suddenly, he kicked Popeye once more, then stepped aside. Pattie discerned that to mean he was through inflicting his brutal assault. She helped Popeye get off the concrete and led him to her car.

Soulja stood in silence, watching them leave, then he walked, entering a passage behind the apartment complex. Later that night, a little after nine o'clock, Soulja knocked on the door of a local crack cocaine dealer. A short-hair, brunette woman opened the door smiling.

"What's up, Soulja!" the woman asked as she held the door open for Soulja to walk inside the house.

"What's up, Nikki?" Soulja replied. "Where's Fat?"

"He in the back," Nikki said as she walked over to a black living room table to retrieve a blunt, marijuana rolled in cigar paper, from an ashtray atop the table. She took a long puff of the blunt and held the smoke inside before she slowly exhaled, releasing smoke, then asked, "You need something?"

Soulja could hear hip-hop music playing from one of the rooms in the rear of the house. He momentarily watched Nikki shake her small twenty-nine inch waist and thirty-six inch hips to the rhthm of the music. Nikki stared at him with flirtatious eyes and a tempting smile. Her dark brown skin beautifully glowing.

"I'm straight. I just stopped by to holla at Fat," Soulja said.

"Let me go get 'em fa' ya," Nikki suggested. She had to pass by Soulja to enter the hallway that leads to the rear of the house. As she approached Soulja to walk pass him, she extended her hand in a gesture to offer him a blunt. Soulja declined the offer by shaking his head from side to side briefly. Nikki kept walking pass him, bouncing and rhythmically moving her body.

Soulja sat down on a nearby chair. Looking at the house from the outside, one would think that the house may crumble if you close the entrance door too hard. Once you are inside the house, it's easy to forget about the outside. The house has black furnishing with gold trimming. The walls have a glossy blend of black and gold paint that keeps the interior looking fresh. The thick, black carpet beneath Soulja's feet made his boots appear to be a faded color of black. A half-buff and half-chubby man entered the living room.

"What's up, Soulja!" the man said as he shook Soulja's hand, making a clapping sound when their hands contacted. Fat sat on the couch.

"What's up, Fat?" Soulja said. "Let me get one of them halves."

"Half-ounce of what, youngsta?" Fat's voice was hoarse and deep.

"Weed, nigga!"

"Look here ol' young ass nigga, you ain't gone be buyin' all my muthafuckin' weed, man! I sell crack! I don't sell no muthafuckin' weed! I ain't gon' keep tellin' you da same ol' shit over and over eitha!" Fat yelled with frustration covering his face. "Nikki!"

"Ain't nobody else sellin' right now."

"Nikki!" Fat yelled again. "Yo' lil ass stay outta trouble you could get somebody to trust you enough not to be scared of you. Them niggas down tha street got weed, but they ain't gon' sell it to you 'cause they thank you gon' rob 'em or somethin'." Nikki walked in the room while Fat was in mid-sentence.

"Baby, go get me an ounce of weed."

Nikki turned around and walked to the rear of the house again.

"Look here, youngsta. C. T. and Tate in tha back. They tol' me about what you did to Popeye. They say it look like you shot him in tha chest."

"I don't know where I shot playa. I really didn't care where I shot 'em. I just wanted to make sure I did shoot him."

"You think you killed 'em?" Fat asked in a low tone.

"I don't know. He was livin' when Pattie took 'em to da hospital."

"Oh, Pattie took 'em to da hospital?" Fat asked with surprise.

"Yeah."

"That's good. Pattie went to school wit' me. We graduated together. She's always been down. She hip to da game. She ain't gon' let

Popeye snitch on you and she ain't gon' snitch on you. Even if that nigga die."

Soulja sat there silently looking at Fat. Suddenly, Fat looked up at Nikki as she entered the room again, this time, with a clear bag of marijuana. She raised the almost full bag in the air as she approached Fat.

"Give it to Soulja," Fat said plainly. Nikki stopped and turned to Soulja, extending the bag to him. After giving him the bag, she took a seat on the couch beside Fat. Soulja opened the clear bag, putting his nose in, taking a sniff.

"What I gotta give you for this right here?" Soulja asked.

"Give me fifty."

Soulja reached in his pants pocket and pulled out a fold of money. He passed ten and twenty dollar bills as he flipped through the money until he saw a fifty dollar bill. He gave the fifty to Fat and began to stand to his feet.

"Hold up for a minute," Fat said, extending his hand in a gesture for Soulja to stop.

Soulja lowered himself to the chair again. He hadn't fully stood to his feet.

"Let me share somethin' wit' cha," Fat said.

"Shit. Let me go," Nikki said sassily as she raised herself from the couch quickly and walked in a fast pace to the back again. She knew Fat wanted privacy.

"Got a job fa ya. My girl's car need some new parts."

"You want me to steal another car fa ya," Soulja said.

"Yeah. I already know where tha car is and everythang. You come wit' me tonight and get it. I'll give ya two ounces of crack and a half pound of weed."

"Damn, nigga. You want this done bad."

"What about it, youngsta? You gon' do it or not?"

"Hell, yeah! I'm ready now!"

"Let me get my keys and holla at Nikki."

Fat stood to his feet taking off the gold and black sports jersey he wore over a black t-shirt. He walked to the rear of the house and returned with a black headband on his head and a thick green sports jacket. Fat and Soulja pulled out of the driveway in a black four-door luxury vehicle with gold flakes in the paint. The music in the car thumped with hip-hop beats as Soulja rolled a blunt, then lit it taking a long drag. They rode around until they had smoked the blunt completely. Suddenly, Fat turned the music off.

"You ain't too high to do this, huh?" Fat asked.

Ignoring the question, Soulja asked, "Where ya tools?"

"In tha trunk. Hold up a minute," Fat said, entering an apartment complex with beautiful exterior. The parking lot was lined with luxury cars. "You see that gold sports car on the end. That's the one."

"Open tha trunk," Soulja said.

"You open it. Push tha button in tha glove compartment."

Soulja pushed the button in the glove compartment, exited the vehicle and retrieved a flat-head screwdriver from the tool box in the truck. He closed the trunk with a gentle push. Fat sat in the car watching as Soulja quickly paced to the gold car on the end of the parking lot. He could see him checking the doors to see if one would open. He saw Soulja enter the car from the passenger's back seat. Within a minute and a half, Soulja was backing the car out of the parking space of the parking lot. Fat backed his car out of the apartment complex. Soulja backed out of the apartments also. Outside the apartment complex, Soulja trailed Fat.

"Soulja! Telephone!" a little girl yelled.

"Angel, I just got out of the bath tub! Who is it?!" Soulja yelled.

"Who is this?" the little girl asked.

"Who is this?" a young woman on the phone asked.

"My name is Angel. I'm Soulja little sister. Now you have to tell me who you is."

"Who you are. You're supposed to say,' tell me who you are'," Soulja instructed his little sister.

She looked at him with a playful smile. "Ok," she said to Soulja. "Tell me who you are," angel said into the phone.

"My name is Veronica."

"I like yo' name."

"Who is that Angel?" Soulja asked.

"Veronica," Angel said as she passed her big brother the phone.

"Hey. What's up, Veronica?" Soulja asked. "Hold on for a minute." Soulja pushed the mute button on the phone. "Angel, you were supposed to say, 'I like your name!'"

"I like your name."

"Right. Come give your brother a kiss."

Angel kissed her brother on his jaw, then ran to the back of the apartment.

"Veronica?"

"Yeah. What's up, baby? Where you been all day? I missed you," she said girlishly.

"You missed me, huh?"

"Yeah."

"Well, I missed you too. How about you get wit' me tomorrow after school? We can do whatever."

"There's an assembly for the seniors tomorrow, so the whole school is gonna be in the auditorium between first and third period. I was thinking about skippin' the assembly and leaving school until the assembly is over. You gon' come wit' me?"

"Shit, I'm game. That's three free hours. I ain't even know about the assembly."

"You gon' bring some of yo' friends? Some of my girls said they were gonna skip too."

"I told you I don't have any friends. I got potnas. But, yeah. I'll round-up some of them niggas."

"Ok. Don't get but about two or three people though. We gon' all come to my house. I hope you ready fa this."

"You need to be asking yourself whether you're ready for me," Soulja said boastfully.

"We'll see tomorrow."

"Alright then."

They both hung up the phone. Soulja could picture Veronica right now. Her short hair, full lips, and thick hips. She was two years older than he was, but she didn't mind and neither did he. Soulja laid in bed and drifted off to sleep.

The morning air provided a chilling atmosphere. The windows of cars were frosted, the water on the ground was frozen, and C.T. and Tate searched the area of the apartment complex with their eyes. They suddenly saw Pattie and Popeye pull into the driveway of the parking lot. C. T. and Tate couldn't easily be seen because they stood between two apartment buildings that were far pass the apartment building that Pattie lives in. They watched Pattie help Popeye out of the car and into the apartment. Tate began to giggle as he pulled two blunts out of the inside pocket of his white and red sports coat. He passed one to C. T. and placed the other one in the cuff of his red sports skull cap. C. T. lit the blunt and they both walked toward a heavily littered playground nearby and took a seat on a wooden bench inside the playground. As they sat there, a woman in a thin jacket and jeans approached them.

"Ya'll workin'?" she asked
"Yeah. What's up?" Tate asked.

"I need somethin' for thirty," she said, flashing a twenty dollar bill and a ten dollar bill. Tate reached in his inner coat pocket and pulled out a clear plastic sandwich bag containing crack cocaine. He gave her one big piece of the white rock looking substance. The woman walked away satisfied.

"Where you get these lame ass niggas from?" Veronica asked. She watched the two young men sitting next to her two friends showing little interest in entertaining the young women.

His arms already around her, Soulja said, "You know what I want to know?" He leaned in close to her ear, running his hands up her wool sweater, touching her breasts. "Where is your bedroom?" he whispered.

Veronica pulled Soulja's hand from under her sweater and held it as she stood to her feet and let him to the back of the house. Soulja looked around at the elegant paintings on the hallway walls.

"My room is down that hallway," Veronica said, pointing to her right. "Let's go in here," she said, entering another bedroom.

As they entered the bedroom, Soulja immediately noticed the huge bed with flower coverings and dark pine, polished, wooden posts. The room was decorated with an entertainment center facing the bed and a dresser mirror on the left. An exquisite marble vase and lamp sat on top of the night stand on the right of the bed, close to a window.

"This way I can tell if my mom or dad comes home early," Veronica said, looking at the front yard through the window.

"I thought you said they never come home from work early," Soulja said with concern and alertness.

"I don't want to take any chances," Veronica said as she pushed Soulja onto the huge bed.

Soulja reached in his pocket pulling out three condoms.

"You gon' use all three?" Veronica asked as she climbed into the bed with Soulja.

"Can you handle all three?" Soulja asked as he tore one from the three and put the other two on the night stand beside the bed.

"I can handle anything," Veronica said with a confident voice and seducing smile.

A few minutes later, their brown bodies were completely naked under the covers on the bed. Soulja pumped fast and hard into Veronica. He had her legs stretched almost directly beside her head. Veronica released grunts of discomfort and pain. "Ahh! Ahh! Ahh! Oooh! Shit!" Veronica screamed. "Um. Um. Um," she muffled, trying not to be so loud. Her loud grunts only fueled Soulja to pump faster and harder. As he still pumped fast, he came closer and closer to climax. He finally reached climax and rolled off of Veronica. As he laid next to her, she breathed heavily for a moment, then rolled over on top of him. She leaned her head forward to kiss him, but Soulja turned his head to the side.

"Oh, you ain't gon' kiss me?" Veronica asked, looking offended.

"I don't like to kiss," Soulja said plainly.

"Man, you wrong fa that. That's bullshit."

"Hey," Soulja said.

Veronica looked at Soulja in anticipation for his response. Soulja kissed her softly on her lips.

"You a trip," Veronica said.

Soulja reached for another condom and shook it in front of Veronica's face like a piece of candy. She smiled and began to kiss Soulja on his neck.

"How long will it take ya boy to put tha parts in my girl car?" Fat asked a light skin man walking towards him.

"Come back in about an hour," the man said, looking at the highway behind Fat.

"I appreciate it, Caesar," Fat said as he slapped hands with Caesar, forming a hand shake.

"Check this out," Caesar said. "I got a serious lick set up, man. All I need is two more people. I was thinkin' you, me, and Soulja. I know Soulja gon' be down fa anything. I just wanna know if you wit' it."

"Yeah. I'm wit' it. I know if you settin' it up it's a lotta money involved."

"This a money and dope lick."

"Money and dope? What you need dope fa? You work for Rome. Rome give you plenty of dope to sell. Yo' brotha ain't gon' let you hurt fa nothin'."

"Yeah, you right. But this nigga we goin' to get deserves this. He tried to cross me. So I wanna punish 'em a lil' bit."

"Shit, I'm cool wit' it. How much we talkin' 'bout?"

"Probably about a kilo of powder and fifty thousand. We'll split whatever we get evenly. Everythang that comes out odd we'll use it to throw a party or somethin'."

"Bet that up. Just let me know when you ready."

"I'ma holla at Soulja today. We can do this tomorrow night."

"Ah'ight."

"I'ma get back wit'cha."

Fat got in his car, cranking his music up as he pulled away and drove down the highway. Caesar could still hear the thump of Fat's speakers as he walked back into the junk yard.

"So, I'll call you later?" Veronica said, standing in the school hallway with Soulja.

"Yeah. Call me."

As they began to walk away from each other, a young man walking pass Soulja knocked his sports cap off his head. Soulja didn't think twice about his sports cap. The young man that knocked it off kept walking as if nothing had happened. Soulja walked up behind the young man in a fast pace. People in the school that saw the young man knock Soulja's cap off of his head followed Soulja because they knew Soulja's reputation and wanted to see the fight.

Soulja touched the young man on the shoulder. When the young man turned around,

Soulja asked, "Why did you knock my cap off of my head?"

"Nigga, fuck you!" the young man said loudly.

Soulja stared at the young man eye to eye for a brief second, then exploded with a flurry of punches. Soulja punched until the young man fell to the school hallway's tile floor, then he began to stomp and kick the young man. As Soulja was stomping and kicking, Veronica and some of Veronica's friends grabbed him, pulling him away from the young man on the floor.

"Stop! Stop! Soulja! You gon' kill that boy! Hear come tha principal!" Veronica and her friends screamed.

Soulja was in a rage. Nothing anyone was saying registered to his brain. He broke away from Veronica and her friends and began to inflict more pain on the young man by continuing to stomp and kick him.

Veronica and her friends finally got his attention with the help of a few guys that knew Soulja. They pulled Soulja away from the young man on the floor and led him away from the scene of the assault.

"Let me get you away from school," Veronica suggested.

"No. I'm going to class. If I leave now the security guards will see us and they'll automatically say I did something. I don't think anyone will tell."

Veronica and Soulja went their separate ways again, going to their respective class.

Chapter 2

Veronica and Soulja walked toward the student parking lot. The crowded parking lot was filled with students entering their vehicles leaving the school premises, and some just standing around listening to the sound system in other cars.

As Veronica and Soulja approached her small sports car, they noticed a few guys walking their way. Soulja quickly realized what was about to happen when he recognized the young man he had beaten to the floor earlier inside the school.

"Get in the car and leave," Soulja said hastily, but still calmly.

Veronica held a complex look at Soulja.

"Get in the car now! Lock the doors and leave!" Soulja said pointing to the car.

Veronica nervously and quickly ran around the car to the driver's side, entered and locked the door. The young man Soulja beat up earlier approached him.

"What's up, now? Huh?" the young man said with his hands in his pants as if he had a gun.

"So, what? You gon' shoot me now? Weak bitch," Soulja said just before unleashing a flurry of punches on the young man.

Apparently, the young man didn't really have a gun. The young man tried to fight back, but Soulja was punching him so fast that he couldn't see straight. Someone hit Soulja from behind, then someone else hit Soulja from the side. Another young man was trying to get in Veronica's car. She ignited her car and reversed out of her parking space, nearly running over another young man, then she sped out of the parking lot. Soulja noticed that more and more people were coming to help the young man he had beaten up earlier and was beating up again. He swung three more times, hitting three different young men, then he ran toward the buses in the opposite direction of the parking lot. The young men chased him, but couldn't catch him.

Soulja got on the bus breathing hard. The distance from the student parking lot to the bus area was quite lengthy. He had to run very fast to get there before the buses drove away. Soulja sat down on the bus beside a young man that lives in the same apartment building as he does.

"What's up, Box?" Soulja greeted in a gasp.
"What you breathin' so hard fa?" Box asked with a grin.

Controlling his breathing pattern, Soulja responded, "Some niggas just jumped me."

Box laughed lightly. "Stop lying. Ain't no muthafucka crazy enough to jump on you."

Soulja looked at Box with a sincere expression of seriousness; an expression that most people familiar with him were acquainted to seeing. He almost always looked serious and took situations that occurred seriously.

"Yeah. Well, some niggas did."

"They didn't do anything to you. You ain't swold up or nothin'."

"They didn't get but a few licks on me. They hit like bitches. It felt more like they were pushing me with their fist instead of hittin' me," Soulja said calmly, looking out of the window of the bus as it drove away from the school premises.

"What you gon' do? You know who these niggas is?"

"Yeah. I know who they are. I'll handle it," Soulja said, bobbing his head slowly for a brief moment.

"You want some help?"

"Nope. I'm straight. I'll handle it."

The school bus arrived to the apartment complex. Soulja, Box, and some more people exited the bus. Soulja glanced around for Tate and C. T., but he saw Caesar standing on the sidewalk. He walked up to Caesar slowly.

"What's up, Soulja?" Caesar asked, stretching his arms high in the air as he smiled delightfully.

Soulja could see a machine gun sticking out of Caesar's black vest. As he got closer, he noticed the machine gun strap around Caesar's zip-up red and black sports sweater.

"What's up, man?" Soulja asked, stopping directly in front of Caesar.

"Come ride wit' me."

They both walked to a glossy, white SUV with tinted windows. Riding down the street, listening to hip-hop music, they smoked a blunt. The music was low enough for them to talk at a regular tone and hear each other. As Caesar turned onto the highway, he passed Soulja the blunt.

"So, check this out," Caesar said. "I got this lick I wanna hit. I need two people wit' me though. Now, I already holla'd at Fat. He say he wit' it. I figured you would be down for it too."

"Yeah. When we gon' do it?"

"Tomorrow. Tomorrow night," Caesar said, grabbing the blunt as Soulja extended it to him.

"Just let me know what time and where you gon' pick me up."

"Just make sure you go over to Fat house before night time. I'ma come over there and get both of y'all."

"Ah'ight."

Veronica laid in her bed on the phone, trying to contact Soulja.

"Hello," a squeaky voice said on the phone.

"May I speak to Soulja?" Veronica asked. She noticed her two friends in the room with her had begun to chuckle.

"He not here right now. Who is this?"

"Is this Angel?" Veronica asked curiously.

"No. This Chris."

"Oh, are you Soulja's little brother?"

"Yes. Soulja not here. Who is this?"

"Tell him Veronica called ok," she said. Her voice searched for certainty.

"Ok."

"Now, what's my name?"

"Veronica."

"Ok. Bye-bye, Chris," Veronica said sweetly.

"Bye-bye," Chris said.

Veronica hung up the phone and angrily asked her friends,

"What's so damn funny?"

"Girl, you trippin'. We laughin' about what happened today," one of the girls said.

"What about today?" Veronica asked even more angrily.

"Girl, you know," the same girl said.

"You just tell me. Then we won't be wonderin' whether or not I know," Veronica said.

"Girl, you know them boys jumped on Soulja today," the other girl said with a giggle. "Bitch! Fuck you! That shit ain't funny!" The two girls stopped giggling. Their facial expressions revealed their regret for making fun of Veronica's boyfriend.

It was still daylight. Caesar sat in the living room of a house, sipping from a cup of brandy liquor. The tan leather chair he sat in blended with the cream painted walls and off-white light beaming down from the chandelier in the center of the room. A slim man wearing ivory colored corduroy pants walked through a bricked arch entrance to the living room. He took a seat on the tan leather couch.

"So, what are you going to do?" the man asked Caesar.

"Everything is ready."

"Keep me posted. I want to know exactly what happens."

"Rome, don't worry. These people I'm doing this with wanna do this," Caesar emphasized.

"Ok," Rome said with an exhalation. "I have a meeting. If there is something you need just call me.

Rome raised himself from his seat and grabbed a brown leather trench coat from a coat hanger near the door before walking out of the house. Caesar sat there in the comfortable chair continuing to sip his brandy and contemplate, looking up at the high ceiling of the home.

Fat and Soulja sat in Fat's house smoking a blunt. Music played from the rear of the house. The rhythm and blues beat carried a mellow sound that had Fat and Soulja sitting silently until Fat spoke.

"Say, man. What's wit' this shit I hear about some niggas jumpin' on you?"

"That happened at school today... in the parking lot."

"They didn't do a muthafuckin' thang. You ain't swold up or nothin."

"Yeah. Them niggas weak. Wanna be real type niggas."

"You gon' let it go?" Fat asked with surprise.

"Nope." Soulja said.

"What you gon' do?"

"Shiit. Let's go handle it now. You know where them niggas cut at?" Fat asked anxiously.

"Yeah. I know where they hang out. I'm straight though. I got it. I'ma handle this." Soulja looked at Fat with a stare.

"Say, man. Check this out. I seen you come a long way. I look at'cha like a lil' brotha. A nigga fuck wit' you a nigga fuckin' wit' me. I'm not askin' you to let me help you. I'm tellin' you them niggas fuck wit' tha wrong youngsta and I'm gon' straighten 'em with or without you."

Soulja looked at Fat with a stare, contemplatively. He respected the way Fat felt about the situation. It's the same way he would feel if something happened to Fat.

"Ok. Wait until night time," Soulja said.

"We need to get a car now," Fat emphasized.

"I stole one earlier today. Everything is already set. I'm just waiting for night time. I was gonna leave from here straight to handle them niggas. We can just go together."

They sat in the house smoking blunts, listening to music, and drinking a little liquor until the sky was completely dark. Walking down the street to a little trailer park circle, they remained silent. They got into a car parked in the trailer park circle without being noticed. Soulja drove directly to his destination without hesitation or pause for conversation. As Soulja approached a brick apartment complex with a parking lot of about ten guys standing around, he noticed three of the young men that jumped on him.

"That's some of them niggas right there. See that nigga wit' that light blue sports coat on. That's the nigga that started all this shit," Soulja explained. Soulja drove into the parking lot and parked about six cars away from the crowd of young men. He noticed more faces as he parked the car. The crowd of young men didn't even pay attention to the car or that Soulja and Fat occupied the car. Soulja put a ski mask over his face and Fat did the same. Soulja opened his door slightly and stuck one leg out of the vehicle. He reached in the front of his pants and pulled two nine-millimeters out, holding one in each hand as he got out of the car slowly. He ducked out beside the car next to him, then quickly ran out toward the crowd of young men, shooting both guns. He shot three of them immediately. Fat quickly followed behind Soulja. Making sure Soulja wasn't in the way, Fat began shooting a forty millimeter. He shot two people immediately. Some of the young men in the crowd got away, but not before Soulja shot three more of them. As the men laid on the ground, Soulja shot them in rotation until his guns were unloaded, then he began to slide another clip of bullets in each of his guns.

"What the fuck you doin' nigga? We gotta get away from here," Fat said anxiously.

Soulja seemed not to hear Fat. As soon as he put the clips in his guns, he began to shoot the six men on the ground in rotation again. As he continued to shoot, he backed away from them in the direction of the car. Soulja saw Fat taking money and drugs out of the pockets of the two men not amongst the six Soulja shot. They were the two men Fat shot. As Soulja walked pass Fat, Fat left the men on the ground alone, but Soulja began to shoot at the two men Fat shot as soon as Fat stepped away from them. Fat grabbed Soulja and pulled him to the car. Soulja got in the passenger's seat and Fat drove, speeding away from the scene of eight men lying on the ground critically wounded and possibly dead.

The next day, at school, Veronica approached Soulja, looking sort of sad and concerned.

"Why didn't you call me last night?" she asked.

"I fell asleep," Soulja said plainly.

"Look, I wanna know if you mad at me fa drivin' away yesterday."

"I told you to drive away, but you were too scared to listen," Soulja said mockingly with a sly smile on his face. He kissed her on the tip of her lips and said, "You didn't do anything wrong. I wanted you to leave because I didn't want you to get hurt." Soulja noticed that Veronica stilled looked worried or concerned about something. "What's wrong?" he asked.

Veronica grabbed Soulja around his waist and pulled him close to her. She looked into his eyes and said in a whisper, "I heard somebody say that boy you got to fightin' wit' got killed last night."

"Who told you that?"

"Ain't nobody tell me. I told you, I heard some people talkin' about it."

"I didn't know that," Soulja said sincerely. He didn't know and didn't care. It didn't matter to him if all of the young men he and Fat attacked with their pistols died.

"So you didn't have anything to do with it?"

"Did someone say I did?"

"Nope. They say some boy he was selling dope fa came and shot him and his friends while they were outside. They said one of his friends died too."

"Oh, yeah," Soulja said without expression of concern.

"Yeah, but I don't believe that. I think you did it."

"Would it matter? Would it matter if I did do it?" Soulja asked calmly, searching Veronica's eyes.

"It wouldn't matter. He shouldn't have tried to jump on my baby," Veronica said with a smile, then kissed Soulja on the lips. "The first period bell gon' ring in a little while. I'll see you later."

Soulja watched Veronica's hips sway from side to side as she walked away. The snug pants she wore revealed the sculpt of her body. Soulja momentarily thought about asking her to skip school with him today, but decided against it and headed to class.

Caesar sat in a steaming, bubbling jacuzzi with a beautiful brown skin woman straddled on top of him. Leaning her head back as she slowly rotated herself on his dick. Her long strands of hair were tucked behind her ears, and her hands clenched the edge of the perimeter of the jacuzzi as she frowned slightly with pleasure and exhaled softly. Caesar reveled in the wetness and warmth provided by the jacuzzi, including the rhythmical motion of her small size twenty-eight waist. He wrapped his lips around her thirty-four B-cup breast and grabbed her lovely size thirty-four hips to push her down on his penis. As Caesar penetrated deeper into her, he called out her name in the ecstasy he felt. "Rachel," he mumbled. He immediately began to slurp on her breast again. They were both misty wet from the steam of the jacuzzi. "Rachel," Caesar said again, whispering in her ear. The pleasure he felt escaped his voice. "Yes," she responded keeping her rhythm and still clenching the edge of the jacuzzi. "Faster. Go faster," Caesar said. Rachel rubbed her hands over Caesar's shoulders slowly, making her way to his chest. Then she grabbed Caesar's long, straight, black hair in one motion. She pulled on his hair, causing Caesar to lean his head back. Rachel kissed Caesar's neck and throat passionately, then kissed him in his mouth, leading with her tongue. As her tongue entered Caesar's mouth, she began to speed her rhythm. Her movements became faster and faster as she kissed him. The kiss muffled Caesar's groans. He could feel Rachel's vaginal muscles snatching on his penis. He couldn't believe it. The experience was new and unbelievable, especially since they were in the jacuzzi. Rachel began to arch her back, causing her firm, round butt to move up and point out of the water, also giving her leverage to move up and down on Caesar with long strokes of her hips and pelvis. She moved up and down, hard and fast, simultaneously pulling Caesar's hair harder and harder as her moans released into his mouth. Caesar was in so much pleasure, he couldn't tell she was pulling his hair so hard. Rachel felt him getting close to climax. She stopped kissing him and he took a deep gasp for air. He breathed heavily and grunted in deep moans. Rachel knew he would climax in a matter of seconds. Caesar couldn't control himself any longer. He climaxed with a long, deep growl. As he climaxed, Rachel wrapped her arms around him and made deep, hard thrusts down with her waist, and made slow-gripping muscular tensions with her vagina as she came up with her hips.

Rachel kissed Caesar's neck, then leaned back, looking at the exhaustion on his face as she smiled. "I thought you wanted me to go faster," she said mockingly and playfully.

"Yeah. I did," Caesar said with a fatigued expression and a shortness of breath. "What were you trying to do, kill me?" he questioned, pausing for a second. "My head should be bald from the way you pulled my hair. It didn't seem like you were pulling so hard."

"Well, it couldn't have mattered too much. Or else you would have stopped me," Rachel said with a sassy smirk.

"Yeah," Caesar said, brushing his hair back with his hands. "You good. You real good."

"Don't I know," Rachel said with confident attitude as she stood up to get off of him, then stepped out of the jacuzzi. Her naked body glistened from the water and the high quality white lights in the room. She walked over to the shower, only a few feet away. Rachel turned around and faced Caesar, but his back was turned to her as he sat in the jacuzzi. "You want to see if you still have enough strength to do me in the shower," Rachel said seductively, putting her hands on her waist. She pretentiously flaunted her five-feet, ten-inch frame, her round breast glossed with water, and her hips, giving her a tempting figure.

Those words were more than enough to get Caesar's attention, but he honestly didn't know if he could last another round of sex with Rachel.

"How about you go ahead and I'll come in a minute or two," Caesar said.

"What's wrong? You afraid of me now?" Rachel asked with more sass.

"Uh, uh. No," Caesar said, looking at Rachel, still sitting in the jacuzzi. "I'm not afraid. I'm coming."

"Ok," Rachel said as she slid the glass doors of the shower back and stepped in.

Caesar thought to himself, "What the fuck did she do to me. I ain't ever been this tired after fuckin' no bitch.

Chapter 3

Tate and C. T. stood on the sidewalk of the low-income apartment complex they lived in. Tate kicked an empty beer bottle off the sidewalk and onto the grass. C. T. noticed a medium-sized moving service truck coming their way. Tate looked up, noticing the service truck, then began to step backwards. Caution covered Tate and C. T.'s face. Tate pulled his knit cap down to fit snug on his head and zipped up his resin-coated jacket. C. T. tightened his black leather belt looped around his khaki pants. They were ready to run, considering the possibility of the service truck being an undercover vehicle for the police detectives and narcotics agents.

The truck parked and two women exited, one from the passenger's side and one from the driver's side. The two women wore ski coats and jeans. They were parked in front of the same apartment building Pattie lives in. The two women walked toward the building and went to the door of a vacant apartment directly in front of Pattie's apartment. Tate and C. T. knew that the apartment was vacant. When they saw the two women enter the apartment, they were confident those two women were moving in.

"Let's go over there," Tate said with a sly smile on his face, looking at C. T.

"Shit. You know I'm game," C. T. said.

"Nigga, you don't know how to pull no bitch," Tate said with a frustrated expression.

"Ok. You just peep tha game as I play it."

Tate and C. T. walked across the street over to the apartment the two women just entered. C. T. knocked on the door.

"Yes, I'm coming," one of the women said with proper pronunciation.

Tate and C. T. stood at the door in anticipation. A short, brownish vanilla skin woman answered the door. "Hi," she said cheerfully. Her hair was pulled away from her face, but a few strands still fell over the front of her face.

"Are our neighbors at the door?" the other woman said with the same pronunciation as the first. The second woman opened the door wide so that she could stand beside the short woman. She seemed taller than five-feet, six-inches standing beside the short woman. They shared the same skin complexion.

"Oh, hi," the second woman said. Her hair was bobbed. It seemed to accent her face.

"Hey. What's up?" C. T. said with a smile. "My name is C. T. and this is Tate," C. T. said, motioning his head in the direction of Tate, standing beside him.

"Hi. My name is Tia," the short woman said, extending her hand, shaking C. T.'s. "This is my sister, Amanda," Tia said with a gesture of both of her hands pointing at the other woman. Tia looked a few years younger than Amanda.

"So, y'all movin' in here, huh?" C.T. asked.

"Yeah," Tia answered.

"Where y'all from? Y'all got this accent like y'all from California or somethin'," Tate said with curiosity in his voice.

"We're from Michigan. Detroit, Michigan actually," Amanda responded sweetly with a grin across her face.

"So, where do you two live?" Tia asked, looking at C.T. and Tate in alternative motions of her head.

"Oh, I live right there," Tate said, turning his body slightly, pointing at an apartment building three buildings down from Amanda and Tia's apartment building.

"And I live in the building right across from that building," C.T. said, turning around for a brief moment.

"So, y'all got a lot of stuff to move?" Tate asked.

"Not really," Amanda replied with an uncertain expression on her face.

"Well, check this out. Y'all ain't gotta move none of it," Tate said.

"Oh really," Amanda said, surprised with Tate's statement. "How's it gonna get moved then," she asked.

"Oh, don't worry. I gotta potna that owes me a fava. He gon' handle this while we all get to know each other betta. What you thank about that?"

Amanda appeared flattered, flashing a smile as she stepped outside the apartment closer to Tate. "I think that's cool, but the inside of the apartment is a mess, so it has to be cleaned before any furniture is placed inside," she said.

"Don't trip," Tate said reassuringly. "My potna's gon' handle all that. And guess what?"

"What?" Amanda asked, still smiling.

"You got chairs in tha truck right?" he asked. Noticing Amanda shake her head in an affirmative gesture, he said, "Well we gon' sit right out here and supervise so we can make sure it's done the way you want it."

"Ok," Amanda agreed with a giggle. "Where are these partners of yours?"

"I'll go get 'em right now. C.T., you gon' stay here till I get back or what?" Tate asked.

"Yeah. I'ma keep our new neighbors company," C.T. responded, eyeballing Tia.

Tia seemed to like the attention. She smiled girlishly, then asked "Do you want something to drink, C.T.?"

C.T. turned his head slightly, noticing Tate walking in a fast pace down the sidewalk. He was considering asking to bring some alcoholic beverages.

"Yeah. What you got?"

"Liquor."

Veronica drove Soulja to the entrance of his apartment complex residence. Soulja was about to step out of the small sports car.

"Hey!" Veronica said, getting Soulja's attention. "Don't I get a kiss or somethin' before you get out?"

Soulja leaned over to her and kissed her on the tip of her lips.

"Wait a minute," Veronica said, expressing obvious dissatisfaction. "I'm not talkin' about that kind of kiss. I wanna real kiss."

Soulja leaned over to her and kissed her again, this time sticking his tongue in her mouth. They kissed for about five seconds, then stopped.

Veronica smiled while she looked at Soulja admiringly.

"What are you doin' this weekend?" she asked.

"I don't know. Me and some of my potnas might throw a party. I'll call you to let you know," he said with one of his legs sticking out of the car.

"Ok. Just let me know. I'll bring some of my girls."

"Ah'ight. I'll see ya," Soulja said, acknowledging her wave her hand in a departing gesture.

Soulja watched Veronica drive out of the apartment complex, then began to walk down the sidewalk. He intended to walk to Tate's apartment. As he walked down the sidewalk, he heard someone calling him.

"Soulja! Say, Soulja!" C.T. yelled through the bedroom window of Amanda and Tia's apartment. "Say. Y'all mind if I call my boy over here. I want y'all to meet him anyway."

"No. I don't mind," Amanda said, looking at Tia to see if she shows any signs of disapproval.

"Why don't you go outside and get him?" Tia asked, looking out the window at Soulja standing on the sidewalk. "He probably thinks he's going crazy. Someone calling him that he doesn't see."

"Soulja!" C.T. yelled again. "This C.T.! Come over to Pattie house!" he said. He noticed Soulja crossing the street, headed for the apartment. C.T. looked at Tia and said, "I'll be right back."

C.T. stepped out of the apartment, meeting Soulja just before he walked to Pattie's apartment door.

"What's up, nigga? We over here," C.T. said, pointing at Amanda and Tia's apartment door. "Some jazzy ass bitches just moved in today," he said in a whisper of excitement.

Soulja remained silent as C.T. opened the door to Amanda and Tia's apartment. Soulja followed C.T. inside the apartment. Soulja noticed a wood and iron dining set on his left and a casual wheat brown colored camel-back sofa and living room set with the same style and color. The portraits on the hallway walls leading to the bedrooms missed his attention. As Soulja entered the bedroom after C.T., he noticed Tate, Amanda, and Tia sitting on the queen sized bed. Soulja took a seat on a recliner a few feet away from the bed. C.T. plopped down on the bed beside Tia.

"This is Soulja," C.T. said, looking at Soulja.

"Hi. I'm Amanda."

"And I'm Tia."

Soulja nodded his head in acknowledgement, as he looked at both of them momentarily.

"So, this is your friend?" Tia asked C.T.

"We all grew up out here in the projects," Tate said, answering for C.T.

"Fire up one of them blunts, man. I know you got some," Tate said, showing minimal excitement.

"You smoke weed?" Soulja asked Tia.

"Hell, yeah! She smokes, Amanda said cheerfully. "We both smoke."

Soulja reached in his inner coat pocket and pulled out a medium-sized clear bag, half-filled with marijuana.

"Either one of you know how to roll?" Soulja asked both Amanda and Tia, alternatively observing them.

"Yeah. We know how to roll," Amanda responded.

Soulja reached in his inner coat pocket again and pulled out seven cigars. He gave each one of them a cigar.

"We'll each have our own blunt," Soulja said.

"Wait. I have a chopping board in the kitchen. You can put the weed on top of it," Amanda said, standing to her feet. As she walked out of the room, Soulja sat up straight in the recliner chair to adjust it for his comfort. Amanda returned with a bottle of gin liquor and five cups on top of the chopping board. She balanced the liquor and cups on top of the board like a waitress balancing a food tray at a diner.

"I didn't know whether or not you drank, but I brought you a cup just in case," Amanda said, pacing her way to the bed. She placed the board on the center part of the bed.

Soulja stood up and walked over to the bed. He reached in the clear bag and pulled out a hand full of marijuana, then placed it on the board. Soulja grabbed one of the tall glass cups off of the board.

"Yeah, I drink," Soulja said plainly. As the rest of the group grabbed a cup, Soulja reached in the clear bag for another hand full of marijuana and placed it on the board with the first hand full, then placed the remaining two cigars he had on the board also. "It's your liquor, you pour it," Soulja said to Amanda. "It's ok. You can pour your own. I don't mind," she said.

Soulja broke the seal on the bottle of gin liquor, then poured himself some in the glass. They all began to break their cigars open down the center, in one line. The tobacco was covering one section of the board as they dipped their hands in a separate section of the board, picking up marijuana, filling their cigar paper with it. They all sat in silence as Soulja pulled out his lighter and lit his blunt. He took a long drag, then passed the lighter to Tate and let Tia use his blunt to put fire to her own blunt. They drank and smoked as they conversed casually, listening to medium volume mellow beats of music. The conversations continued for a couple of hours. Suddenly, Soulja stood up.

"I have to go," Soulja said, tugging on the hem of his coat for comfort.

"Oh, why?" Amanda asked, showing disappointment on her face. "We were just beginning to get you to talk to us more. I was enjoying it."

"Yeah. Why are you leaving?" Tia asked sweetly.

"I'll leave the weed," Soulja said as he glanced at the remaining marijuana on the chopping board, "but I have to go check on something."

"Ok. Just make sure to come visit us again," Amanda said sincerely.

"Yeah." Tia added, sharing Amanda's sincerity.

"I'll holla. I'm in tha hood," Soulja replied.

"Ah'ight, bra!" Tate said loudly.

"Holla at'cha," C.T. said.

"I'll walk you to the door, so I can lock it after you leave," Tia said as she stood to her feet, walking towards Soulja. Tia and Soulja walked to the door. Tia opened the door and Soulja walked out. "See you around," Tia said, giggling.

Soulja kept walking. He was about to leave until a little girl ran out of Pattie's apartment, calling him, "Soulja!" the little girl screamed. Tia heard the little girl scream and opened the door to a cracked view, wide enough for her to look outside. Soulja turned around and walked toward the little girl. The little girl stood almost exactly in the center of the distance between Pattie and Tia's apartment. Soulja kneeled down to the little girl.

"How are you doing this evening?" Soulja asked the little girl, emphasizing proper pronunciation.

"I'm fine. I'm going to the store," the little girl responded.

Soulja zipped her little pink coat and asked, "What are you going to buy?"

Tia stood at her door, straining her ears to listen out of curiosity.

"My momma going to buy some food. You gon' buy me something?" the little girl smiled.

"You're supposed to say, will you buy me something," Soulja said.

"Ok. Will you buy me something?"

Soulja cracked a smile, then noticed Pattie and Popeye walk out of her apartment. Soulja stood to his feet with his attention on Popeye. Popeye held a walking cane.

"Go get in tha car!" Pattie said with a demanding voice to the little girl.

"Soulja finna buy me somethin' ma," the little girl whined.

"Just go to the car like you mother said. I'll give her the money for you ok," Soulja assured.

"I wanna give it to her," the little girl whined more.

Tia watched Soulja reach into his pocket and pull out a fold of money. She saw him take one of the bills from the fold of money and give it to the little girl. The little girl, in turn, gave the money to Pattie.

"Now go to tha car," Pattie demanded of the little girl.

The little girl ran to the car, swinging her little arms. Soulja began to walk away.

"Wait a minute, Soulja," Pattie said with a desperate expression on her face that Soulja noticed as soon as he turned to face her.

"What's up?" Soulja asked, looking at Popeye eye to eye.

Tia stared out the crack in her doorway wondering what the obvious tension between Popeye and Soulja was all about.

"I got yo' money, man," Popeye said nervously. "I didn't tell the police you shot me."

"He's right. He didn't snitch," Pattie said, confirming Popeye's statement. "We just want to get this debt cleared that he owes you."

"I don't have any beef with you, Pattie," Soulja said.

"I know. I just want you to take the money. That way I know he's out of yo' debt. I told him not to play with you," Pattie said.

"What did you tell the police?" Soulja asked.

"I told them some guys in a dark blue, old model car shot through the windows and hit me then jumped out of the car and stomped me,"

Popeye explained, holding a roll of money in his hand.

"Just take the money, Soulja," Pattie urged him.

Soulja took the money from Popeye's hand, then walked away. Tia closed the door completely as she frowned in contemplation of what she just heard.

Soulja walked promptly to Fat's house. The sun was setting and the darkness of night would soon cover the sky. He looked up at the changing colors of the sky as the sun set.

Fat heard a knock at his door and immediately thought of Soulja. He grabbed a black skull cap from the sofa, then opened the door. Seeing Soulja standing at the door, he stepped out of the house and closed the door behind him.

"You ready fa this lick tonight, nigga?" Fat questioned expressing anticipation.

"Yeah. Caesar should be here in a lil' while," Soulja said, looking at Fat.

"Speakin' of tha money-man… there he is right there," Fat said. "Let's roll, my nigga."

Fat and Soulja jumped in a four-door red, box shaped vehicle with Caesar sitting on the driver's seat. Fat sat on the front passenger's seat and Soulja sat on the back seat. Caesar had already explained the plans to Fat and Soulja. Caesar drove directly to their destination. They entered a brown wood and stained brick house approximately thirty minutes before a car pulled into the driveway. The bald-headed, tall, dark slim man entered the house alone. Soulja stood behind the door. As soon as the man stepped completely in the house, Soulja pushed the door shut and pointed a nine millimeter pistol in the man's face.

"Get yo' ass on tha flo' nigga!" Soulja said aggressively.

A mask hid Soulja's face and he wore a black one piece janitor's uniform over his regular clothes. Fat and Caesar did also.

Soulja pressed his gun hard against the man's back while he used his free hand to search the man. Soulja pulled a chrome nine millimeter pistol from the space between the man's navel and belt buckle. He placed the chrome weapon on top of the man's back, then continued to search him. He pulled a fold of hundred dollar bills from one pocket and a pair of car keys from the other. Soulja put the money and car keys in his pocket.

"Where that money and dope at, nigga?! Huh?!" Soulja asked, then immediately aimed at the man's thigh and pulled the trigger of his gun.

The man screamed in anguish and physical pain as Soulja picked up the chrome weapon on the man's back.

"It's in the back, man!" the man said in fear of his life.

"Where in the back?!" Soulja asked.

"In... in the bedroom! On the right!" the man said.

Soulja looked up at Caesar standing on the right side peeking from behind the wall of a hallway as Fat peeked from the left side. Fat ran to the bedroom on the right as Caesar stepped into the living room with Soulja.

"Where in tha bedroom, nigga?! Don't make me bust yo' bitch ass again!" Soulja asked.

"Under the mattress and behind the dressa mirror!" the man responded.

"Look under the mattress and behind tha dressa mirror, man!" Soulja said loud enough for Fat to hear him.

"Get up on yo' knees, nigga!" Soulja demanded.

The man kneeled on both knees and after looking a Caesar, he immediately knew who he was, obviously, the mask wasn't enough to hide his identity.

"Caesar! Caesar, don't let 'em kill me, man! I'm sorry! I'm sorry fa what I did, man! I ain't gon' do it no mo'!" the man cried.

Caesar was stunned. Fat came from the back holding up a pillow case, bulging with contents.

"I got everything. Let's roll out," Fat said.

"Wait a minute," Caesar said. "You know what bitch?" Caesar said, pointing his gun at the man kneeling on the floor. "I know you ain't gon' do it no mo'," Caesar said, holding his gun to the man's head. He just held it there, listening to the man weep.

"Shoot tha muthafucka so we can go, man," Soulja said.

"I'll give you my cut if you kill 'em Caesar said to Soulja.

Soulja looked at Caesar eye to eye and said, "I want it as soon as we get out of here," then shot the man in the back of the head.

Caesar, Fat, and Soulja exited the house through the side door. They jumped the side fencing of the house and got in the red vehicle, parked on the lot of an abandoned building, then Caesar sped off. He drove to a vacated bushy area, they all got out of the car and Caesar opened the trunk. They all took off the uniform that covered their regular clothes and threw them in the trunk.

Caesar took a five gallon tank of gas from the trunk and poured it all over the clothes, the interior of the car, and under the hood, leaving a trail of gas a few feet away from another four-door, yellow, small sports car. They all entered the small vehicle just after Caesar lit the trail of gas, setting the red vehicle to blazes of fire.

Soulja walked around the apartment complex sidewalks as if nothing had happened. It was about midnight. He looked down on the far end of the projects. He could see some of his partners just standing around down there. Soulja preferred to be alone at the moment. He enjoyed seclusion.

"Hey," said a woman wearing a long, white sweater pulled down just above her butt cheeks, black python boots that reach above her knees, and a gray and white knit jacket.

Soulja turned to his right, then completely toward the woman, looking her up and down. "What's up?" he asked.

"You holdin'?" the woman asked.

"What you trying to get?" Soulja asked.

"Well, I don't have any money, but…," the woman stopped her sentence, gapped her legs open, and raised the front of her sweater showing her vagina as she stood. "Don't you think we can work somethin' out," she said sexily.

Soulja looked at this woman, definitely in her thirties, aroused by her gesture. Seeing her vagina and small size thirty-six hips, her dark tan legs, and beautiful face. Soulja looked at her for a second longer, admiring her sexiness in the clothes that seemed to be fresh from the mall. He turned away from her and began to walk away.

"Where you goin'?" the woman asked.
"You ain't got no money. I'm finna go."
"Oh, what you saying, you don't want none of this?" the woman questioned flamboyantly.
"Oh, you jazzy as a muthafucka. You just ain't got no money," he said. "Go down on the other end of the projects. Them niggas down there'll fuck wit'cha." Soulja began to walk away again.
"Hold up," the woman said, getting Soulja's attention again. "Ain't you Black Sunday's son?" she asked.
Soulja looked at the woman with a frown of curiosity and frustration. "Yeah. How do you know him?" he asked.

"My name is Precious. I used to work fa yo' daddy when I was younga. You look just like that nigga too."

"Yeah, whatever. What kinda work did you do for him?"

"I used to be a prostitute."

"Used to be? What you doing now? Seem like you still workin' tha track."

"Nah. I stopped workin' about seven years ago," Precious said.

"So, what were you gonna work out wit' me?" Soulja asked.

"I wasn't. I was gon' trick you. I was gon' get you to give me tha dope first, then tell you to go get some condoms. When you went to go get tha rubbers, I was gonna leave."

Soulja muffled a giggle, then said, "That's slick but it wouldn't have worked because I already got rubbers and I wouldn't leave you here while I went to get some if I didn't. Unless I didn't give you any dope."

"You smart. You ever thought about doing what cha daddy did? You know, pimpin'?"

"I ain't wit' whoppin' no nigga over no bitch!" Soulja said disapprovingly.

"You ain't wit' it, huh?" Precious questioned as she eyeballed Soulja. "You sell crack, right?"

"Yeah. You still need some money."

"Just listen. Do you credit dope to people!"

"Yeah."

"When someone owes you money fa yo' dope, you expect them to pay, right?" Precious asked, walking closer to Soulja, and recognizing his affirmative nod. "When they don't pay, what do you do?" she asked, waiting for a response.

"It depends. Sometimes I whop 'em, sometimes I use a stick or somethin', sometimes I pistol whoop 'em or shoot 'em," Soulja said calmly with a gesture of warning.

"Ok. You do all of that fa yo' money. You do all of that because somebody got yo' dope and didn't pay, right?" Precious questioned, recognizing Soulja nod, affirmatively again. "It's tha same way when you pimpin', nigga! Just like that crack brings you money, and you flip about yo' money when you credit crack. You suppose to flip on any nigga that don't pay yo' bitch! Because yo' bitches bring you money just like yo' crack! When a nigga take from yo' bitch or cheat yo bitch, he cheatin' you too, he takin from you," Precious emphasized, calming down. "Pussy is just a little more addictive than crack."

Soulja stood there, listening to Precious. She gave him an entirely different perspective.

"Well, I don't have any bitches anyway."

"Oh, so you would pimp if you had tha bitches, huh?"

"Well, what you just told me is true. I just never really looked at it that way."

"Would you do it?"

"Yeah. If I had the bitches to do it."

"If you willin' I'm forgivin' and ready to do some dealin', Precious said rhythmically.

"What?" Soulja asked, not clearly understanding what she meant.

"I got what you need. The bitches, the house, everything," Precious said putting her arm around Soulja, leading him away from the projects. "I'm gon' be tha madam of the house, you gon' be tha pimp. I been lookin' fa somebody like you.

Chapter 4

The days of cold mornings and nights passed, leaving only an occasional light breeze as the sun beamed in the day and the moon gleamed at night. In the months that passed, a lot had changed for Soulja that he was unaware of and more changes would come that he wouldn't have ever predicted. Soulja stood at Veronica's door, knocking mildly with his knuckles. His white and green sports cap fit perfectly on his head. His white tank top was tucked under his green boxers and green pants. Veronica opened the door, throwing on a smile as soon as she laid eyes on Soulja. Soulja stepped in the house, taking off his cap with one hand and rubbing his low-cut waved hair with the other hand. Veronica wrapped her arms around him, then kissed him on his lips.

"You wanna go somewhere with me?" Soulja asked as he held Veronica's hands in front of him.

Veronica ran her eyes across Soulja's muscular frame and said, "I can't. My uncle is on his way over here." Her facial expression changed suddenly. "You have to leave! If he sees you in here, he'll flip!" she said frantically, pushing Soulja backwards out of the door.

"But I wanted you to-"

"No! You have to go now!" she said nervously as she continued to push Soulja out of the door. "I'll call you later," she said.

"Ok," Soulja acceptingly said, outside the door just before Veronica closed it.

Soulja felt a vibe of suspicion running through his entire body as he walked to his glossy coated, green painted, four-door luxury car. The glossy coat and chrome show car rims flashed a shine like diamonds in the sun. The green paint seemed to be swirls of hidden black. Soulja got in his car and pulled out of Veronica's driveway with the music inside the flashy, green vehicle thumping mildly. He drove four houses down the street, then took a left onto a by-street, but before he got half-way down the by-street, he stopped his car. The suspicion, obviously stronger now, had built curiosity in him also.

Soulja stepped out of his car and walked back down the by-street toward the street Veronica's house is on. Before he could get ten feet away from his car, he saw a vehicle that looked much too familiar to him pass by the by-street, going in the direction of Veronica's house. "That's C.T.'s car," Soulja thought to himself.

C.T. couldn't have seen Soulja unless he looked to his right, down the by-street Soulja stood on. Soulja began to walk faster. As he approached the end of the street, he saw Veronica run out of her house in a short summer dress and enter C.T.'s dark purple, two seat, sports car. Soulja frowned slightly, turned around running back to his car, and quickly entered. He drove backwards out of the by-street, barely catching a glimpse of C.T.'s car turn on another street in the opposite direction of him. Soulja straightened his car and stepped down hard on the accelerator, heading in the same direction as C.T. He followed C.T. and Veronica to a casual restaurant. Seeing them enter the restaurant seconds before he parked on the lot. Soulja reached to his back seat, grabbing a white T-shirt, then put it on quickly. Soulja got out of his car and walked into the restaurant. He didn't see Veronica and C.T. sitting to his right as he walked in, but Veronica's seat faced Soulja. Veronica saw Soulja as soon as he entered the restaurant. She was shocked and absolutely frightened with her mouth dropped wide open. She couldn't hide; she couldn't run, the only thing she could do now is face Soulja. She wasn't prepared to do that.

"What's wrong wit' you, man?" C.T. asked Veronica in a concerned tone, noticing she seemed frozen in her seat. "What you see?" C.T. asked, turning his head in the direction Veronica's eyes were focused only to find Soulja walking toward their table.

Soulja pulled one of the vacant seats from another table over to Veronica and C.T.'s table then sat down with a drop of his body on the chair.

"What's this all about?" Soulja asked, looking at C.T. and Veronica alternatively. "This yo' uncle that's gon' flip, Veronica?" he asked, with a mocking tone of voice, looking deep into her eyes.

"This what you lied to me in my face about? So, what's going on?"

Veronica was still shocked and frozen, but began to loosen up as a tear began to roll down her face. C.T. sat speechless, uncertain of whether or not he should say something.

"How did you know we were here?" C.T. asked.

"Fuck that man! You muthafuckas supposed to be people I could trust to a certain extent. So, right now, all I wanna know is what's going on?" He was convinced an affair was in act, he just wanted them to admit it.

"We just been spendin' some time together. That's all," C.T. responded.

"Don't try to play me nigga! Come real wit' this shit. Just say what it is!" Soulja said, piercing C.T. with his eyes.

"Alright. We been-"

"We been havin' sex!" Veronica exploded, then dropped her head in sobs and tears. "I'm sorry."

"How long this been going on?" Soulja asked.

Veronica kept her head dropped in sobs and tears.

"Check this out. You need to stop cryin' and talk, Veronica!" Soulja said with mild aggression in his voice.

"For about three weeks," C.T. answered. "We been together for about three weeks," C.T. said with a slightly trembling voice.

Soulja looked at C.T. eye to eye, then slowly turned his head and eyes to Veronica.

"Veronica. Veronica, look at me!" Soulja said demandingly. "Veronica," he said, putting his hand underneath her chin, pushing her head up so that he could make eye contact with her. "This is what you lied to me about," he said, looking into her tear-filled eyes. "This is why you rushed me out of your house? Afraid you would get caught?

Isn't it?" Soulja pressured, waiting for a response from her. "Isn't it?!" he said again.

C.T.'s entire body tensed up, not knowing what to expect of the situation.

"Yes," Veronica replied, weeping, as she stared at Soulja's raging eyes. "I'm sorry. I'm sorry."

Soulja looked at Veronica with a strong stare, then looked at C.T. with the same steady gaze. A waiter approached the table.

"Will you be having breakfast with the couple sir?" the waiter asked Soulja.

Soulja gave no reply. He just got out of the seat and exited the restaurant. The waiter watched him leave, standing dumb-founded to what just occurred before he arrived.

Caesar sat on a white and tan detailed sofa with one arm wrapped around Rachel as they watched the big screen television positioned on the entertainment center in front of them. Her flowery, peach colored blouse revealed her cleavage. Rome entered the room, fastening the wood-stoned buttons on his double-pocket twill shirt. He approached Caesar and Rachel, taking a seat on the stylish white and tan detailed chair near them.

"Don't forget what we talked about," Rome said to Caesar and Rachel, interrupting them as they watched television.

"Don't worry, Rome. I won't let him forget," Rachel said reassuringly.

"Ok. Because these people moving into the area are very powerful. They're at least as powerful as I am in the business. This is a very serious issue," Rome emphasized.

"We've talked about this all morning. I'll be on the look-out. I'll talk to some people personally," Caesar said, obviously annoyed.

"Don't fuck around with this situation, Caesar! I'm serious!" Rome said angrily.

"Calm down, man. I'm takin' this serious," Caesar responded.

Rachel looked at them both, then said, "Come on, man. You both are getting too stressed out about this. We know this is a serious issue. He won't forget and neither will I. We'll tell you everything we find out."

Rome calmed down, then stood to his feet, tucking his shirt in his brown pants as he said, "I'm going to talk to a few people now. I might be able to find out a few things."

Soulja sat in his room, on his bed with the telephone pressed against his ear listening to the line ring in anticipation of someone answering.

"Hello," a female voice answered.

"Tia?" Soulja asked.

"Yeah. Good morning. What are you doing?" Tia asked.

"I'm about to take my little brother and sister swimming. You and Amanda wanna come?"

"Hold on for a second," Tia said. "Amanda! Soulja wants to know if you wanna go swimming!" she yelled at Amanda.

"No! I just got my hair done! Maybe next time!" Amanda answered.

"She says she doesn't want to because she just got her hair done," Tia told Soulja. "But I'll go. Just let me get a swimsuit and a towel."

"Ok. That's cool. I'm about to leave the apartment in a few minutes."

"I'll be ready. Just come get me."

"Ok. I'll be on my way."

Soulja hung up the telephone, then walked across the hall to his younger sister and even younger brother's room. He swung the door open and said, "Come on to the living room," then closed the door. He walked to the living room where his mother sat on a dark brown worn down couch.

"Ma, you ready to go?" Soulja asked.

She stood to her feet, standing five-feet seven-inches, only a few inches shorter than her son. They shared the same brown skin complexion. She paced her medium sized frame over to Soulja.

"I'm just waiting on you."

Soulja saw his siblings, Angel and Chris, running from the back of the apartment to the living room.

"Let's go," Soulja said.

Soulja drove to Tia's apartment building. She was already standing outside waiting on him wearing a white halter top and blue jean shorts. She swung her towel in her hand as she jogged to the car.

"Hi, Ms. Walsh," Tia said, flashing a smile as she entered the car, then sat on the back seat.

"Good morning, Tia. How are you, baby?" Soulja's mother asked in a sweet, motherly tone as Soulja began to drive out of the projects.

"Oh, I'm fine. Are you going swimming with us too?"

"I'm going to the grocery store. Y'all will go swimming after you drop me off."

"Well, actually, I have something to show you first, then I'll take you to the grocery store."

"Well you need to hurry up, because I don't want to be caught in that grocery store traffic," Ms. Walsh said with the same calmness Tia is accustomed to seeing in Soulja's character. It was obvious that the tranquil gene came to him from his mother.

Soulja inserted a blues CD in his car CD player and allowed the music to play at a low volume. The drive was longer than Ms. Walsh anticipated. She became confused when Soulja drove to the closed entrance of gated community of an elegant apartment complex. Soulja stopped next to a security dialing booth and pressed numbers on the dialing board to open the gate. To Ms. Walsh and Tia's surprise the gate swung open and Soulja drove inside the apartment complex. He made a few turns in the apartment complex, then entered a parking space.

"Come on. We're here. You have to get out to come see, ma. Come on y'all. Y'all get out too," Soulja said to his siblings and Tia.

"Boy, I'll be late messing with you," Ms. Walsh said with a perplexed expression still covering her face.

Tia noticed a pool in the distance ahead of them, but they walked onto the porch of one of the apartment buildings before they got close to the pool. Soulja approached one of the doors, pulled a pair of keys out of his pocket, then he unlocked the apartment door and walked in.

"Come in," Soulja said with an inviting gesture of his hands.

They all walked in behind Soulja in hesitation.

"Ma, you see all of this?" Soulja asked. He looked at his mother as she glanced at the stain effect, dark brown, leather living room set with plush oversized seats. "This is all yours!" he said with moderate excitement.

Ms. Walsh couldn't believe what her son just told her. She held her mouth open as she walked around the apartment. She entered the kitchen. The oak colored, square dining table and chairs caught her attention immediately. The apartment was an enormous upgrade from the low-income apartment complex she just left.

"Look in the refrigerator, Ma," Soulja said.

She opened the wide refrigerator. It was packed with food.

"These are all the items I normally buy at the grocery store. This is really my apartment?"

"It's all yours. Here are the keys. Rent is paid for a year. You have more in the back of the apartment. Come on," Soulja said, leading Ms. Walsh to the back of the apartment.

Tia smiled in amazement. She began to follow Soulja and Ms. Walsh to the back, noticing Soulja make a gesture with his hand for her to come. Tia gently pushed Soulja's siblings in front of her, saying, "Come on."

As they got to the end of the hallway, Soulja said, "That's Chris and Angel's room," pointing to a bedroom on the left, "and this is your room." They all entered the bedroom on the right side of the hallway. The bedroom was furnished with a cherry wood style bedroom set. A queen sized bed sat in the center of the room with a small entertainment center, similar to the larger one in the living room, facing the foot of the bed. Both entertainment centers were fully equipped with a television, video cassette recorder, DVD, and stereo system. "Come to the window, Ma," Soulja said. "Tia, Angel, Chris, come'ere," Soulja said. They all stood at the window as Soulja opened the window blinds.

"You see that silver looking sports car with the big sign in the windshield that says, I'm yours."

"Yeah. I see it," Tia said energetically.

"I see it, son," Ms. Walsh said.

"It's yours too," Soulja said, pulling out another pair of keys from his pants pocket. "It's fully paid for," he said, giving his mother the keys.

Ms. Walsh looked at her son intimately. Her eyes watered and a tear fell down one side of her face.

"I see it! I see it!" Soulja's siblings screamed with delight.

Soulja wiped the tear away from his mother's face with his thumb as he said, "Don't cry. You deserve more," then kissed her softly on her jaw line. "There's cable connected to both TV's. You still need to go to the grocery store?"

"No," Ms. Walsh said softly. She noticed Tia's eyes had become watery. She stood in contemplation briefly. "If Chris and Angel's room is across the hall, where is your room?" she asked Soulja.

"I have my own apartment. It's about three apartment buildings down. I'll show it to you later."

"Oh, ok. I'll see it later, then," Ms. Walsh said in satisfaction.

"You sure you still don't wanna go to the grocery store?" Soulja questioned.

"No. You go ahead. Take Tia and your brother and sister swimming."

"Oh, yeah," Soulja said reflectively, "The apartment complex has a swimming pool. There's a pool for adults, a pool for children, and a Jacuzzi out there. You might enjoy that."

"Maybe some other time."

"Ok. I'm going to the pool. Come on, Tia."

As Soulja and Tia walked out of the apartment, Chris and Angel yelled with delightful excitement and anticipation of swimming. Soulja went to the trunk of his car, put his T-shirt in the trunk and took off his shoes and pants. He had already put on swimming trunks before he left home. After taking off his shoes, pants, and shirt, he pulled a pair of flip flops from the trunk and put them on his feet. All he wore now was a tank top, black swimming trunks, and flip flops. He grabbed a large beach towel just before closing the trunk of his car. Angel and Chris sat in the children's pool. Tia stepped out of the adult pool wearing a white two-piece bikini. Her thirty-four B-cup breast pressed against the top piece, her nipples bulging a print. Her small sized, twenty-six waist and thirty-six inch hips fit perfectly in the bottom piece. She walked over to Soulja and sat down close beside him, swinging her legs in the water with him.

"Have you seen C.T.?" she asked, searching Soulja's face with her eyes.

Soulja looked at her silently, then responded, "Yeah."

"Well, where is he? I've constantly paged him earlier this morning, but he didn't call me."

"He gave her the look with silence again, then said, "He's with a new partner. He'll call you later."

"Ok," Tia said pausing tersely. She slung one of her arms around Soulja, pulling him closer to her, then said, "That was really sweet. What you did for your mom." She pecked him on his jaw with a quick kiss. "Very sweet," she said, then slid into the pool. Turning around to face Soulja, she said, "Get in the pool and race me to the other end."

"What? Can you even swim?" Soulja asked with a playfully mocking tone.

"I can beat you, no doubt."

"Ok. Get out and walk to the deep end with me. We'll race back down to this end."

"Ok," Tia accepted the challenge, pulling herself out of the pool.

Tia and Soulja walked to the deep end of the pool together. They stood on the edge of the pool at the deep end.

"That's deep water, Tia. You sure you wanna do this," Soulja teased.

"Shut up and get ready to swim, Soulja."
"Ok," Soulja said, cracking a sly smile. He stood close to her. Suddenly, he pushed her in the water and laughed at her.

"Why did you do that?" Tia complained, dog pedaling in the water to stay on top.

"You said you can swim!"

"You need to get me out of this water."

Tia began to go under water. Soulja watched as she sank deeper and deeper into the water. Realizing she wasn't coming up, he jumped in the water, swam to the bottom, and saw Tia standing there sticking her middle finger at him. She swam to the top of the water, followed by Soulja. She laughed at him as he stuck his head out of the water.

Chapter 5

Soulja took Tia home later in the day. Entering her apartment Tia saw C.T. sitting in the living room. Soulja stepped in the apartment behind her.

"Hey! Baby, I've been trying to contact you. Soulja told me you were with a new partner so I stopped paging you. I didn't want to interrupt your business," Tia said, standing close to C.T.

Soulja just glanced at C.T. He saw Amanda in the room.

"Amanda, what's up?" Soulja asked with strong focus on her.

"I need to talk to you about something," Amanda said, causing Tia and C.T. to attentively gaze at her. "Tia, Uncle Mike is in the restroom. He said he just settled in today, then came straight over here."

"What?! Are you serious?!" Tia asked with excitement in her voice. "Uncle Mike!" Tia yelled.

"I'm coming out in just a second," a male dry voice loudly traveled from the restroom. Seconds later, a salt and pepper head of hair, tall, solidly built, brown skin man stepped into the living room.

"Uncle Mike!" Tia said, rushing to the man, wrapping her arms around him. "It's so good to see you."

"It's good to see you too, Tia," Uncle Mike said, staring at Tia. He looked at Soulja.

"This is Soulja," Amanda introduced, grabbing Soulja's arm. "Come with me for a minute," she said, pulling Soulja to the bedroom. "Come on, Uncle Mike."

Uncle Mike followed Amanda and Soulja to the bedroom. Amanda and Soulja sat on the foot of her bed while Uncle Mike took a seat on the recliner.

"What's up?" Soulja asked in curiosity.

"I wanted to talk to you about making a deal with my uncle," Amanda said sincerely. "I know you don't know him, but I want you to take what you've learned about me in the past few months and trust me. He's legit."

"Ok. That's cool. But what kind of deal are we talking about?" Soulja asked.

"I have some weapons I'm trying to trade off," Uncle Mike said, observing Soulja.

"What kind of weapons?"

"Machine guns, hand guns, assault rifles… All with ammo and extra clips."

"What are you trying to get for 'em?"

"Combined, the weapons are worth about fifteen hundred dollars to me. Now weed is sold differently were I'm from but Amanda said I could get a good deal from you. She told me how weed is sold around here, so I guess about two pounds would be good."

"You want two pounds of weed for the guns?"

"Yeah."

"Where are the guns?"

Uncle Mike opened Amanda's closet and picked up two large travel bags. He placed them between himself and Soulja.

"They are all hand guns," Uncle Mike said, opening one bag, "and these are all machine guns," he said, opening the second bag. "I have two assault rifles in my trunk."

Soulja searched through both bags, admiring the weapons he held.

"I'll be right back with your weed," Soulja said, getting off the bed. He walked out of the bedroom.

Amanda and Uncle Mike characterized Soulja as straight and definite at that moment. Soulja drove to his old apartment in the projects, got two and a half pounds of marijuana out of his old apartment, and drove directly back to Amanda's apartment building. Soulja knocked on her apartment door.

"Who is it?!" Tia yelled.

"Soulja!"

"Come in!" Tia said. As she watched Soulja walk through the door, she said, "We told you that you didn't have to knock, so why do you still knock on the door?"

Soulja looked at Tia silently, then asked, "Is Amanda in her room?"

"Yeah."

Soulja walked straight to Amanda's bedroom and into the open door.

"Bring the bags outside. We'll make the exchange from our trunks," Soulja suggested.

Uncle Mike didn't disagree. He just grabbed the two bags and went outside with Soulja. Co-incidentally, Soulja was parked next to Uncle Mike's car. They made their exchange, then walked back inside the apartment. Amanda was sitting on the couch between C.T. and Tia.

"Move Amanda," Tia said in frustration as Soulja and Uncle Mike entered the apartment. "We don't meddle with you and Tate when you two get together."

Soulja walked to Amanda, then grabbed her hand saying, "Come with me, Amanda. Let Tia get her smile back." Soulja pulled Amanda off of the couch and led her to her bedroom. "This is yours," he said, pulling two of the four ounces of marijuana out of his pocket. "Put these away. I'll smoke a couple of blunts wit' everybody before I leave, but I gotta go," he said, then walked back to the living room.

Soulja took a seat on the loveseat in the apartment. Uncle Mike sat in a chair observing Soulja with glances. Amanda came out of her bedroom and entered the living room. She took a seat on the loveseat with Soulja.

"If I had to guess for myself, I would say Soulja's your boyfriend, Amanda," Uncle Mike stated.

"No. Tate is my boyfriend. Soulja already has a girlfriend," Amanda said.

"No, I don't," Soulja impulsively said.

"Stop lying!" Tia said.

"I'm not lying," Soulja said, looking at Tia and C.T.

"When did you break up?" Amanda asked.

"Today," he responded.

"You've been with me most of the day," Tia said, skeptical of Soulja's claim.

"Veronica and I broke up early this morning before I came to get you to go swimming."

"I'm sorry. I know you really liked her," Amanda said.

"It's alright. I'm not heartbroken. I've just broken the bond with her."

"Why didn't you tell me earlier?" Tia asked, realizing Soulja was serious.

"It's no sweat. That's why I didn't say anything, Tia," Soulja said as he reached in his pocket and pulled out two blunts and a lighter. Soulja passed Amanda one of the blunts and he puffed on the other. Then he passed Amanda the lighter. They passed around the blunts and conversed. Soulja stood from his seat when both blunts were about half smoked.

"I have to go. I'll see y'all later," Soulja said.

"Where are you going so fast?" Tia asked.

"Business partna. Keep your head up," he said as he walked pass her, tapping the bottom of Tia's chin with his four fingers. "I'ma holla."

Soulja walked out of the door, got in his car, and drove directly to Precious' house. He opened the door with his key and walked into the moderate house. Neither of the seven women sitting around in the living room said anything to him as he closed and locked the door. The women smiled at Soulja as he made his way to the rear of the house. Some of the women sat on the couch wearing only panties and bra's while others wore short shorts or short skirts.

As Soulja passed by one of the rooms in the house, he heard a woman moaning, but he kept walking until he reached a door on the far end of the house. He entered the bedroom and stood in the middle of the floor. Precious was laying on the bed, talking on the telephone.

"Girl, I'll call you back," Precious said, then hung up the phone. "Hey, baby," Precious said cheerfully, getting off of the bed. She hugged Soulja tightly.

Soulja felt her breast press against him. He knew she didn't have on a bra underneath her silky, short one-piece skirt because her breast spread apart as she held him.

"We've been doing good today," Precious said, stepping away from Soulja. "We've made a lot of money already and it's not even completely dark outside," she said. "So, how did your mom and girlfriend respond to the surprise?"

Soulja took a seat in a wooden chair in the room.

"My mom was surprised. She liked it all. I know she appreciates it."

"What about your girlfriend? What did she think of the apartment you got for you two?"

"Veronica isn't my girlfriend anymore," Soulja said with agitation.

"What happened?" Precious asked with concern.

"She been fuckin' one of my partnas for tha pass three weeks," he responded bluntly.

"Oh," Precious responded, disappointed with the news.

Suddenly, a huge grin swept across her face. "Hey, have you ever given Veronica an orgasm?"

Soulja looked at Precious contemplatively, then answered, "No. You think that's why she fuckin' somebody else?"

"Maybe. Have you ever given any girl an orgasm?"

"No. I don't think so anyway."

"You would know if you did. So, you don't know how to give a girl an orgasm do you?"

"Why you askin' me all these questions?"

"Come on. Don't get shy with me. We've talked about things like this before."

"No. I don't know how to give a girl an orgasm. But I'm sure I could," Soulja said with confidence.

"Yeah. I know you could. Especially if you knew how. Why don't you let me teach you?"

"What?" Soulja asked, searching her face to find a clue of her intentions.

"Let me teach you how to treat a girl in bed; let me teach you how to give a girl an orgasm. Drive a girl wild. Don't you want to be able to drive a girl crazy?"

"Yeah, but…."

"Listen. When you and I met I'd just broken up with my girlfriend."

"Your girlfriend?!" Soulja questioned with surprise."

"Yeah. When I stopped working with your daddy it was because I'd discovered a new sexuality in myself. I'd fallen in love with a woman and she wanted me to quit workin' for your daddy. So, I quit. I lived with this woman for years. She kept me straight. Made sure I didn't smoke crack or anything. I was clean the entire time I was with her. I hadn't had sex with men. Only her and other women we agreed to have sex with. Threesomes, mostly. But, anyway. When we broke up, I went lookin' for old comfort. Crack. But instead, I met you. In some way I can't explain, you give me confidence and comfort. I'm still clean. I still haven't smoked any crack and I hadn't really thought about sex with a male until you. It's all because you helped me prove to myself that I didn't need it, because you reminded me of self-comfort." Precious stopped talking to see if Soulja would say anything. She knew he realized she was serious about her proposition. "Please let me teach you. Let me give you something that no one will ever be able to take from you."

"You don't have to do this," Soulja said sincerely.

"That's the point. I really want to do this. Just say yes!"

"Ok. Ah'ight."

"Good," Precious said, standing to her feet. She walked to the door and locked it, then walked back in front of Soulja, smiling. She straddled herself on top of his lap while he sat in the wooden chair. "The first thing we should work on is…," Precious said, discontinuing her sentence, she allowed her arms to rest on Soulja's shoulders as she leaned her body against his, then kissed him with her soft lips. Her agile tongue working in his mouth sent a tingle through his spine.

"Wait," Soulja said, breaking the kiss.

"What?" Precious asked.

"I can't believe you just kissed me. I don't like kissing."

"That's because you really don't know how to kiss. From what I feel bulging through your pants, it seems you liked that kiss," she said with a smile, staring in Soulja's eyes.

"Yeah. I did," Soulja sincerely said.

"Ok. Did you feel the way my tongue and mouth worked at the same time?"

"You mean the sucking and your tongue wiggling or something?"

"Ok. I'm gonna do it again. Don't try to kiss me back. Just pay attention to what my tongue and mouth does."

Precious slowly kissed Soulja again. Her tongue working inside his mouth as she gently sucked on his tongue simultaneously. After kissing him for about twenty seconds, she allowed her lips and tongue to glide down the length of his neck. She caressed his neck with warm, wet, kisses, making her way to his earlobe. She wrapped her lips around Soulja's earlobe and nibbled for about ten seconds. She could feel Soulja's breathing get heavy. He struggled to control his arousal.

"Ok," Precious said, stopping. "You try to do the same thing to me that I did to you."

Soulja began to kiss Precious the way she kissed him, but not quite the same. He ran his tongue down her throat and nibbled on her earlobe. Precious grabbed the hem of her one-piece skirt and lifted it over her shoulders, removing it from her body. She raised one of her thirty-four, c-cup breasts to Soulja's mouth. "What can you do with this?" she asked. Her voice was soft and sexy. Soulja began to kiss on her breast. Precious placed one of Soulja's hands on her other breast and his other hand on her small size thirty-six inch hips, running that hand around her small size thirty inch waist, and continuing to her lower back. "Ok. Stop," Precious said. "You learn fast. The kiss was a lot better. But it needs work. You need to slow down a little. When you touch and rub on a woman the way I ran your hands over me, women like that. And you need a lot of practice on breasts. I feel your dick throbbing. You'll get used to it, because we could be doing this for months. We're gonna keep doing everything I know until you get it exactly right. Tomorrow I'm gonna get a prescription of birth control pills. It'll probably take the medication a while to kick in. Then I'll be ready to let you penetrate me," Precious raised herself off of Soulja's lap, holding his hands, and pulled him to his feet. "For now, I wanna see how good you are with your fingers."

Precious kissed Soulja as she paced backwards to the bed, leading Soulja there. She stopped kissing him when her legs touched the edge of the bed, then she took off his tank top.

Soulja looked at her face to face, unable to deny her beauty; her naked charms; her firm body. Precious rubbed her full, firm breasts against Soulja's chest by stepping closer and closer to him. "Feel what I do to your chest," she whispered to him. She stood at the same height as Soulja until she arched her back and placed her wet lips and juicy tongue on his chest. She folded her lips in, pulling Soulja's nipple into her mouth, then pressed down strongly as she flicked her tongue at the tip of his nipple in her mouth. She used one free hand to rub his other nipple between her thumb and forefinger, gripping it gently. Her other free hand pulled Soulja's body closer to her by pressing his back and caressing it.

Soulja had never experienced such pleasure before. He thought his erection would explode if it got any harder. Precious raised her head to Soulja's ear and said, "Do the same to me," then pulled him on the bed, on top of her. She kissed him again, then said, "Come on. Do what I just did."

Soulja began to mimic Precious, starting by kissing her. He traveled her neck with his lips and tongue just before he fed off of her earlobe. "Yes." Precious said softly, providing encouragement. As he began to work on her nipples, Precious ran one of Soulja's hands down her aerobicized stomach, over her trimmed mound of pubic hair, to the warm wetness of her vagina. She put his thumb on her clitoris and slipped one of her own fingers into her drooling wet vagina. "Ahh," Precious moaned softly. Suddenly, her eyes closed, then opened. Her expression of pleasure disappeared.

"Ok. Wait a minute," Precious declared calmly.

"What did I do wrong?" Soulja asked.

"It's not what you did wrong, exactly. It's what you didn't do at all," she responded with more calmness. "You never want to let a girl lose her arousal. It's more about what you didn't do to keep the arousal than anything else that makes it so wrong." She noticed Soulja's facial expression reveal disappointment and lack of inspiration. "Come here. Lay down beside me," Precious requested. After Soulja laid down beside her, she rolled on top of him, then kissed him for a very long time. After she stopped kissing him, she just looked into his eyes and said, "Don't worry you won't learn everything in one night. You're doing good. We need things to be slow. You'll get it all right. Everything." Her silky voice carried the words, giving Soulja confidence and encouragement. "Ok. Let's try this again," she said.

Rome, Caesar, and Rachel sat at a long, rectangular, retro cherry style, dining table with four side chairs and two matching arm chairs. Rome sat on the arm chair at the end of the table. Caesar and Rachel each occupied a side chair next to each other. They had just finished eating dinner. Half eaten food still on their plates served as evidence. They sipped wine as they discussed the outcome of their day, respectively.

"Were either of you able to find anything out today?" Rome asked.

Rachel and Caesar glanced at each other with an uneasy expression on their face.

"Well, I did warn my rollas," Caesar began. "They know what to expect. I told 'em to tell me the names and places of anybody that offers them a front," he continued, slouching in his seat.

Rome looked at Rachel in anticipation of her news. Rachel nodded her head slightly, acknowledging the fact that Caesar and Rome where waiting for her to speak.

"I talked to most of the girls today. I asked them if any new faces have popped up. I asked them if any unfamiliar guy tried to date them lately. And I asked if any home wreckers have come into their lives. Those questions were enough to stir a hundred conversations. No one has seen anything. Not even a new show car," Rachel revealed, her body language showing that she wished she could say more. Rome took another sip of his wine and released a steady sigh. He rubbed his bald head and said, "I think these people moving into the area are not going to show themselves in the way we expect." He paused, looking at the confusion on Caesar and Rachel's face. "When I left here today, I met with some associates with very reliable sources. They told me, word is these people are capable of supplying the entire southeast with cocaine, ecstasy, whatever."

"That's nothing. You move at least three-hundred kilos of cocaine through three states. These people aren't a threat movin' in southeast Mississippi," Caesar said quickly.

Rome looked at Caesar with a grin as he said, "I'm not talking about southeast Mississippi. I'm talking about the entire southeast of America."

Caesar and Rachel seemed dazed by Rome's statement.

"Do you believe this info is true?" Caesar asked.

Rome rubbed his neatly trimmed beard and disappointingly responded, "All I know is, if this is true, it could cause a lot of problems for me."

"Well what do you want us to do?" Rachel asked with sincere concern.

"Don't stop asking questions; don't stop doing anything you're already doing," Rome cautioned with a commanding gesture calmly. "You should probably be expecting people to propose large fronts to you though. Someone in our click will bite the bait. And whoever bites the bait will bite the bullet. Won't they Caesar?"

Caesar noticed the contemplative expression on Rachel's face and the seriousness on Rome's face. He sipped more of his wine and slouched further into his chair.

Chapter 6

"What's your first impression of Soulja?" Amanda asked Uncle Mike, looking at him as they sat on the couch in her living room.

Uncle Mike deliberated for a second, then responded, "Confident, vigilant, brave. I see a lot of potential in him. He seems honest."

"He is. He's never lied to me. He's actually helped me a lot. He's a lot smarter than he allows people to see."

"Well, I want to examine his character. It's hard to know the intentions of people like him. He has a mysterious silence," Uncle Mike casually remarked. "I'll find a way to get on leveled ground with him."

Soulja walked into his mother's new apartment. His eyes searched the living room promptly. He had changed clothes at his own apartment after taking a shower. Being with Precious was very arousing. Premature semen soaked the front of his boxers and Precious' juices covered the front of his pants after he left her house. Soulja felt refreshed after taking a shower and dressing himself with black jean texture shorts and another tank top.

Soulja locked the front door of the apartment behind him and walked through his mother's living room, down the hallway of the apartment. He checked in his siblings' room, but they were peacefully sleeping.

"Soulja! Is that you?!" Ms. Walsh asked.

Soulja closed his siblings' door and paced quickly to his mother's room across the hall. Ms. Walsh was sitting up straight on the bed when he walked through the door.

"Why didn't you have the front door locked?" Soulja questioned.

"I didn't lock the door in the projects. Why should I lock the door here?"

Soulja walked to his mother, then gave her a hug. He sat down on the bed next to her.

"I just stopped by to check on you," Soulja informed.

Ms. Walsh stared at Soulja admiringly. Her meditative eyes focused on Soulja sternly. She put one hand on his shoulder and kissed him on his jaw.

"You still feel like you have to protect me, don't you?" Ms. Walsh reflectively questioned.

Soulja gazed at his mother in a compassionate character. Ms. Walsh positioned herself to sit closer to her son.

"I know we don't talk about this much, but I know what you did to your daddy hurts you sometimes," Ms. Walsh said. She held Soulja's hand and stared in his eyes as she said, "You've been so strong dealing with it, but you don't have to hide your feelings when you're around me."

"It doesn't hurt, Ma. I'd been waiting to do it for a long time. I never said that to you because I thought it might hurt you."

"I loved your daddy. That's why I could never do what you did to him. I wanted to do it so many times too. The way he used to beat me. You just did something I wasn't strong enough to do. My little soulja. You've always been my soldier. Even when you were a baby you would kick and swing at certain people when they came around me. Everyone thought you were just being a fussy baby, but I knew you were trying to protect me. That's why I started calling you my little soulja."

"Without hesitation...I'd do it again," Soulja assured her as he mentally depicted what he did to his father.

Soulja remembered being twelve years old, listening to his father and mother argue in the living room of the apartment in the projects as she stood at his door. He remembered hearing a loud smack, like a slap, and hearing his mother weep loudly, "You said you wouldn't hit me anymore while the children were here," then his father walking out of the apartment yelling inaudibly, slamming the door behind him. He remembered peeking through his window, watching his father enter the dark alley behind the apartment building. He could see himself reaching beneath his bed for the .32 revolver he hid there, jumping out of his bedroom window, then running into the alley behind his father. "What you doin' out here this late boy!" he remembered his father yell to him just before he pulled the .32 revolver out of his pants, pointed it at his father, then pulled the trigger three times. Soulja shot his father in the chest three times, killing him instantly. He remembered taking the money from his father's pockets and running back to his window and climbing through, being shocked that his mother was standing in his room as he fell in through the window. "What are you doing?" his mother had asked him bitingly. He remembered her anger and how it eased after he admitted to her that he had just shot his father. He could still remember the anxiety on her face as he stood in front of her with the gun he killed his father with and the money he took from his pockets in the other.

"I'll never forget what you did for me, Ma. You kept me from getting caught," Soulja thankfully said.

"I'll never help anyone take my little soulja to jail. Not even for what you did to your daddy."

The phone rang in Ms. Walsh's bedroom.

"You must've had the calls forwarded to this apartment. I've been getting calls from everyone. That girl Veronica has been calling you all night," Ms. Walsh said.

"I'll go in the living room to answer the phone. Good night," Soulja said, then kissed her on the jaw.

Soulja walked to the living room then answered the phone, "Hello."

"Soulja. It's me," Veronica said in a low whimpering voice.

Soulja held the phone to his ear in silence.

"Soulja?"

"Yeah," he said.

"Baby, I love you," she sobbed.

"Man, I don't wanna hear that shit."

"I do. I promise I do. I just…C.T. don't mean nothing to me. I'll stop messin' wit' him. Baby, I just wanna be wit' you."

"Yo' promises don't mean shit to me no mo'."

Veronica cried hard as she begged, "Please. Baby, don't break up wit' me. I love you. Please."

"I don't have to break up with you. I broke up with you. Hear tha break," Soulja declared, immediately hanging up the phone after uttering his last word.

After midnight, Soulja attended a party held at luxury hotel. The party had a multitude of female attendants, walking around in two-piece bikinis, stylish one-piece bikinis, and a variety of casual clothing. Soulja noticed people he knew in a corner shooting dice with people he didn't know. Caesar and Rachel walked toward him. Soulja's eyes fixed on Rachel's burnt-orange tie-dyed tee with lace-up neckline and denim shorts with a drawstring. Her glossy coated toenails drew attention to the leather thong sandals on her feet.

"What's up, Caesar?" Soulja asked as Rachel and Caesar stopped in front of him.

"It's all gravy," Caesar responded enthusiastically.

"How you doing, Soulja?" Rachel asked.

"I'm straight," Soulja answered. "Everything is everything."

"I was tryin' to catch up with you earlier today," Caesar said. "I wanted to ask you if you've seen any new dope boys pop up in the cut."

"Nah. Ain't nobody gon' come in tha projects to sell no dope. I ain't seen nobody nowhere else either though," Soulja responded.

"Ain't nobody tried to front you or nothin' like that, huh?" Caesar questioned as Rachel searched the party with her eyes.

"You know I don't sell dope fa nobody but myself," Soulja emphasized.

"Yeah, I know. But let me know if somebody try to front you or sell you some dope. If it's somebody new to da spot."

"Bet. I got' cha."

"Soulja, you seen Veronica tonight?" Rachel asked.

"Nope," Soulja answered plainly.

"Look over there at the pool. Ain't that her and C.T. over there?" Rachel asked with a shocked expression.

Soulja turned his head to look at the pool. He saw C.T. and Veronica standing beside the pool in a lip-locking kiss.

"Yeah. That's them," Soulja said calmly, turning back toward Rachel and Caesar.

"Damn. My nigga, you ain't gon' do nothin' about that?" Caesar asked as he observed

C.T. and Veronica with a strict expression of anger on his face.

"She ain't my girl or anything. And if she was all I could do is leave her alone and let her be with that nigga," Soulja explained.

"When y'all break up?" Rachel asked.

"This morning," Soulja said, noticing Amanda walking toward him in a fast pace.

Amanda's motion was full of aggression. Caesar and Rachel watched her approach, silently wondering what her intentions were.

"Let me talk to you in private for minute," Amanda said in a commanding tone.

"Alright," Soulja uttered with a concerned expression. "Let me get back wit' y'all later. I'ma holla later on," Soulja assured Caesar and Rachel just before walking away with Amanda.

Amanda led Soulja to one of the accommodating bedrooms on the second floor of the hotel.

"Where we goin'?" Soulja asked as Amanda opened the door to the bedroom.

As soon as they entered the bedroom, Soulja saw Tia sitting at the foot of the bed with her head between her knees, sobbing in tears. From the way she sat, folding her upper body over her lap, the two-piece bikini she was wearing was barely visible. Soulja stared at Tia, then looked at Amanda.

"What's wrong with Tia?" Soulja asked with concern.

"She saw C.T. and your ex-girlfriend together downstairs kissing," Amanda replied, folding her arms over one another in agitation.

"Why didn't you tell me today?" Tia wept. "You could've told me he was cheating on me!" she cried with her head still between her knees, covering her eyes with her hands.

"Did you know about C.T. and Veronica? Is that why you broke up with her?" Amanda asked.

"Yeah," Soulja answered Amanda, noticing an expression of disappointment on her face.

Soulja walked to Tia. Standing in front of her, he said, "Tia, I was just trying to give C.T. enough time to tell you himself. I didn't want…"

"He didn't tell you! Why do you think he would tell me?" Tia screamed from between her knees.

Soulja laid one of his arms around Tia's shoulders as he sat down close beside her. He gently lifted her head up from between her knees with his other hand.

"Take your hands down Tia. Move your hands away from your face," Soulja said calmly, at a low tone. Tia dropped her hands to her lap with a smack on her thighs. Soulja used his hand to gently turn her face toward him.

"If he didn't tell you tonight or you didn't find out tonight, I would've told you tomorrow," Soulja said sincerely as he stared into Tia's tear-filled eyes. "I always thought it would take me years to consider someone my friend, but you and Amanda managed to become my friends in less than a year. I know you would've told me if you saw something like you did tonight. I need you to trust me when I tell you I would've told you tomorrow," Soulja said, pausing only to hear a response from Tia. "Tia, do you trust me?" Soulja asked. Tia released a long sigh and responded, "Yeah. I trust you. I believe you." Tia wrapped both of her arms around Soulja's body and leaned her head on his shoulder. Soulja wiped Tia's tears from her face with his hand. "You shouldn't be crying. You're bigger than what you're going through," Soulja articulately said. "You just learned something that can make you stronger. You know that you're a loyal, honest, respectful, person. That makes you stronger. Come on." Soulja said, standing to his feet, pulling Tia from the bed to her feet as well. "You know what?"

Soulja energetically asked, standing in front of Tia, concentrating on her eyes. "You about to take yo' gorgeous, sexy, intelligent, fine ass back downstairs to the party so you can drink, dance, and be merry," Soulja said with more dynamics.

Tia smiled, then released a light giggle as she hugged Soulja, leaning her head against his chest.

"Have I ever told you I love you?" Tia asked, looking up at Soulja.

"Nope."

"Well, I do," she smiled.

Amanda observed with a smile. She was impressed with the way Soulja cheered Tia up.

"Come on, let's go back down to the party," Soulja suggested.

Soulja led Tia out of the bedroom with his arm around her neck. Outside the bedroom, he put his other arm around Amanda's neck.

"Where's Tate?" Soulja asked Amanda.

"He's downstairs. He's the one that told me to come get you for Tia," Amanda replied.

Downstairs at the party, music thumped, women bounced and shook their bodies, dancing to the rhythm, and guys were slipping in a quickie fuck in the pool. Soulja didn't recognize the guy Tia was dancing with, but he did recognize the young lady approaching him with another young woman. Their hips went from side to side in a hard thrust as they walked. They stopped in front of him.

"What's happenin', Soulja? You just don't fuck wit' cha girl no mo' do you?" the young woman wearing a red two-piece bikini asked with playfully flirtatious attitude.

"It ain't like that, Becky," Soulja assured the young woman in response. "I haven't seen you in the projects in a while," he said, looking Becky up and down. "Damn. You lookin' good as a muthafucka girl! Yo' titties lookin' bigga, yo' hips spreadin' and everything," Soulja said of her size thirty-two A-cup breast and thirty-four inch hips. "Let me see something," Soulja said, putting his hands around Becky's small size twenty-four inch waist to turn her around in a circle. "Yo' ass lookin' good and everything, Becky. What's up?!" Soulja strongly emphasized.

"Shiit. You know me, "Becky said with a smile. "This my partna, Adriana," Becky introduced with a gesture of one hand and a quick dance at the brown skin young woman silently standing beside her.

The two cute women shared an almost identical skin complexion and body attributes except for the shade lighter skin of Becky and the slightly larger breast of Adriana.

"What's up, Adriana?" Soulja asked.

"She been askin' me to let her meet you," Becky promptly said.

"Girrl," Adriana said shyly.

"Girl, Soulja ain't wit' all that fake ass beatin' around tha bush shit," Becky spat. "I'll see y'all later," Becky cheerfully said before walking away.

"You lookin' real good Adriana."

"Thank you," she acknowledged.

"So, why don't we go upstairs and spend some time to get to know each other," Soulja charmed.

"Ok," Adriana agreed with an enchanting smile.

Chapter 7

The seasons changed again from summer to winter. Soulja could remember over a year ago, when he met the beautiful woman Precious. He still didn't feel like his sex sessions with her had been ongoing for more than three months. He had already learned a lot from her about arousing women to the optimal point of orgasm.

Soulja walked down her hallway wearing his black leather jacket, a pair of black wool pants, and black boots. When he opened Precious' door, his face showed perplexed contemplation as he stared in the face of the pale vanilla skin complexion woman sitting beside Precious on her bed.

"This is my ex-girlfriend, Lisa," Precious explained, walking toward Soulja. "Close the door and take off that coat. It's hot in here. I have the heater on, that's why we're only wearing panties and bra."

Soulja closed the door behind him, then took off his jacket.

"Are you two back together again?" Soulja asked.

"No I told you she's my ex-girlfriend. I'm still close with her. I told you that."

"Yeah, I remember."

"Hey," Precious said with a glittery smile, staring at Soulja. "I wanna see how good you are with your tongue."

"Now?" Soulja asked.

"Yeah. Don't be shy. She's…"

Soulja locked his lips on Precious and began to kiss her as he griped her butt cheeks and rubbed his hands all over her.

"Mmmm," Precious released into Soulja's mouth with a tone of pleasure. "Wait," she said, breaking the kiss. "That was very good, but it's not what I was talking about. I was talking about putting your tongue here," Precious said, putting one hand over her vagina.

Soulja looked down, then said, "I've never done that before."

"That's why Lisa is here. I told her I wanted you to watch me eat her and she was fine with it," Precious explained, pulling Soulja closer to Lisa.

The blue eyed woman stood to her feet. She was a little shorter than Precious. The long, straight, blonde, hair on Lisa's head fell over her shoulders and down the palm of her back. Soulja could understand why Precious was attracted to Lisa. Her size thirty-four C-cup breasts and firmly pointed nipples looked soft after Lisa removed her bra. Her size twenty-five inch waist and size thirty-four inch hips were obviously remarkable even before she sat down on the bed, sliding her panties off.

"I want you to pay close attention to my tongue and the way I use my hands while I'm doing this," Precious said sternly to Soulja. "I'm gonna skip the other foreplay and just start." Precious spread Lisa's legs wide. "Come here. Get down here beside me," Precious told Soulja. Precious and Soulja were both on their knees. Precious grabbed Lisa's waist and pulled her cheeks to the edge of the bed. Lisa's butt cheeks hung half way off the bed as Precious began to bury her tongue deep in Lisa's pretty, pink, vagina. Precious used her thumbs to massage the outer tissue of Lisa's private area as she gently wrapped her lips around Lisa's clitoris, then circled her tongue around it. Lisa released a soft moan and began to play with her own breast. Precious stuck one of her thumbs in the succulent, warm hole while she continued to massage with the other thumb and work on Lisa's clitoris, with her skillful lips and tongue. Soulja noticed the humping movements of Lisa's hips as Precious pulled her thumb out of the hot, pink tissue, then entered two arched fingers. Precious slowly rubbed the inside upper wall of Lisa's vagina with her tongue, alternately switching from clitoris to inside upper wall. Lisa's moans became louder. She squeezed on her full breasts. She bucked her hips. Precious felt Lisa's vagina pulsating, felt her walls vibrating. As Lisa climaxed, she moaned "Yeeeahh." Her heavy breathing became soft as she calmed. Precious turned her head to Soulja.

"Did you pay attention?" Precious asked.

"Yeah. I'm right here. I can't help it," Soulja replied.

"I want you to do me the same way I did her," Precious said, raising to the foot of the bed beside Lisa as Lisa rolled out of the bed.

Precious commenced to remove her bra and panties. She threw both to the side of the bed.

"You ready," she asked Soulja.

"Just lay back," Soulja said.

Precious laid back on the bed. Soulja buried his tongue into Precious' vagina the way he saw Precious dive into Lisa's. He moved his thumbs on Precious' outer vagina the way he thought Precious did Lisa. He tried to do everything the exact same way as he had just seen Precious do, ignoring Precious' vaginal secretion covering his upper and bottom lip. Precious couldn't believe how sensitive she felt. Performing on Lisa really aroused her more than she expected to be. Even Soulja's unskilled tongue, lips, and hands felt great to her right now.

She tried not to make it obvious by clenching her mouth closed and breathing, rather heavily through her nose. The harder she tried to hide her arousal, the better Soulja's performance seemed to feel. Her stomach tightened with contraction and quivered spasmodically as she reached an orgasm. Precious quickly pulled Soulja on top of her. She kissed him, releasing a high pitch moan into his mouth. They kissed with passionate slurps and smacking lips. Precious rolled herself on top of Soulja. She took off his shirt, pants, and boxers. Soulja's throbbing penis stuck up like an erected piece of metal. Precious began to kiss Soulja as she enclosed his penis in the warm embrace of her vagina. She slowly slid herself up and down the length of Soulja's penis. Her torso raised as she sat erect on him. She swayed her torso from side to side with pumping motions; her hips bobbed gracefully. Soulja raised to her breast and began to work his mouth on her hard nipples. Precious moaned, "Uhh, Yeah." She wrapped her arms around his neck tightly, performing muscular contractions with her vagina, snatching on his penis as she sped her movements, then slowed down, arching her back to allow him to enter her deeper. Precious' vagina sucked Soulja's full length in as she thrust down on him, then it pulled hard from the base of his penis to the head of his penis. She leaned herself on Soulja, causing him to lay back on the bed. She kissed him on his neck and ear, then placed her lips on his, working her tongue in his mouth. Precious glanced at the chair in the room. Lisa sat there masturbating. Precious kissed Soulja with more passion, pressing her stomach against his, bending her back inward, raising her butt to a position that allowed the hot tissue of her vagina to cover only the head of Soulja's penis. She made three explosive, extremely fast thrusts down on his penis, then slowly swallowed his penis with her wet vagina. She was impressed that Soulja was keeping up with her pace. He hadn't missed a stroke with her. He was meeting her every movement until now, and she knew he wouldn't be able to endure her much longer. Soulja felt that he would burst in climax at any moment. He had never felt anyone move on him like that. Precious subjected him to a different rhythm of sex. She made those movements a couple times more and felt Soulja's penis jerk in quick jumps. Soulja released a deep groan into her mouth as he climaxed. He was drained. Precious kept kissing him. She traveled down to his chest, his stomach, his navel, then she stuck her tongue on the base of his penis and licked it to the head. She could taste the mixture of their passion juices on her tongue. Lisa couldn't resist joining Precious. She paced quickly to the bed with Precious. They both kissed on Soulja's penis, sharing him with their lips and tongue circling him. Their mouths inadvertently touched on occasion as they slid their tongues up and down the length of Soulja's penis simultaneously. Their tongues suddenly tangled, then they began to kiss. Soulja watched silently. He was beginning to be arouse again. Precious broke her kiss with Lisa.

"Oh, I'm sorry," Precious said to Soulja. "None of this was part of the plan for tonight," she sounded regretful.

"Don't worry. It doesn't bother me," he assured.

"What is it?" Lisa asked.

"The only reason I wanted you to let him watch me eat yo' pussy was because I want him to be able to use what he sees me do," Precious explained.

"I don't have a problem with that. Maybe he could watch me too, and use what he sees me do to you?" Lisa questioned.

Precious looked at Soulja for a sign of disapproval.

"That's up to you, Precious," Soulja said without anxiety.

"Ok," Precious smiled at Lisa. "Then you can stay for the rest of the night?"

"Sure I can," Lisa replied.

"After we take a shower you'll be ready for another round or two or three," Precious smiled.

"Whatever you want me to do," Soulja answered.

The cold day was filled with cars traveling the streets and highways. Car mufflers exhaled clouds of steam as Tia sat in the passenger's seat staring out of the window at the other moving cars. The young man driving reduced the volume on the stereo system in his car.

"Tia, I need you to do me a fava," the young man said, glancing at Tia.

Tia looked at him and asked, "What kind of fava?"

"I owe some people a lot of money. I need to pay 'em befo' they try to do somethin' to me."

"How much do you owe?" Tia asked with concern.

"It don't matter. I know how I can get 'em to leave me alone."

"How?"

"I need you to do somethin' with 'em."

"Something? Something like what, James?" Tia asked in an offended tone.

"Man, you know what I'm talkin' 'bout."

"You want me to fuck somebody for your debt?"

"Yeah."

"Boy, you crazy as hell. I don't do nothing like that. Don't say anything like that to me again," Tia said strictly.

"Oh, you gon' do it like that?"

"How much do you owe? I can probably get you the money, James."

"Nah! Fuck that!" James aid angrily. "You gon' do a muthafucka like that," he said, punching Tia on the side of her head. "Bitch! Get cho ass out of my car!"

Tia looked at James with tears in her eyes.

"You think I'm playin' bitch!" James said, pulling his car to the side of the street. "Get cho ass out!" he said, taking his keys out of the ignition and stepping out of the car.

Tia sat in disbelief, watching James walk around the car to the passenger's side. James opened Tia's door.

"Bitch! I said get out!?" James said as he grabbed Tia's arm and snatched her out of the car on her butt.

"James. I'm a long way from home!" Tia wept. "Don't leave me out here!"

"You shoulda thought about that shit!" James said as he got in his car.

James sped off, leaving Tia standing on the side of the street, wearing a thin, purple jacket, purple pin-striped shirt, and purple denim pants. The air was cold. She rubbed her jacket against her skin to keep warm. Tia remembered seeing a sequence of stores down the street. She knew there would be a telephone booth on one of the lots.

Tia walked to one of the stores and used the pay phone to call Amanda. Eventually, Amanda arrived to take Tia home. She got out of the car with Amanda, walking with her head hanging low. Amanda walked in front of Tia to the door of their apartment. Amanda's countenance reflected sorrow as she held the door open for Tia to enter the apartment. Tia lifted her head once she entered apartment. She quickly scanned the living room with her eyes, seeing Tate, her uncle Mike, and Soulja sitting on the furniture. She felt mortified and afraid. She knew they were going to ask a lot of questions and her answers to their questions would bring a lot of trouble to James' life and a lot of trouble to her heart. She didn't want James to be physically injured, but she couldn't lie to her friends and her uncle.

"What happened, Tia?" Mike asked, showing concern.

"I really don't want to talk about this right now," Tia said lowly.

Mike walked toward Tia. "Tia," Mike said, standing in front of her, "you can tell us what happened."

Mike raised his hand to Tia's head to brush her hair down with his fingers in a comforting effort. As he pressed his fingers against Tia's hair, she breathed a sigh of pain, "Ah," then pushed Mike's hand away. It was obvious her head was injured.

"Please. I'll be fine. I just need to find some aspirin," Tia said, then walked toward her bedroom.

"Tia!" Soulja yelled, stopping Tia in her steps. "Just tell us who did it," he pleaded.

"James," Tia said simply, then continued to walk to her bedroom.

"Amanda, what happened, man?" Tate asked.

"She was with James," Amanda began to explain. "He tried to get her to have sex with his friends, but when she said no he punched her on the side of her head a few times, then pulled her out of the car and left her on the side of the street."

"What?!" Tate said loudly, with disbelief.

"I have to get her some water and some pain pills. She probably won't swell, but I know her head hurts," Amanda said, then paced to the kitchen.

"James?" That's that nigga she met at the party a few months ago ain't it?" Soulja asked Tate.

"Yeah. He one of the Corner Ave. boys," Tate answered.

"Come on, man. We finna go find this nigga," Soulja said, raising out of his seat.

"Soulja," Mike said. "This is my niece we're talking about. This involves me. We'll do this my way."

"Alright. We'll take yo' car. Let's go," Soulja said with eagerness.

"Where are we going? We haven't made any plans yet," Mike said.

"We don't need a plan to go over here on Corner Ave. and blast every weak bitch we see," Soulja said with enthusiasm.

"Do me a favor?" Mike calmly asked. "Sit down. Listen to me."

Soulja stared at Mike for a moment with an uncertain expression. He took a seat, although he didn't understand why Mike was obviously trying to quiet him. Tate seemed uncomfortable.

"We're not going to blast anyone," Mike emphasized, looking at Soulja. "The only person we need to find is James. Now, do you know where he hangs out or where he lives?"

"I know where Corner Ave. is," Soulja replied with calm composure.

"I know where that nigga sit in da cut at. I know what his car look like and everything," Tate assured.

"Good. This is what we'll do. We'll check for his car at his home, where he hangs out, then on the streets until we find 'em. Then we'll take him to this abandoned house I saw a few days ago. Let's go," Mike said.

"I need to change shirts. I'll be right back," Tate said, removing a multi-colored cotton shirt as he walked to the rear of the apartment.

"Soulja. Don't make me regret giving you gun range training," Mike whispered.

"What?!" Soulja frowned.

"I'm not giving you gun range training so that you can abuse it."

"Man, I'm not abusing anything."

"I don't want you to do any shooting," Mike strictly remarked. "We're gonna do this my way."

"Damn, Mike. I said alright."

"I just want to be clear," Mike said as he turned his head toward the hallway of the apartment. Tate approached, wearing a black leather zip-up coat.

"What's with the black jacket, man?" Mike asked with curiosity.

"It's a project thang," Tate answered.

They walked out of the apartment. Soulja sat on the passenger's side of Mike's gray, old model car, while Tate sat on the back seat. They listened to an old blues tape Mike played on his car stereo while he drove. The search for James had lasted a couple of hours. Tate was slouched on the back seat, tired of being driven around on the streets and highways of Jackson. He sat erect, contemplating whether he should suggest they end the search now or wait a few minutes then make the suggestion. Suddenly, a white and blue blended paint coated short-frame luxury vehicle obtained his attention.

"Say, jack! There that nigga car right there!" Tate excitedly said.

"Where?!" Soulja asked.

"Right there," Tate said, pointing at the white and blue blended vehicle at the turning interval of a four-way intersection. "That's James! That's James!"

Mike switched lanes, driving into the turning lane behind James. When James turned, Mike turned behind him.

"The next time he stops I'ma go get that nigga," Soulja said calmly.

"How are you gonna do that?" Mike asked.

"When I put this nine in his face he gon' scoot over," Soulja said, slightly raising the nine millimeter weapon on his lap.

"No shooting. Don't shoot him," Mike cautioned as he kept his focus on following James.

"I won't shoot unless he reaches for something."

"Say, jack. Hold up. I just said I'll help you find 'em," Tate anxiously said. "Y'all can just let me drive back in this car and y'all take that nigga car."

"Nigga, what?!" Soulja spat aggressively. "Tia's Amanda sista! They been like family to yo' ass. How da fuck you gon' let this nigga treat yo' family like that, nigga?!"

Tate sat silently, exhibiting frustration.

"Tate, I thought you said you wanted to marry Amanda?" Mike questioned.

"Yeah. That's why I proposed to her," Tate answered nervously.

"Then you have to do this for your fiancé. You have to do this for Amanda.

Tate slowly shook his head in disagreement.

"Man. Check this out! If you don't keep yo' ass in this car and ride wit' us...I'ma treat you like one of these niggas in da streets next time I see you! Now that's real!" Soulja declared.

"Damn, dogg. It ain't gotta be all dat," Tate said.

"You're not going anywhere, Tate. Just stay in the car," Mike said.

James turned on a by-street, unaware that he was being followed. His music pounded loudly from the speakers in his car and he puffed on a blunt as he stopped at a stop sign at the corner of the by-street.

Soulja quickly exited Mikes' car before Mike could even stop the car's motion completely. He ran to the driver's side of James' car, pointing his gun at him. Soulja's gun was pressed against the window as he simultaneously opened James' door. "Scoot cho bitch ass over," Soulja demanded.

James was confused, afraid, and shocked as he moved himself to the passenger's side of his car. Mike drove around James' car and Soulja followed Mike.

"Let the seat all the way back bitch!" Soulja told James, hitting him across the head with the butt of his gun. "I want you to do anything, so I can knock yo' weak ass off!" he said, looking down at James as he laid all the way back on the passenger's side with blood gushing from his head.

When they arrived to the abandoned house, Soulja parked the car beside Mike's car. As Mike stepped out of his car, he peeked into James' car, noticing James laid back on the passenger's seat. Mike opened the passenger's side door.

"What did you do to him?" Mike asked Soulja noticing the dry blood covering the cuts on James' close texture hair styled scalp.

"I just busted 'em upside the head a few times. He ain't dead, he just unconscious," Soulja answered. Mike re-adjusted James' seat so that he sat erect. He pulled James out of the car as Soulja pushed him out from the inside. Soulja exited the car from the passenger's side simultaneously lifting James to help Mike carry him into the abandoned house. Tate observed the remote distance between the abandoned house and the last house they passed by on the way. As Tate opened the door to the abandoned house, he frantically stared into the empty house waiting for Soulja and Mike to completely enter with James before he closed the door.

"This way," Mike said, directing their steps with a tug of James' unconscious body.

They entered the hallway to their right then entered the kitchen on the left side of the hallway. They sat James in a single, wood, arm chair in the otherwise empty kitchen. Mike went to a drawer in the kitchen as if he was familiar with the house. In haste, he retrieved a long coil of rope, rushed to James, and commenced to take the rope out of a coil. As Mike cut the rope in sections, he passed Tate a piece, saying, "Tie his wrists to the arms of the chair." Mike watched Tate tie James' arms to the chair while he tied James' body to the chair.

Soulja watched Mike attempt to enliven James with slaps to his face. Suddenly, Soulja walked close to James and slapped him vigorously, saying, "Wake yo' chump ass up!" James' eyes busted with blinks as he gained consciousness. His eyes immediately focused on Soulja.

"Man…Man…what I do to you?" James asked fearfully, realizing he was restrained with rope.

Soulja struck James again with a violent blow on the center of his face, rocking James' head back.

"You've made a very serious mistake today, James," Mike said to him. "You see…you tried to force a young woman to do something and when she refused to, you beat her, then put her out of your car," Mike continued calmly.

"I'm sor-," was all James could manage to get out of his mouth before Mike struck him with blows to his head.

"I don't want to hear any apologies! I don't want to hear shit from you right now! You just listen!" Mike demanded.

James peered at Mike with reverence as he watched Mike fiddle with a large hunting knife.

"I know where you live," Mike uttered in a tranquil voice. "If you ever come near Tia again, I will not show mercy to you or your family. When you see Tia, I want you to run not walk in the opposite direction. Do you understand?"

James shook his head in a gesture of affirmation.

"Let me give you something as a reminder," Mike said as he clasped James' fingers down on the left side of the arm chair, then compellingly pierced James' hand with the knife. Mike twisted the knife in James hand as he listened to James scream and cry in agony. Soulja watched, holding his regular composure of silent attentiveness, but Tate seemed to be uncomfortable and paranoid.

Mike used the knife to cut the ropes fastened around James' hands, then stood behind him to cut the ropes that were fastened around his body. "Stand up," Mike commanded James. "Hold your head down." Mike grabbed James neck and led him out of the house, followed by Soulja and Tate. Mike led James to James' car and opened the passenger's side door, saying, "Keep your head down, facing the floor of the car as you step in and sit down." Soulja entered on the driver's side of James' vehicle, "Lay the seat back bitch," Soulja said to James, hitting him on the head with the butt of his nine millimeter as each word came out of his mouth. Soulja glanced at James, laid back on the passenger's seat, and remarked, "I'm still waiting fa you to do something so I can knock yo' bitch ass off." He watched Mike and Tate reverse out of the two-way driveway in Mike's car, then he reversed out himself, then followed Mike's car.

Chapter 8

Caesar and Fat sat in the living room of Fat's home. Caesar sat with an upward slope, leaning toward the slip-on cover chair Fat sat on, angled opposite the couch in the room. Caesar re-adjusted himself on the far end of the sofa, closer to Fat.

"You sure you don't want to do this?" Caesar asked.

"If I'd known you were gon' ask Soulja ta pop that boy last time I wouldn'ta went. I thought we were just gon' take some money and dope," Fat explained.

"I'm tellin' you...there's more money and dope on this lick than the last one," Caesar emphasized.

"Nah! You and Soulja gone do this by ya self," Fat said.

"I don't even know where Soulja is. This gotta be done tonight," Caesar stressed.

"You paged him? He gon' call back," Fat assured Caesar.

Soulja and Mike stood in front of Soulja's vehicle in the projects. Very few people were standing outside because of the cold weather.

"Before you leave, I need to tell you something," Mike sincerely said, observing Soulja's accreting attention. "I want you to enroll in a martial arts class."

"What?!" Soulja asked with curiosity.

"I want you to enroll in a martial arts class. It'll help you enhance your gun range training."

"How?!"

"There's a lot of hand and eye coordination involved in martial arts. You need that training."

"Man, I don't need that shit. I know how to fight," Soulja replied with frustration.

"I know you can fight. This is about your training. You wanna be better or not?"

"Yeah, I wanna be better," Soulja confirmed.

"Ok. You go to the class. If you don't like it you can always quit. If you're afraid, don't worry about it."

"I'm not afraid of anything. And I don't quit," Soulja contemplatively informed. "How long do I have to go to the class?" he asked.

"I'll sign you up for a year."

"How much does it cost?"

"The instructor owes me a favor. You won't have to pay for anything," Mike said. "I'll handle everything tonight, show you where the place is tomorrow, and tomorrow night you can attend your first class."

"Alright," Soulja agreed, shaking Mike's hand. "I gotta go. I gotta emergency page a little while ago."

"Is everything alright?" Mike asked with concern.

"I can handle it," Soulja said as he sat in his car.

Soulja left the projects and drove directly to Precious house. His concern grew as he approached the driveway. Soulja entered the house only to find the numerous women sitting in a state of fright. Precious rushed from the rear of the house.

"He tryin' to rape everybody," Precious declared, continuing to rush toward Soulja.

Soulja had never seen Precious so worried.

"Where is he? Who?" Soulja questioned.

"He said he gon' save me for last. He back there raping Kim!"

Soulja pulled out his gun and commenced to walk toward the rear bedrooms of the house.

"He got a gun, Soulja!" Precious warned.

"Just stay in here."

Soulja continued to walk to the bedrooms. He held his gun tightly in his hand as he approached the bedroom door on his left in the hallway. He heard crying and a male voice mumbling. Soulja kicked in the bedroom door with the gun pointed in the room. As soon as the door swung open, Soulja saw a tall dark skin man pointing a gun at the head of the woman on her knees. Reflexively, Soulja shot the man four times before he could even turn to see Soulja. The tall stranger fell over, the woman remained on her knees in shock, and Soulja rushed to the man. He stood over him and grabbed the gun off of the floor beside the man. The man squirmed around on the floor. Precious and a few of the girls ran from the living room to the door of the bedroom.

"What tha fuck is wrong wit' you, nigga?!" Soulja yelled. "Who the fuck-," Soulja stopped his sentence and began kicking the man on the floor.

"He raped me too!" one of the girls standing at the door yelled.

Soulja looked back at her quickly, then started kicking the man more. Precious ran into the room and pulled Soulja away from the man.

"We gon' take you to the hospital, but if you tell the police who shot you or anything else, I'ma tell them you raped two women in this house," Precious said to the man.

"Fuck this nigga," Soulja said aggressively to Precious as he aimed his gun at the man's head and pulled the trigger, but missed because

Precious pushed his hand to the side, causing him to shoot the floor instead.

"Man…What the fuck wrong wit' you, Precious?! This nigga just-"

'I can't have you kill anyone in my house, baby. Please. Don't shoot him no mo'," Precious begged. "Let me take him to da hospital," she said. "Y'all pick him up and take him to my car," Precious signaled to the women standing at the door.

Precious held Soulja's arm, contemplating a way to distract him. She wanted to keep his attention off of the man being lifted from the floor by the other women. She just stood in front of Soulja, staring at his face, desperately hoping he would respect her wishes as she held his arm tightly.

"You need to keep this," Soulja told Precious, handing her the .38 revolver he picked up from the floor. "If anyone else comes in here like that, you need to unload it on 'em," he said instructively. "I need to use your phone," Soulja noted as he walked out of the bedroom with Precious.

Soulja walked into Precious' bedroom to use the telephone. Caesar's cell phone number was in Soulja's pager too. He went to Precious' house first because the page denoted emergency needs. He called Caesar and waited for him to answer.

"What's poppin'?" Caesar answered his cellular phone."

"This Soulja."

"Damn, nigga. You got good timing! Magical!"

"What's up?"

"We need to talk face to face. Meet me at Fat house."

"Ah'ight. I'ma go over there now."

"Bet. Hurry up. This shit serious."

"Ah'ight."

Soulja disconnected with Caesar on the phone. As he walked out of the bedroom, he noticed that everyone was gone. No-one was in the house anywhere. The only car in the driveway was his own. Soulja drove to Fat's house speedily.

When Soulja arrived to Fat's house, Caesar's white SUV was already parked in the front yard. Soulja walked to the front door and knocked lightly as he yelled, "Soulja!" Fat opened the door and Soulja walked in.

"What's up, bra?" Fat asked.

"You tell me," Soulja replied frankly.

"Check this out, bra." Caesar cheerfully said as Soulja sat next to him. "I gotta lick that got'cho name on it."

"Oh, yeah. What kind of lick?" Soulja asked.

"This nigga got at least five kilos and two-hundred thousand dollars on 'em. All we gotta do is go get him."

"What, you talkin' 'bout now?"

"Yeah!"

"Shiit. Let's move," Soulja suggested standing to his feet.

"We can go in my ride," Caesar said.

Soulja and Caesar left Fat's house in Caesar's SUV. The banality of Soulja's face always impressed Caesar. As they drove to their destination, Caesar lowered the volume of the music.

"Do you remember what happened last time we went on a lick together?" Caesar asked, focusing on the highway.

"Yeah, I remember."

"If you do it this time, you can have everything. All the money. All the dope. Everything," Caesar promised shifting his focus for a glance of Soulja's physiognomy.

"Ah'ight," Soulja agreed without hesitation.

Caesar continued to drive until they reached the parking lot of a ten-story high hotel. He drove slowly pass the parked cars until he saw a navy-blue, four-door SUV. Caesar beeped the vehicle's horn once, stopping directly behind the SUV, then he slowly kept driving pass the navy-blue vehicle to a parking space ten cars away from the navy-blue SUV. Caesar and Soulja exited the white SUV and walked to the navy-blue SUV. Caesar entered the front passenger's seat and Soulja entered the rear seat.

"Shiit. I almost left," the brown skin man with a medium sized afro declared. "That's ya front man," he said, looking through the rear-view at Soulja.

"Yeah. I tol' you I was comin'," Caesar said.

"Yeah. Here," the man said with agitation, passing Caesar a brown paper bag.

Caesar opened the bag and began searching the contents.

"I see seven kilos, but how much money is this?" Caesar asked.

"Three hundred. Don't worry about that. I told Rome what I was spending. You just betta hope ya boy back there can handle that seven ki front cause…if he can't I'ma have to have that ass. He gon' get fucked off."

"He can handle it," Caesar said." I told him to bring somethin' fa you, bra. A lil' gift to show appreciation for frontin' 'em, ya dig."

"I'm straight. I don't need shit, but fa you ta bring me my shit after you holla at Rome and that nigga back there ta flip my dope," the man said angrily.

"He gon' give it to you anyway. Soulja, give da man his gift."

Through keenness of insight, Soulja knew what Caesar meant. He quickly pulled his nine millimeter and shot the man in the back of the head.

Caesar and Soulja simultaneously exited the vehicle. Caesar opened the door to a black minivan next to the navy blue SUV.

"Soulja! Where you goin' Get in the van," Caesar said.

Soulja entered the van from the driver's side. Caesar entered the van, reaching in his pocket for keys. He placed the brown paper bag in Soulja's lap, ignited the van, and then reversed out of the parking space.

As they left the parking lot of the hotel, Soulja peeked into the bag. He fiddled around, searching the contents. Caesar drove onto the highway with paranoid eyes.

Underneath an illuminating brass chandelier in the dining room, Mike sat at an antique dining table with detailed carving across from a chunky bodied man.

"He's going to martial arts class tomorrow night. I told Clarence to make her his assistant," Mike told the man.

"And you think this will work?" the man questioned.

"Charles, he's the person for her. He's got all the props," Mike spoke in a convincing tone.

"Ok. We'll know for certain soon enough," Charles said.

The day's atmosphere provided cool, still air. Moisture lingered in the air from the late night rain the night before. Becky primly walked the sidewalk in the projects. The knit skull cap pulled neatly over her head touched the midsection of her ears. Her straight, brunette hair hung just above her shoulders with the ends curled to the jawline of her cute face. She took her hands out of the pockets of her beige pants and began to wave them in the air as she noticed Soulja driving into a parking space in front of Tia and Amanda's apartment.

"Soulja!" Becky yelled as she watched him exit his green vehicle. "Holla at me, nigga!"

Soulja immediately walked across the street to the sidewalk Becky stood on.

"What's jumpin', nigga?" Becky asked with interest.

"I'm just rollin' through."

"Man, we need ta kick it, fa real."

"What's up? Tell me something."

"Man, you drivin' my girl crazy, man. She don't talk about nothin' but Soulja. I don't know what you did to her, but she talkin' 'bout getting' yo' name tattooed on her and everything," Becky explained. "I told her ain't no dick that good," she giggled.

"Who you talkin' 'bout?" Soulja curiously asked.

"Adriana, nigga! You know who I'm talkin' 'bout."

"I know what…She don't need to get my name on her nowhere. That's fa sho'."

"I tol' dat bitch you don't want her," Becky stressed "Check this out, though. Smoke somethin', nigga," she said, noticing Veronica and C.T. approaching in Veronica's car.

Becky observed Veronica and C.T. as they gained closer. Soulja's attention shifted to the object of Becky's distraction. He shared observance with Becky as C.T. exited Veronica's vehicle. C.T. peered at Soulja momentarily as he closed the passenger's side door on Veronica's car. Veronica looked through her rear-view mirror at Soulja across the street standing on the sidewalk with Becky.

"Man, don't tell me y'all still beefin' 'bout that bitch, man!" Becky's voiced filled with disappointment.

"There was no beef to start wit'," Soulja replied as he watched C.T. walk away from Veronica's car. Veronica drove out of the projects. "How do you trust someone that lies to you about a bitch if he supposed to be yo' potna?" Soulja asked Becky as he put one arm around her neck and began to slowly walk with her across the street. "You don't trust no muthafucka that break tha pact, baby. That nigga know he was supposed to tell me he was fuckin' that bitch. That's all he had to do. That nigga didn't stay loyal to da pact. Ain't no love lost. I just don't trust 'em no mo'," Soulja explained.

"So if he woulda tol' you he was fuckin' Veronica, you would still trust 'em?"

"Yeah 'cause he woulda been showing me that that bitch ain't loyal. But all he did was show me that he ain't loyal and Veronica ain't loyal eitha."

"Ok. That's real," Becky acknowledged as they stopped beside Soulja's car. "Where you thank you takin' me?" Becky asked.

"Man, get cho ass in da car. You said you wanted to smoke somethin'."

Becky took off the beige jean vest she wore over the thermal shirt as she walked to the passenger's side of the car and entered. "Oh. You already smokin'?" she said, noticing a blunt in Soulja's ashtray.

"I was gon' wait until I left the projects to smoke it."

"But you gon' smoke it wit' me, huh? Nigga, you need to gon' head on wit' that game."

"Damn, Becky. You think everything I say is game?"

"Oh, nall. I know you about business nigga, but tha game just in ya. It might come out when you don't know it 'cause you did somethin' to my girl," Becky giggled.

"Fire da blunt up," Soulja suggested.

Becky reached in her pocket for her lighter and took short puffs from the blunt as she held the fire from the lighter in front of it. She took a moderate puff and held the smoke in her body, then exhaled the smoke.

"Man, you got tha projects on lock. When you gon' let me work fa you?" Becky asked as she gazed at Soulja's face, then took another puff from the blunt.

"Nigga, you don't wanna sell no dope."

"Shiit. Yes I do," Becky promptly verbalized as she passed Soulja the blunt.

"Why you wanna do something like that?" Soulja asked, intently concentrating on Becky, then puffed the blunt.

"Why do you sell dope?"

"I know why I sell dope. I'm talkin' about you, though. Why you wanna do that?"

Becky stared at Soulja as she answered, "I want my own shit. I want my own money, so I can buy my own clothes. I wanna buy a car. I'm tired of drivin' everybody else shit. I just want my own shit."

Soulja took another puff of the blunt before passing it to Becky.

"Do you know how to sell dope?" he asked.

"Man, you trippin'. I been livin' in tha projects like you. I been around niggas sellin' dope long enough fa me to know how."

"But you ain't never sold befo'."

"That don't mean shit. At one time you didn't sell dope until you started. Now you one of da biggest dope boys in da projects," Becky stressed.

"I ain't no dope boy."

"What are you then? Coulda fooled me," Becky said with sass, then puffed the blunt.

"Ah'ight. I don't want you to sell dope fa me."

"Why not?"

"Hold up. I'm gon' give you some dope. Don't tell anybody where you got it from. I'm not gon' front you no dope. I gotta go somewhere. When I come back to da projects, I'ma have something fa ya. Now tha money you make, you can buy some dope from me or go to somebody else," Soulja explained, accepting the blunt from Becky.

"I'ma spent wit' you, nigga. Don't play me now Soulja cause I'm serious."

"I got you, baby girl," Soulja remarked as he ignited the car.

"Where we goin'?"

"Nall, I'm just finna' turn on tha heat," he said as he started the heater in the vehicle.

"You might as well turn tha radio on. Pop in one of them CD's," Becky energetically suggested.

Soulja turned on the stereo system in his vehicle and the music began to play loudly.

Caesar, Rachel, and Rome sat in the living room discussing additional information pertaining to the new organization of drug dealers in the area.

"My girl, Pam, said she been dating this guy that says he just moved here. She said she went to his apartment and it's laid out wit' all kinds of expensive furniture and when she asked him where he works he told her da streets."

"So, does she still date him?" Rome asked anxiously.

"Yeah. I tol' her to keep 'em cause she might be able to get 'em to buy her some expensive stuff. She ain't nothin' but a pretty girl. Anyway, she said his car straight factory except fa da radio system."

"This cat might just be a wannabe. That nigga probably ain't neva been on da streets," Caesar offered.

"Ok. Tell Pam to ask him if he has any friends, because you wanna meet one," Rome told Rachel.

"Yeah. Then I can find out if he a wannabe or real dope-boy."

Caesar's face frowned with disapproval of the notion. Rome noticed Caesar's disapproval.

"Can you handle Rachel doing this, Caesar?" Rome voiced concern.

"Yeah. Yeah, I can handle it. Baby part of da team too. Right now she da only one that can check this cat out."

"What's his name? Did she tell you his name?" Rome asked eagerly.

"She said his name is Legend," Rachel said.

Rome contemplatively said, "If we knew exactly where this new click was coming from it would help, but we don't know where they came from exactly because as far as I know they came from a lot of different states. Try to find out where he's from though."

"Alright," Rachel agreed, shaking her head in an affirmative gesture.

"We need to go somewhere," Rome said as he stood to his feet and grabbed the blue corduroy jacket from the backrest of the sofa.

"Yeah, I'll holla at you lata," Caesar told Rachel, then raised from the couch and walked toward the door.

As Rome and Caesar walked the brick covered passageway to the driveway, Caesar thought of the reward he would soon receive for the job he did with Soulja last night. After entering Rome's glossy cream painted sports car, Rome placed the key in the ignition and leaned back on the seat.

"Last night…you did a good job. There's no-one else standing in your way. You have control of west and east Jackson now. But if this cat, Legend, is a part of this new click…I don't know, but you might have to kill him too. Right now…all the dope boys in west and east of the city owe you. They work for you now," Rome explained.

Caesar was overwhelmingly satisfied with his reward, but concealed it with a smile.

The night air was clear as Soulja stepped out of his car with a black duffle bag strapped over his shoulder. He briefly amused himself with the gunmetal BMW parked directly opposite his car. He looked up at the sign on the adjacent building on the lot.

"Taiwan Dojo," Soulja said to himself before walking toward the entrance of the dojo.

After entering the dojo, he stood still, looking around at numerous people on the floor stretching while others sparred, and yet others did calisthenics. One older Asian man walked toward Soulja grinning.

"Hello," the Asian man said to Soulja, extending his hand. "My name is Clarence. Is there something I can do to help you?" he asked as he shook Soulja's hand.

"My name is Geronimo Walsh," Soulja introduced himself. "Mike told me-"

"Yes. I talked to Mike on the phone. He told me about you. It is good to have you join us. Mike says you're a good street fighter with a strong mind. You are just the kind of student I like in my class. I need more street fighters here. You can put your bag down over here," Clarence instructed, directing Soulja to a nearby bench. "Excuse me for a moment. I'll be right back."

Soulja dropped his duffle bag, sat down on the bench, and unzipped his tracksuit jacket. He tugged on the tracksuit pants as he watched Clarence talk to one of the female students. Her copper, gold, auburn, and semi-brown straight textured hair was pulled into a ponytail. Clarence and the young woman conversed as they walked toward Soulja, but became silent as they approached him.

"This is Breanna Stiles," Clarence introduced the beautiful young woman. "And Breanna, this is Geronimo Walsh," Clarence introduced Soulja.

"Hi. Nice to meet you," Breanna said, extending her hand to Soulja.

"Hey. Nice to meet you too," Soulja said as he shook Breanna's hand.

"She is my highest ranking student," Clarence announced proudly. "She's a third degree black belt. Oh, Breanna. Geronimo is a street fighter.

"Another street fighter," Breanna articulated with interest. "Now we have two."

"Breanna will be assigned to assist you," Clarence informed Soulja. "She will be a terrific sparring partner for you, but first I would like to use you for a demonstration in the class."

"Ok," Soulja agreed, wondering to himself if the short man, Clarence, will try to embarrass him.

Soulja and Breanna stood before the class with Clarence. All eyes in the class were focused on Clarence, Breanna, and Soulja.

"This is Geronimo," Clarence introduced Soulja to the class. "He has agreed to assist me in a demonstration. Geronimo has the skills of a street fighter. Timothy! Come forward."

A tall, thick bodied, pale face young man raced to the front of the class and stood in front of Clarence.

"Will you participate in this demonstration?" Clarence asked Timothy.

"Yes," Timothy answered.

"Excellent! Timothy will be participating in the demonstration. As you all know, Timothy is a student that also has street fighter skills.

Timothy and Geronimo, I want you to punch with about this much pressure," Clarence informed, punching Soulja's chest mildly. "Timothy, you know what to do."

Soulja and Timothy stood facing one another. Timothy's height exceeded Soulja's by three inches. Clarence stood between them.

"You will start when I say, Start!" Clarence informed. "Punch each other below the neck only," he explained. "Start!"

Timothy and Soulja stood still momentarily. Suddenly, Soulja released a flurry of punches to Timothy's ribs and stomach. He shocked Timothy with his speed. Timothy tried to move backward, away from Soulja, but couldn't get away.

"Stop!" Clarence demanded, stepping between Soulja and Timothy with a foot and an arm. "That was good. Now I want Timothy to use the art he has learned since attending the class while Geronimo continues to street fight. Ready. Start!"

Timothy tried to sweep Soulja, but Soulja reflexively tangled his leg with Timothy's and clipped Timothy off of his feet.

"Stop!" Clarence demanded. "That was good class. This was an example of how important the application of the art is. Learn to apply the art to yourself. Don't just learn the art."

After class, Breanna and Soulja walked to the parking lot in the same direction.

"You did very good in class today," Breanna complimented Soulja. "I think you'll learn fast.

Soulja looked at Breanna's beautiful face intently, noticing that her hazel brown eyes looked much darker than her caramel complexion under the parking lot light pole.

"I think I just have a good sparring partner," Soulja flirted.

CHAPTER 9

Adrianna primly walked through the crowded hallway of her high school. She saw Soulja taking a few school books out of his locker and immediately sped the pace of her steps toward him.

"Now, I know you ain't takin' them books home wit you," Adrianna communed, cracking a wide smile at Soulja.

"Today da last day of school. What I look like taking books home?"

"You wouldn't take books home if it wasn't tha last day of school," Adrianna mocked.

"I'm making passing grades. As long as I graduate," Soulja said as he walked away from the locker.

"So, where you goin'?"

"Take these books to da teachers."

"I know you ain't stayin' at school all day. You gon' let me leave wit' you?" Adrianna flirtatiously asked.

Soulja glanced at Adrianna's face and the sexiness of her body filling out the navy blue and minimal white and red halter top and hip-huggers.

"I gotta handle something," Soulja replied.

"You can't go handle somethin' after handlin' me?" Adrianna seductively asked.

"Nall. I gotta handle this myself."

"Soulja, I don't know why you keep treatin' me like this," Adrianna whined. "What I do to you?"

"You ain't did shit to me. You ain't my girlfriend or nothin'. What you trippin' fa?"

"I told you I love you," Adrianna said sadly.

"You love me?" Let me handle my business and we'll get together another time."

"Man, you full of game," Adrianna voiced with disappointment as she stormed farther down the hallway from Soulja.

Caesar swam in the pool behind the house as Rachel walked through the glass doors that open onto the concrete covered patio leading to the pool. Her vest style top displayed her navel and her breasts threatened to bounce out of its V-neck. She walked closer to the pool as Caesar's head emerged from the pool. He watched Rachel walk toward him, admiring the sexy energy that surrounds her mere existence.

"He's ready to deal. Legend finally gave in. He wants you to come by his apartment," Rachel informed Caesar as she stood at the edge of the pool.

Caesar was positioned directly beneath her. He looked under her skirt. "You don't have on panties," Caesar acknowledged.

"You know I rarely wear panties in the summer," Rachel responded. "What do you want me to do?" Do you want me to tell him to meet you somewhere else?"

"Nah. His apartment, huh? When?"

"He didn't say. I'll see him tonight, though."

"You spend a lot of time wit' this nigga. You wit' 'em more than Pam ain't it?" Caesar voiced bitterly.

"I might spend a lot of time with him, but you know why, baby," Rachel consoled. "Legend know Pam is just a pretty girl and I'm the real deal. That's why he's attracted to me. I'm like his boss bitch dream. He fuckin' Pam. But you fuckin me." Rachel said with sexual arousal as she removed her vest, then pulled her skirt over her head. Rachel stood, making a pose for Caesar, then squatted in his face. She slid in the pool with Caesar and wrapped her arms around his neck.

Precious and Lisa sat on the bed in Precious' room conversing at a low tone. When Soulja stepped through the door, they immediately stopped talking and sat silently.

"What's up?" he asked, closing the door behind him. "Y'all talking about me ain't it? I can tell, so you might as well tell me."

"Yeah, we were talkin' bout you," Precious admitted as Soulja took a seat on the chair in the room.

"So, what about me?"

"I asked her if you would mind if we kept our little threesome going," Lisa intervened bluntly.

"That's cool. I thought y'all said I was good at everything though?" Soulja questioned.

"Well, yeah," Lisa said.

"Yeah. You're real good, but I didn't think there would be any harm in still havin' a little fun with it," Precious smiled. "You know they say practice makes perfect."

"Yeah. And. You make me feel a lot younger," Lisa volunteered.

"I…We need to talk to you about somethin' else too, though," Precious said with uncertainty.

Soulja stared at them with calm anticipation.

"You and me been makin' a lot of money, but I think we can make a lot more doin' something else," Precious said.

"What you mean?"

"Ever since that man came in here wit' that gun and tried to rape all us, the girls been kinda scared to come and I been tryin' to figure out a safer and better way fa us to make some money," Precious explained with concern. "Lisa said she'll help me open a strip club, but...I still need more money to do it right. So, what I wanted to know is if you want to go in on the club wit' me too?"

"What I gotta do?" Soulja asked contemplatively.

"Well...really, all you have to do is have your part of the money ready. I was thinkin' you could put yo mama's name down fa part ownership wit' me and Lisa."

"Alright. Let me holla at my mom first, right? Then you can just let me know how much money I gotta put up."

Later that night, Soulja attended a party at a luxury hotel. People crowded the upstairs and downstairs accommodations of the section of the hotel approved for the party. The swimming pool was filled with women in bikinis and some of them were completely naked. Amanda and Tate stood side by side as Soulja approached them.

"They got Tia playing spin da bottle," Soulja informed as he leaned against the upstairs railing beside Amanda, looking down at the pool. "She gon' be drunk as a muthafucka."

"Where are they?" Amanda asked with concern.

"They sittin' on the floor right over there," Soulja pointed to a corner on the far left side of the downstairs area.

Amanda stared momentarily at Tia and said, "She'll be OK She'll only pass out after she drinks so much."

"You ain't drinkin' or nothin'?" Tate asked, peering at Soulja over Amanda's shoulder.

"I got some cognac I'm sippin' on," Soulja replied, holding up a bottle he retrieved from the back pocket of his pants.

"I got some gin fa me and Amanda. We gon' catch a room in a minute. Leave you wit' this shit out here," Tate communed, referring to the carousal surrounding them.

"You ain't gon' leave me wit' it. I'ma dip in a minute myself."

"Who you leaving with?" Amanda asked with interest.

"Shit, I don't know. I might leave dis muthafucka by myself," Soulja responded as he searched the rave with his eyes. "Aye, I'ma holla at y'all lata, man. I need ta holla at Becky right quick," Soulja said, eyeballing Becky as she walked up the stairs alone.

"Ok. We'll probably be gone, but we'll see you tomorrow or something," Amanda said.

"Alright."

Soulja primly walked toward Becky, meeting her as she stepped to the upstairs floor.

"What's up, Jack?" Becky asked with a smile. Her short-shorts and stomach revealing shirt fit her body with moderate snugness.

"Aye, I was gonna wait until tomorrow to holla at cha, but what's up?"

Becky swung one arm around Soulja's waist and pulled him close to her and said, "I just wanna spend five g's wit' you."

Soulja put one arm over Becky's shoulders and said, "Just …Just … I'll getcha tomorrow morning. Be outside in da projects in da morning. When I come through … just come get in da car."

"Alright. You know Caesar lookin' fa you?"

"Nall. Where he at?"

"Downstairs sittin' by da pool," Becky said, pointing to a set of beach chairs and tables surrounding the pool, positioned in a semi-circle.

"I'ma go holla at 'em. Don't forget about tomorrow morning, though," Soulja cautioned.

"Nigga, I ain't gon' fa'get."

"Alright. I got'cha in da morning," Soulja assured Becky as he commenced to walk down the stairs.

Soulja took a good view of the drunken activities as he walked down the stairs. The music seemed to animate the event as he watched people dance to the rhythm of the fast pace beats. A group of women bounced their butts in union.

Stepping through the crowd downstairs, Soulja glanced at Tia, observing that she was still playing spin-the-bottle. As he passed by, Tia was hastily drinking a glass of liquor. Just before he approached Caesar, he noticed Veronica in the pool with an unfamiliar young man. Veronica and the guy seemed to be having sex in the pool, judging by the way her body kept rising up and down against the young man's as they stood in the pool. Soulja acknowledged their sexual engagement, but disregarded it. He sat down at the beach table next to Caesar after removing his bottle of cognac from his back pocket and setting it down on the table.

"What's up, bra?" Soulja asked.

It's all gravy, baby," Caesar responded. "I got anotha lick," Caesar said, peering at Soulja. "It's just a lil' different this time, because I'ma have to throw you somethin' myself."

"I thought you said it was a lick," Soulja asked with obfuscating physiognomy.

"Check this out. Ah'ight. Really … I just … you know what I'm sayin' … need you ta knock this nigga off, man."

"Oh, Ok. Who is it?"

"Really… Just this nigga that thank he can't be handled, you know. They call da nigga Legend, you know what I'm saying, but this nigga just don't know."

"Legend? I don't know 'em."

"Nall. You don't know 'em," Caesar confirmed as he leaned across the table from his seat, closer to Soulja. "You know, Rachel done slid up under tha nigga. She don set 'em up fa tomorrow night. So, me and you gon' get together tomorrow evenin', right. I'ma page you and come get you. Then we gon' go over ta da nigga crib and you can handle da nigga," Caesar explained.

"Ah'ight, but what you talkin' about giving me for this?"

"I'll give you ten ki's, you know what I'm saying'. All you gotta do is handle up. Then I'ma come clean."

"Bet," Soulja agreed.

Chapter 10

Rachel laid in bed naked beside a brown skin man with a low-cut, box-top hair style. She stared at the ceiling with a meditative guise. The phone on top of the dark stained wood night stand rang, breaking the silence that previously conquered the room. The man reached for the telephone.

"Hello," the man answered the telephone with a sleepy tone.

"Legend, this Pam. Did I wake you up?" the low toned voice asked.

Legend sat up straight in the bed, leaning his back against the solid headboard of the bed.

"I was almost asleep," Legend lied.

Legend gazed at Rachel. Rachel was motioning with her lips, "Is that Pam?" Legend shook his head affirmatively. Rachel suppressed a laugh with the palm of her hand pressed against her mouth.

"Oh. Well, I didn't mean to wake you up," Pam remarked as she walked her five-feet-five inch frame to her bed, fiddling with one of the braids angled off her beautiful face.

"Well, what is it?" Legend asked.

"Nothing, really. I guess I just wanted to talk," Pam explained as she sat on her bed.

"Oh. Well, why don't I call you in the morning before I leave the apartment," Legend offered as Rachel rubbed her hand over his chest, then traced her fingers down to his penis to play with it.

"You gon' take me to the mall tomorrow?" Pam asked.

"Yeah," Legend answered as Rachel began to caress and kiss on his stomach. "Let me get some sleep so I can be ready to come get you tomorrow," Legend suggested, trying to subdue the expression of pleasure he felt from Rachel's sensual kisses and massaging hands stroking his penis and alternately squeezing his scrotum.

"Alright, baby. I'll see you tomorrow," Pam exclaimed blithely before disconnecting with Legend.

Legend hung up the telephone and asked, "Are you crazy?" with amazement escaping from his voice.

Rachel kept kissing on his stomach, unaware that Legend's eyes were closed, enjoying the sensation of her lips and tongue rolling over his stomach. She looked up at him and laid her head on his chest. "You want me to stop," she bantered.

"You're even crazier if you think I want you to quit."

Soulja relaxed on a bed in one of the bedrooms of the hotel. He could still hear the music playing downstairs. Suddenly, Tia burst into the room boisterously laughing. He stared at her with concern, watching her close the door behind her and stumble toward him in the room.

"What the fuck are you doing up here all alone, Soulja?" she asked, lethargically standing in front of Soulja as he sat erect in the center of the bed. "Is that yours?" she asked, eyeballing the half bottle of cognac on the nightstand.

"Yeah," Soulja answered, watching Tia stumble a few steps to the bottle. "Give me that!" Soulja said, slightly raising his voice. "You're drunk!" he said as he pulled the bottle away from Tia's guzzling mouth.

"I'm not drunk," Tia replied, gazing at Soulja as he put the cognac back on the nightstand.

Tia jumped in the bed with Soulja, pushing him on his back as she mounted herself atop him.

"Tia, what--," Soulja began his sentence.

Tia began to kiss Soulja. Reflexively, Soulja kissed her back the way Precious taught him to kiss. As his tongue flicked and twirled in Tia's mouth, she started humping against him. She released a moan in Soulja's mouth as the suction from the kiss slightly tugged her tongue. Soulja pushed Tia's shoulders softly, breaking the kiss.

"What … What are you doing?" he asked.

Tia smiled and leaned her head down to his ear whispering "I want you to fuck me." She began to kiss him on his neck.

"No. No!" Soulja hastily said as he pushed Tia to the side and rolled off of the bed. "You're drunk, man. You need to lay down," he suggested, walking backward from the bed.

"Well, come put me to bed," Tia enticed. "Come on. Just lay here with me," she suggested as she laid her head on one pillow and clasped another close to her body. She closed her eyes.

Soulja slowly paced to the bed.

"Tia, I don't want to do this. We're supposed to be friends, man," Soulja emphasized. "Tia," Soulja voiced, noticing she hadn't responded. "Tia," he pronounced.

Soulja realized Tia had passed out. He picked up his bottle of cognac from the nightstand and took a long swig as he sat on the side of the bed.

The next morning, Soulja drove through the projects. He flipped the hydraulic switches in his vehicle as he slowly rode through, glancing at some of the children running up and down the sidewalk on both sides of the street. The front end of his car bounced high in the air as Becky stepped from the middle of two apartment buildings. Soulja's car lifted up one wheel as the other three guided the frame of the glossy green vehicle into a parking space in front of Amanda and Tia's apartment building.

Becky opened the passenger's door to Soulja's car and entered. She immediately reached into the front pocket of her pants and pulled two bulged folds of money, then passed it to Soulja.

"You wanna count it?" she asked.

"Nope," Soulja answered, stuffing the money into his two front pockets. "You said you wanted to spend five-thousand wit' me. I believe it's five-thousand."

"It is," Becky assured, watching Soulja reach into his pants crotch and pull out two large blocks of crack cocaine in a clear plastic bag.

"You wanna put it on a scale, baby girl?" Soulja asked, playfully mocking.

"Hell, nall! How much is this?!" Twelve ounces or something?!" she asked with excitement.

"That's eighteen ounces. You been doin' some real hustlin'. I just wanna help you out a lil' bit. You know you my potna," Soulja explained.

"Damn, man. I'ma come up wit' this, fa real," Becky smiled.

"I wanna see ya come up. Just handle business and keep hustlin' hard. I'ma keep lookin' out on ya 'til you can buy you a couple ki's," Soulja communed. "Ey. Check this out. I know we got this lil' treaty wit' them Corner Street boys, but I want you ta have somethin' wit' you when you on the cut. Look in my glove compartment.

Becky opened the glove compartment, immediately noticing a sleek nine millimeter pistol.

"You talkin' 'bout this?" Becky asked as she grabbed the weapon.

"Yeah. That's too big fa you ta handle?" Soulja asked.

"I can handle it. You know these niggas in da projects wouldn't help me find a gun," Becky voiced with disappointment.

"A few people told me you were tryin' to buy a pistol. But I believe you can handle it. I'll rather see you cap one of these niggas on the streets than see one of these niggas do you some harm."

"I want it. What I gotta give you for it, though?"

"All I want you to do is use it. That's yours. It's another clip in there. You don't owe me nothin'."

"Ok," Becky said, reaching for the extra clip for the weapon. "I'm finna go cut up my dope and go ball, playa," she said as she stepped out of the car, stuffing the weapon in her pants before she completely exited the vehicle.

Soulja exited his glossy green vehicle and walked to Amanda and Tia's apartment door. Tia answered to his knocks on the door.

"Who's there?!" she yelled.

"Soulja!"

Tia opened the door wearing a T-shirt and shorts.

"Come in," Tia told Soulja as she held the door open. "I need to talk to you," Tia said in a low tone. "Last night, I was really drunk," she began as she closed the door, then walked to the couch to sit beside Soulja. "I remember what happened. I knew what I was doing. Even if I was sober, I would've – you're someone that I would definitely have sex with. I mean, if we weren't friends, I'd have sex with you. And, I guess that kind of came out while I was drunk. But, I'm glad you didn't take advantage of me. I wouldn't have been able to talk to you ever again," Tia explained. "So, I'm sorry for how I acted."

"It's ok

. You just need to learn how to control your liquor," Soulja suggested.

"Yeah. Because I can be a total drunk."

Chapter 11

Pam sat in a chair on the front porch of her brick home, peering at the four-door blue-green sports car entering her driveway with Legend at the driver's seat and Rachel on the passenger's seat. Pam's pink, side lace-up tank top seemed to raise her size thirty-six C-cup breast and revealed her brown stomach. As she stood, her loose fitting jeans gave no sculpt to her twenty-nine inch waist and thirty-five inch hips. Pam turned to the carved wood design front door of her home, stuck her head in the house, braids swinging, and said, "He's here, mom," to the similar framed woman sitting on the couch.

Pam's mother pulled her contoured cut, round neck shirt down just below her beltline as she rouse from the couch. She walked out of the house onto the porch. Rachel exited Legend's vehicle and waved one hand in the air to Pam's mother, saying, "Hey, Rose. What you doin' this morning, girl?" in a graceful, girlish tone.

"Hey, what's goin' on?" Rose responded in the same courtesy as she approached the passenger's side window next to Pam.

"You could've stayed in the front seat," Pam offered, noticing Rachel beginning to enter the rear passenger's seat.

"Girl, shit. That's yo' man. You sit in tha front seat wit' 'em," Rachel verbalized. "He drive like a bat outta hell anyway. I need to be in da back seat, shit. It's safer. That nigga can't drive. See ya, Rose," Rachel smiled as she sat on the back seat.

"Where you takin' my baby?" Rose asked.

"I'm taking her to the mall. I want to buy her some shoes and an outfit," Legend explained. "You can come if you want to."

"Yeah. Come with us, mom," Pam urged excitedly.

"I'm not comin' wit' y'all ta be walkin' around," Rose said.

"I'll buy you something too. Buy you an outfit or something," Legend assured.

"Girl, come on get cho ass in this car and chill wit' us today," Rachel encouraged.

After hesitating a bit longer, Rose finally agreed. "Let me lock up my house. I'll be right back," she said as she walked to the front door.

"Thank you for picking up Rachel for me," Pam sweetly said to Legend.

"No problem, baby. My girl always gets her way."

Pam smiled at Legend, then leaned into the car and kissed him on the tip of his lips. Rose walked back to the car.

"I'm ready. Wine and dine me, baby," Rose playfully said.

"Mom, get in the front seat," Pam insisted as she entered the rear passenger's seat behind Legend.

Nikki walked into the living room of her home while Fat and Soulja sat on the couch casually conversing. She sat on the arm of the chair beside Soulja and placed her hand on his shoulder.

"Soulja, I got a girl fa ya. She on her way over here. I just got off the phone wit' her about twenty minutes ago," Nikki informed.

"Who is it, Nikki?" Fat asked.

"Ayesha," Nikki answered.

"Oooh," Fat approved with excitement.

"What she look like Fat?" Soulja asked.

She tight, bra. She thick … big ass titties … booty bouncing, dancer-type ass. She tight, fa real," Fat emphasized.

"Nigga, I ain't gon' hook you up wit' no wildebeest," Nikki assured, playfully slapping Soulja's shoulder once with mild force.

A knock on the door grasped their attention. "Who is it?" Fat yelled.

"Ayesha!" the knocker answered.

"Come in!" Fat yelled.

Ayesha opened the door and stepped into the house. "Hey. How y'all doin'?" she asked.

"What's up girl? This Soulja," Nikki introduced as she raised from the arm of the chair. "Soulja was just askin' what you look like."

"I look like the woman gettin' ready ta sit wit' her new man," Ayesha said sassily as she strutted to the chair Soulja sat on.

Ayesha wore a front lace-up wrap-on peach colored shirt that covered her breast and exposed the rest of her upper body. Her hips swayed from side to side as she strutted.

"Is that your car sittin' outside … tha shiny lookin' one?" Ayesha asked as she sat on Soulja's lap and wrapped her arms around his neck, pulling his face close to her breasts.

"Yeah. You wanna go for a ride or somethin'?" Soulja asked.

"It depends on where you trying to take me, baby," Ayesha noted seductively.

Soulja whispered in her ear, placing one hand over his mouth and her ear, "I wanna take you to a place we can be alone so I can give you a fuck you'll never forget," then stuck his tongue in her ear softly.

"Oooo, shit," Ayesha burst with amusement. "You hard to handle ain't it."

"Why don't you find out?" Soulja said temptingly.

Ayesha rose from Soulja's lap, taking his hand in hers as she paced toward the door with Soulja behind her. "Girl, I'll be back. Let me go for a ride 'til I whoop me one," Ayesha said to Nikki with a giggle.

"Ah'ight, girl," Nikki approved.

"Everything is set up?" Rome asked Caesar, sitting across from him in the living room.

"Yeah. The nigga was supposed to pick Rachel up this mornin' from her house," Caesar assured.

"Sometimes, I forget Rachel has her own house. She's here so much."

"Yeah. She called me this morning and told me da nigga was on his way to come pick her up."

"She really wrapped this cat around her finger, huh? Does that fuck with you?"

"Nall. She ain't fuckin' da nigga or nothin', you know what I'm sayin'. She just gamin' on da chump."

"Well. If Legend really ready to sell you fifty ki's, then he won't be a chump on da streets if he gets a chance to put it out there. He could give you some serious competition."

"Oh. He ain't gon' get a chance, 'cause I'm gon' squash all dat tonight."

Mike and Charles sat on stools at the granite top island in the kitchen sipping drinks. The two stained trim doors to their left lead directly into the living room, but to their right were glass doors that gave them a view of the patio and the open backyard. A ceiling fan hung above them from the decorated stained beaded board ten-foot ceiling.

"I'm going to Chicago in about an hour," Mike informed, checking the time on his watch.

"Is this for the arms trade?" Charles asked, taking a sip of his drink afterwards.

"Yeah. Our buyers from New York agreed to conduct the trade there. We'll come out of this with two million clean."

"Do our Chicago people agree on maintaining a steady course of purchase with our New York buyers?" Charles asked with concern.

"I intend to negotiate a bargain that will provide benefits for all parties," Mike assured. "I'll be back tomorrow morning. I'll see you then," Mike said, just before a short, one-hundred and twenty-five pound woman walked through the two doors on their left. She entered the kitchen in haste.

"Oh. Mike, I didn't realize you were here," the woman said, slowing her pace as she approached the island, close to Charles' stool.

"It's alright, Asia. How are you?" Mike asked.

"I'm fine," Asia assured.

"Listen. I don't mean to run, but I have a meeting to attend," Mike informed.

"Ok. I'll see you another time."

"Soon. I'll stop by, maybe tomorrow," Mike communed as he walked out of the kitchen through the doors she had just entered.

"What was he in such a rush for?" Asia asked suspiciously.

"You know how Mike is. Always in a hurry. Won't except being late for a meeting," Charles said quite frankly before turning to Asia and kissing her on the cheek of her face. "You came through those doors pretty fast. What were you in such a rush for?"

Asia wrapped her arms around the broad shoulders, medium sized Charles and responded, "I was about to take our daughter to the salon, then I remembered leaving behind my car keys on the kitchen counter."

"Well, you don't want to keep her waiting. She becomes brutally irritated when she loses patience."

Asia pecked Charles' lips with her own then said, "You're right." She walked to the kitchen counter, retrieving her car keys. "She gets that from you," Asia smiled.

"So, what happened?" Nikki asked Ayesha as they sat alone in Nikki's living room.

"Shit. Girl, I thought that nigga was just talkin' shit. But he held up for everythang he said."

"What he do, girl? What he say?"

"You know when he whispered in my ear?"

"Uhm-huhm."

"He said he wanted to give me a fuck I wouldn't fa'get. That nigga was not lying girl. I ain't gon' never fa'get how that nigga fucked me. I'm have ta get me some of dat dick der again! Ain't no secret! Ain't no doubt!" Ayesha exclaimed.

"Ooooh, girl, what he do?! Nikki asked with interest. "He eat cho pussy?"

"He ain't put tha tongue on me, but he did some shit wit his lips and tongue on my neck and my nipples … oooh, girl! That nigga just know what to do. I thought I was gon' pass out. I ain't had multiple orgasms wit' nobody but myself until today!"

Chapter 12

Soulja walked to his ringing telephone in his apartment bedroom. He sat on his matrix black bed and answered the telephone.

"Hello."

"Hi. This Breanna. What are you doing?"

"I just got out of the bath tub."

"Oh. Do I need to call you back?"

"No. No. Don't worry about it. I can put on my clothes and talk at the same time."

"Good. I'm bored," Breanna sighed.

"Oh. It's like that ... You can only call me when you're bored?"

"Nooo! That's not the only time I call you. I call you sometimes when I want to vent my anger, don't I," she bantered.

"Yeah. Did private school do that to you? You know ...turn you into an angry madwoman?"

"You know I'm not always angry," Breanna giggled. "Just when those stuck up students try to pass judgment on people."

"You know they just wanna come to the dojo. Get 'em in class and drop 'em fast. I'll help you. You've been helping me learn the art so, we'll drop 'em together."

"Yeah, maybe I should," she laughed. "What I really called for though was to get some company."

"What do you mean? You want me to come to your house?"

"Yeah."

"What?!" You mean to tell me you ready for me?" Soulja joked.

"Geronimo. I told you I'm a virgin. And, you're not even my boyfriend," Breanna said defensively.

"Calm down. I was just messing with you. You are a mad woman."

"I'm sorry. I just feel stressed out. A lot on my mind, that's all.'

"It's ok. How do I get to your house?"

"No. I have to come get you," Breanna insisted.

"These apartments have a security gate. You can't get in without the code."

"Then give me the code. I already know where those apartments are. All I need is your code and the number of your apartment building."

Soulja gave Breanna the information she needed to come and pick him up. Soulja slid on a black sports jersey over a white shirt.

As Breanna drove onto her driveway in her BMW, Soulja examined the huge house.

"This is where you live?" he asked.

Breanna nodded her head affirmatively and said, "Come on. My parents are gone."

Soulja admired the black front door, trimmed in gray stone carvings. They entered the wide framed door. He looked up at the railing that lined the stairs leading to the second floor of the house.

"Come on. My bedroom's upstairs," Breanna said.

They stepped up the hardwood staircase to the second floor as Soulja glanced at the numerous pictures and artwork on the walls. The chain rail molding above the hall to Breanna's bedroom was impressive. As they entered Breanna's room, Soulja stared at the wide crank windows, but Breanna led him by the hand to the balcony just beyond the glass slide doors next to her bed.

"Have a seat," Breanna suggested, referring to the two soft textured chairs on the large semi-circle balcony. "Do you want something to drink?" she smiled.

"Ah. Yeah."

Breanna paced to a personal refrigerator in her bedroom and returned with a bottle of juice." All I have is juice and water, so, I got you Kiwi Strawberry juice," Breanna explained, noticing Soulja enjoying the view of land in front of him.

"You only brought one. You didn't want anything to drink?" he questioned.

"Oh, yeah. You don't mind sharing do you? I'm not a poisonous creature, you know," she flirted.

"No. I don't mind."

"Here. You take a drink first," Breanna offered, passing Soulja the bottle of kiwi strawberry juice.

Opening the bottle to take a sip, Soulja suggested, "Why don't you tell me what is really bothering you? You said you're stressed out."

Breanna stared at the setting sun as she said, "I don't know if I should talk to you about this. It's probably just gonna bug you."

"I wanna hear it," Soulja assured her.

"Can I have some juice?" Breanna asked, accepting the bottle as Soulja passed it to her. She took a sip then said, "I have this ex-boyfriend. We broke up about a month before I met you, but I did have feelings for him. Anyway, the only person I kinda considered a friend is dating him now."

"If the relationship is over, why are you upset because she's with him? Do you want him back or something?"

"No. That's not it. I'm not mad because she's with him. It's just that, when I broke up with him she was with me. We both walked up on him kissing another girl at school. And, she was like, 'I would never be with someone like him!' And now, she's his girlfriend."

"So, you feel like she betrayed you?"

"Well, yeah. Wouldn't you?"

"Yeah! I've been through something like that myself, but I didn't let it stress me. It was a lesson. It let me know that my partna wasn't loyal. Well …my situation was a lil' different because I was still with the girl when my partna started fuckin' her. But, I think it all boils down to what's most important. The lesson or how you feel.

"What's most important to you?" she asked.

"The lesson."

"No. I mean …like in relationships," Breanna clarified as she stared at Soulja.

Soulja stared at the sun as it continued to set while he spoke, "With me …the important thing is honesty and loyalty, and faith because if I can't trust a girl, I don't want to be her boyfriend. But, if she's tellin' me the truth, and she's being loyal and faithful, then I can trust her and our bond will never break as long as she remains trustworthy."

"Well, what about love. Love isn't important to you?" she asked with concern.

"Yeah, it's important. But even if I loved a girl …if I can't trust her, I don't need to be with her because all I'll be doin' is settin' myself up for her to betray me. Why should I go through that? Why should I wait for that?"

Breanna raised herself from her seat and paced to the railing on the balcony as she said, "You know what? I've never thought about relationships in that kind of detail."

Soulja walked to the railing on the balcony and stood beside her, then asked, "Why not?" enjoying the beautiful color of the sky as the sun positioned half past the horizon.

"I guess I just kind of feel relationships instead of thinking about them. But you feel relationships and think about them."

"What's wrong with that?"

"Nothing," she replied. "I like that. It makes a lot of things clear to me," she said, staring into Soulja's eyes as they leaned against the balcony.

Soulja slowly leaned his body toward her and kissed her slowly, deeply, and steadily for about a minute and a half. When they stopped kissing, they stared into one another's eyes.

"You've never let me kiss you before," Soulja noted.

"You've never tried. But I'm not having sex with you. I told you –

"You're saving your virginity for someone special," Soulja completed her sentence. "And I'm not your boyfriend, right?"

"Well, maybe you should be," Breanna suggested softly.

"Maybe you should let me be."

"Ok You're my boyfriend. But, I'm still not having sex with you. But you can still kiss me," Breanna smiled.

Breanna and Soulja began to kiss again. The sun had set and the darkness of night covered the sky.

Later, after midnight, Rachel sat on Legend's bed wearing a short skirt and blouse. Legend walked into the bedroom, stood in the doorway and stared at her.

"What's wrong?" Rachel asked.

"Nothing. I was just thinking about how good it feels to be around you," Legend answered.

"You mean how good it feels to be around me, or how good it feels to be in me," Rachel tempted with a smile.

"No," Legend said, walking toward her. "I'm talking about the way I feel when I look at your pretty face. The way you smile at me. The way you look at me," Legend paused in contemplation. "It makes me feel good."

"Well, you know what you can do to make me feel good, don't you," Rachel further tempted with a seductive voice.

"We can't. Your friend is on his way over to make the deal."

"Yes we can. Come here."

"No. We don't have time," Legend said as he stood directly in front of her.

"Come here," Rachel said softly, pulling Legend closer to her by tugging his shirt collar with a strong grip. "Just a quickie. It'll be fun, baby," she said as she began to kiss him on the left side of his neck with one hand in her purse.

Rachel stood to her feet, continuing to kiss Legend on the left side of his neck as she held a knife in her right hand that she retrieved from her purse. She held the knife close to her thigh as she listened to Legend's breathing became heavy, slowly raising the knife. Rachel noticed that Legend's eyes were closed. Suddenly, with one quick hard thrust, she stabbed Legend in his throat. She backed away from him, watching him bleed vigorously from his throat. Legend gagged just before hitting the floor. He stopped gagging as his corpse fell on the floor face down.

Someone began to knock at the apartment door. Rachel quickly paced to the door and looked through the peek-hole. Relieved at seeing Caesar, she opened the door and immediately turned to go back toward the bedroom. She couldn't wait to show Caesar her gift to him. She didn't see Soulja, who had stepped into the room after Caesar.

"I killed him baby!" she said after taking a few quick steps ahead him toward the bedroom. She turned to take in his expression at this revelation. "You don't have --," Rachel stopped mid-sentence as she turned around and saw Soulja standing in the room. "What is he doing here?" Rachel asked hotly. "Why is Soulja here?!"

"He was gonna help me carry the body," Caesar lied. "And, what do you mean, you killed him?! You were supposed to be gon' by now!"

Soulja frowned at the thought of Caesar telling Rachel he was there to help carry the body.

"Where is he?" Caesar asked.

"He's in the bedroom. He's dead," Rachel assured Caesar excitedly as she continued to walk toward the bedroom.

Caesar and Soulja followed Rachel. They all glanced around the room before focusing their attention on Legend's body lying on the floor.

"Yeah. He's dead," Soulja said after quickly examining Legend and the blood soaked carpet around his body. "Let's get out of here," he said urgently.

"What … What about the body? I thought you were going to carry the body out?" Rachel nervously questioned.

"Don't worry about that. I didn't want you involved in this like this, Rachel," Caesar stressed.

"Well …, now I'm already involved!"

"Ey. Y'all can settle this later at home. Let's get the hell out of here," Soulja calmly demanded. "We need to leave … now," he insisted as he turned, but not before he noticed Rachel and Caesar following his lead out of the apartment.

The next morning, Mike was back at Charles' house, sitting in the living room on an antique, wood trim sofa with fringed pillows. Charles sat on a similar styled chair in front of a marble top table setting on top of a very expensive porcelain rug. The sun, shining through the four, double-hung windows, gave light to the room.

"We have a problem," Charles said simply.

"What?" Mike asked.

"Our cocaine dealer was killed last night."

"Legend?"

"Yeah. He was running a test. He was supposed to make a deal for fifty kilos to see if he could wiggle into the business down here. He was gonna offer a front for one-hundred kilos, if this buyer could pay for fifty."

"You have any idea who did it?"

"No. But he kept talking about this girl. I didn't ask for any details about her, though. I just told him to be cautious. He was confident he had it under control."

"Find out what happened, Mike. In the meantime, I'll send for another dealer to take Legend's position here in Mississippi."

"Ok. The trade in Chicago went smooth. Everyone agreed to accommodate our needs for building property in their territory. Construction is being planned as we speak."

"Good. Because if that --,"

"Hey, Mike. You're back already?" Asia asked as she walked into the room.

"Yeah. I'm here to stay for a little while."

"Would you like something to drink?"

"Sure. I'll have a glass of orange juice."

"Ok. You want something, baby?" Asia asked Charles.

"Yeah, baby. Give me a shot of gin from the bar."

"I will not. I'll be right back with your juice, Mike," Asia smiled.

"Just be sure we're protected," Charles said to Mike after Asia walked away.

"Why do you have such a large bed?" Breanna asked, bouncing her butt on the edge of Soulja's bed.

"It's comfortable. Lay back on it," Soulja suggested, already lying on the bed himself.

Breanna lay down beside Soulja. "It is comfortable," she said, turning her head toward Soulja. "Do you really live here all alone?"

"Yeah," he answered, admiring her gorgeous face.

"How do you afford it?" Breanna's hazel brown eyes searched for Soulja's.

Soulja moved himself closer to Breanna, then he began to kiss her.

"Mmmm," Breanna muffled beneath the kiss. "Why do you keep ignoring that question?" she asked after breaking the kiss.

"I just think it's better if we don't talk about how I get my money." He touched her soft caramel skin. He loved her soft skin and lips. She was so beautiful. "I don't want to hurt her," he thought.

"Ok But, you know, eventually you're gonna have to tell me something."

"You gon' make me or something?"

"Yeah. I'll shoot you or something. My dad has these two colt .45 automatics. I'll just get one and shoot," Breanna joked. "Am I making you afraid?"

"I am not afraid of anything."

"Yeah, right. That's what all guys say, but really on the inside they're scared little bitches."

Soulja slowly rose himself from the bed and walked toward his closet.

"What, are you mad at me now? Did I hurt your little ego? You don't want to be around me now?" Breanna questioned hotly.

Soulja pulled an AK-47 from his closet and said, "I'm not mad at you. You know what this is?"

Breanna looked confused and slightly nervous. "It's a rifle," she said.

"It's an AK. Let me show you how to use it," he said approaching Breanna. Soulja stood beside Breanna, then cocked the rifle, saying, "Did you see that bullet go in the chamber?"

"Yeah."

"This is the trigger," Soulja said, putting Breanna's finger on the trigger. Soulja stood in front of Breanna and grabbed the barrel of the rifle, pressing it to his chest, then said, "Now all you have to do is pull the trigger."

Breanna stared at Soulja as her eyes began to water with tears. She threw the rifle on the bed and broke to her knees with tears running as she cried out. Soulja put his arms over her shoulder and asked, "Why are you crying?"

"Don't you ever do anything like that again! I could have killed you! You scared me, you …you …," Breanna exclaimed, then began to cry again.

Ok. Ok. I didn't mean to scare you. Come here," Soulja said, pulling Breanna to her feet. "Don't cry, baby," he said as he hugged her tightly. "Don't cry. I'm sorry," he comforted her.

Chapter 13

Caesar and Rachel dressed themselves in the bathroom. They both stood in front of the double-wide mirror checking their attire.

"You can't tell Rome that Soulja was wit' us last night."

"I won't tell, baby. I just want Rome to know that I'm true to da click. I want him to know that he doesn't have to wait for me to leave every time he wants to talk about something," Rachel explained.

"You can't tell 'em you killed Legend eitha," Caesar stressed. "He thinks I was gonna do it."

Rachel positioned herself close to Caesar and rubbed her hands across his chest as she said in a soft, comforting voice, "Baby, you were going to do it. Rome knows you'll kill fa da click. Now, he'll know I'll kill fa da click two."

In the living room of the house, Rome sat on the chair looking at Caesar and Rachel as they walked to the loveseat and took seats side by side.

"Rachel, you're looking sexy as always, but where are you going this morning dressed like that?" Rome asked as he examined the manner in which the dark red split seam dress clasped to her body.

"You like it? This is the dress Legend bought me at the mall yesterday. I'm wearing it so I can say I wanted him to see how it fits me today," Rachel rationalized.

"That's slick. I like the way you're thinking," Rome approved. "Let me talk to Caesar for a minute."

Caesar glanced at Rome and Rachel in alternate succession, then said, "Let'er stay."

"No. I need to talk to you about some details on something," Rome cautioned.

"I know, but Rachel, uhm …Rachel got all tha details you need."

Rome looked at Caesar in ponders trying to determine what Caesar meant. He focused in on Rachel's eyes and Rachel calmly peered at him in return. Caesar's discomfort was obvious by his perpetual blinking and his hesitation to speak.

"Before Caesar made it to Legend's apartment, I'd already handled everything," Rachel stated.

"I know you set everything up, but …"

"I didn't just set everything up," Rachel clarified. "I killed Legend too. I did it before Caesar got there. I stabbed him in his throat."

Realizing Rachel was serious, Rome responded, "Why the hell would you get involved in something like that! It's why you never know details!"

"Because I need to prove my loyalty! I needed to show you I'm not some little pretty girl that needs to be protected!" Rachel answered hotly.

"I never questioned your loyalty. But, you're right. Now, I don't have to."

The winter weather froze water on the ground in unidentified geometric crystallized shapes. The rustic surroundings of cars in the projects were covered with thick white frost. The bedlam of people chattering and kids playing didn't exist in the ambiance of the empty sidewalks and playgrounds. The heated comfort of Soulja's car protected Tia, Tate, and Amanda from the unrelenting frigidness of the weather as Soulja drove out of the projects.

Soulja drove into a junkyard owned by Caesar. He exited his car, leaving the engine ignited so the heater could continue to blow for the perpetual comfort of the occupants of his car. Soulja ran to the garage section of the junkyard. He knocked on a door to his left. Caesar and Rome sat in the office-type room behind the door. They were conversing, but stopped at the sound of the knock.

"Come in!" Caesar yelled.

Soulja walked inside the room slowly, asking, "Where da bodyguards? I don't see nobody out there."

"They next door. On the other side right there," Caesar answered, pointing to the opposite side of the room. "It's cold as a muthafucka out there, playa. They need ta be somewhere warm. They knew you was on yo' way. If it was anybody else comin' in da the junkyard …they woulda stopped 'em," Caesar assured with confidence.

"Street Soulja, I've been receiving impressive news about you," Rome said sincerely.

"I haven't heard anyone call me that since I was about thirteen years old," Soulja said.

"I'm used to calling you Street Soulja because that's what we all called you. You used to fight in the streets everyday out in the projects. Now you're putting dope on the streets."

Soulja stood, silently concentrating on the comments Rome made.

"What did you come fa is time?" Caesar asked.

"I want twenty," Soulja replied.

"Caesar …No. Soulja, listen. You wanna buy twenty ki's. I've known you since you were a kid," Rome emphasized. "I wanna do something for you. When you buy from Caesar from now on, he's gonna give you five ki's for every ten ki's you buy," Rome explained. "So, Caesar, when Street Soulja comes to get his twenty ki's, you give him ten extra."

Caesar stared at Rome intently. He couldn't imagine what would make Rome display the generosity just extended to Soulja.

"Alright," Caesar agreed. "I'll page you later, Soulja. I'll have that fa ya in a few hours."

"Ah'ight. Aye, good lookin' out, Rome," Soulja complimented. "I appreciate it."

Soulja commenced to exit the room.

"Hold up, Street Soulja," Rome said.

Soulja turned away from the door and faced Rome. "What's up?" he asked.

"I know you work for yourself and I respect that," Rome expressed. "Normally, the only people that come to my Playa's Ball are the people that work for me. But, I want you to come. I'm not trying to get you to work for me. But tell me what you think about working with me."

"Work with you," Soulja simply reiterated. "I don't have no problem wit' dat. But what you want me to do?"

"You'll do what you do now. Just ...You'll get better deals on your purchases. You'll be introduced to a few people when you go places with me. I just want you on my team," Rome explained.

"I'm down wit' it," Soulja responded.

"Good. The Playa's Ball is tonight at my club. Don't bring anyone with you."

"Ah'ight," Soulja agreed, then walked out of the door and ran to his car.

"Why you do dat, man?" Caesar asked with irritation permeating his every fiber.

"For all the reasons I said and then some," Rome answered.

Soulja pulled into the driveway of the brick house with red-wood trimming. The moderate size lawn wrapped around half of the front of the house to the backyard. The other half of the front of the house was the driveway and garage. Tia, Amanda, Tate and Soulja exited the car.

"Looks nice," Soulja said, following Tate and Amanda with Tia walking beside him.

"All of the houses in this neighborhood are pretty," Tia observed.

"Amanda used a key to open the front door of the house. They all entered the house with wondering eyes.

"What's that smell?" Tia asked.

"That's fresh paint," Tate answered, recognizing the cream colored walls.

They all stood in the unfinished family room examining the hardwood floors and eyebrow arched windows.

"Let's go see what our bedroom looks like, baby," Tate suggested to Amanda.

Amanda and Tate walked out of the family room, leaving Tia and Soulja alone.

"You're sure you wanna live here with them?" Soulja questioned Tia.

"No. They just got married. They're gonna be fucking like crazy because they're supposed to be like on a honeymoon, but they're just in a new house. I know I don't want to stay in the projects by myself, so I'll just stay here until I can find my own, one bedroom house or apartment," Tia explained.

"You remember I told you I bought my mom a house a couple of weeks ago, right."

"Yeah. I remember."

"The apartment she was livin' in vacant."

"Oh. Ok Now, I wouldn't mind living in those apartments. Those are some very nice apartments."

"Well, yeah. See, I was paying my mom's rent by the year. So, it's still somethin' like nine months' rent paid on it already. You can live in dat apartment. All you gotta do is stay there until the rent need to be paid again and like I said, that won't be for about nine mo' months."

"Tisss," Tia sighed.

"What?" Soulja asked.

"You serious?!" Tia asked in disbelief.

"Yeah, I'm serious. What? You don't wanna live there or somethin'?"

"Oh. No. I mean, yeah. Yeah, I wanna live there," Tia voiced with cheer. "You've never done anything like this for me …Amanda either. I thought you might be joking."

"Nall, man. You need somewhere to stay. Nobody livin' there. What's the use of havin' money if you don't help tha people you care about."

"This'll help me save a lot of money," Tia expressed with a huge smile. "Thank you," she said, embracing Soulja.

"It ain't nothing'. The furniture still there though. We don't know what to do with it. You can keep the furniture that's there fa yourself or you know, whatever," Soulja informed Tia.

Becky drove into the driveway of a green painted wood house. The small house was in poor condition. As she sat in her red two-door sports vehicle, a young man exited the house wearing a puffy yellow coat and navy blue pants. He jogged to the car and opened the door.

"What's the word, boo?" Becky asked the young man as he sat in the car closing the door.

"You know I love you," the young man said as he leaned over to Becky, then covered her smile with a kiss. "Did you bring it?" he asked.

"Yeah, I got it. What you gon' give me for it?" Becky asked playfully.

"You got me. That ain't enough?"

"Nall, nigga. You need to give me something else."

"I'ma pay. Where da package at, though."

Becky looked down at the crotch of her pants and rubbed one hand over it, then smiled, asking, "you gon' put cho hand down there ta get it?"

The young man reached over to Becky and unbuttoned her brown wool zipper front pants. He slid his hand into her pants and retrieved a clear plastic sack containing four irregular shape blocks of crack cocaine.

"This don't look like four ounces," the young man said.

"Oh, its four ounces," Becky assured. "I gotta go. Give me my money."

"Damn, Becky! You act like I ain't gon' pay you or somethin'," the young man said angrily.

"Nigga, don't you be getting mad at me about my own money. I just told you ta give me my money so I can go. Now, come on," Becky stressed.

"Man, fuck that! This mine," the young man said as he stepped out of the car.

"Becky reached under her seat and pulled up the nine millimeter pistol. She stepped out of her car with it by her side.

"Nigga, you need to pay me right now!" Becky screamed.

Two more men suddenly exited the house, pointing revolvers at Becky as one yelled, "Bitch, get cho ass back in dat car and get the fuck away from here."

Becky quickly entered her car and reversed out of the driveway. She drove at high speed looking for the nearest pay phone. She drove her car onto the lot of a convenience store. Becky used the pay phone to call Soulja. No one answered, so she got back in her car and drove to the projects.

As she drove into the complex, Soulja was driving out. Becky honked her horn and flagged her hand at Soulja. They both stopped and rolled their windows down.

"Man, this nigga just robbed me," Becky told Soulja.

"Who?" Soulja asked. "Hold up. Park right there," he asserted, pointing to a parking space on her right.

Soulja parked backwards beside her. He got out of his car and got into Becky's.

"Who robbed you?" Soulja asked again.

"My boyfriend."

"What?" Soulja asked with minimal confusion.

"Well, he really just took my dope. He was supposed to pay me for it, but when I gave it to him, he got all mad when I asked fa my money and he just got out tha car talkin' 'bout the dope is his. Then, when I pulled out my bitch, his two lil' friends came outside pointin' they guns at me and shit," Becky explained as her anger increased.

Soulja focused on Becky's face. The frown on her face depicted the anger she felt.

"You remember when you first talked to me about sellin' dope?" Soulja asked calmly.

Noticing the affirmative nod of Becky's head, he continued, "I didn't wanna front you no dope because I know I would make you pay me if you felt like you didn't have to because we potnas. Now, you gotta make this nigga pay."

"How, though?"

"Where da nigga at?"

"He at home."

"Is his mama there?"

"Nall. His mama don't live wit' him. It's just him and his partnas in there."

"Oh, we gon' make 'em pay fa real then. I'll be right back," Soulja said as he stepped out of Becky's car.

Soulja went to the trunk of his vehicle and grabbed an AK-47 and an extra clip. He walked back to Becky's car and entered again, laying the rifle upright between the door and passenger's seat. He held the extra clip in his hand as he removed his nine millimeter from the clasp of his belt and pants.

"You use my gun and your gun. I'll use the AK. Let's go," Soulja said.

Becky backed out of the parking space without hesitation. She drove back to the little green house.

"That's the house right there," Becky said, looking at the little green house.

"Beep yo' horn," Soulja directed.

Becky honked her horn a few times. Suddenly, the young man that took her dope peeked out of the square windows of the house.

"That was him! That was him at the window!" Becky acknowledged excitedly.

"Get out," Soulja instructed as he stepped out of Becky's car stuffing the extra clip into the sleeve of his jacket and grabbing the AK with the other hand.

Soulja aimed at the door knob of the front door, then he began to unload the AK-47. His first shot blew away the little house's door knob. Soulja gradually stepped closer to the house as he continuously shot the rifle, changing his aim from the door to the square windows, and from the square windows to the side of the house. As the bullets from the AK shattered the glass windows and destroyed the television, picture frames, and refrigerator in the house, Becky unloaded the two nine millimeters in her hands on the opposite side of the house. She shot through the windows on the left side of the house while Soulja paced his way to the front of the house again, aiming directly at the door until he completely unloaded the AK-47. While exchanging the empty clip in the rifle for a full clip, Soulja walked backward to Becky's car. His eyes searched for Becky and canvassed for any surface of the occupants of the house. The young man that took Becky's dope and his two minions laid flat on the floor in a bedroom in the rear of the house. They were afraid and fearfully locked their hands around their heads. The shooting suddenly stopped, but the young men remained on the floor. Soulja and Becky entered her car. Soulja rolled down the passenger's side window and pointed the AK-47 out of the window as Becky backed her car out of the driveway. Before she had completely backed out of the driveway, Soulja began to shoot at the house again. He continued to fire the rifle at the little green house until Becky drove away.

Becky passed Soulja his pistol while simultaneously looking through her rear-view mirror. She felt paranoid and still maladapted to the extremities of Soulja's action. Soulja stuffed his pistol into his pants.

"Becky, I'ma have somethin' fa ya tomorrow, ah'ight," Soulja announced. "Them niggas that took yo' dope might be dead now. But if they ain't, they ain't gon' wanna see you no mo'. Don't ever let nobody get away wit' anything. They always got to pay. Them niggas just paid the price fa fuckin' wit' you. But, you have to realize that you just did something. And …sometimes …you come across niggas that feel like you gotta pay for something you did. So …they come back to make you pay. That's why I hope them niggas dead. So, they can't come back for you. But, if you see them niggas again you need to be ready to kill. These niggas out here in da projects always screaming, 'Ride or die.' But …the way I see it …when you wit' me …its die or kill. You need ta be ready. Watch who you fuck wit'. I gotta go. I'ma holla," Soulja communed.

At least two-hundred people danced to the music in the club. The colossal floor space in the club provided room for the tables and chairs close to the bar, all occupied by spectators of the dance floor. The party lights flashed the spectrum of colors at various angles. Soulja sat alone at a small circular table. He sipped from a glass of liquor as he eyeballed the carousal. Rose noticed Soulja sitting alone and immediately began to scrutinize his presence from a seat five tables away. She raised herself from her seat and began to walk to Soulja's table. The teal color sleeveless dress with zipper detail snugged the small frame of her body as she stood next to Soulja.

"You look to young to be in here," Rose stated.

Soulja peered up at her from his seat then took another sip of his liquor as he shifted his focus back to the dance floor. "What are you doing in here?" Rose asked Soulja.

The music was loud, but the volume didn't prevent Soulja from hearing Rose. He just wasn't concerned with her question, so he didn't answer.

Rose became annoyed with Soulja ignoring her. She angrily grabbed his arm.

"You come with me!" she demanded.

Soulja snatched his arm from her grip and said, "Don't touch me! You need to leave me alone!" he said as he stared furiously into her eyes.

Rose couldn't believe what was happening. She could actually feel the rage inside Soulja's calm presence. His eyes seemed to burn clear through her. Rose stood in shock and admiration of Soulja's defense mode.

"Rose," Rome said, suddenly standing beside her. "It's good to see you," he commented as she turned to face him. Rome embraced her then put one arm around her shoulder as he led her away from Soulja saying, "Rachel's been asking about you all night. She said she hasn't been able to contact you all day." He said as he led her to a table where Rachel was seated.

"What's up Rose?" Rachel greeted zestfully.

"Oh, I'm alright, baby," Rose replied. "You been lookin' fa me, girl?" Rose asked as Rome departed their company.

"Yeah. I ain't been able to get in touch wit' you or Pam all day.'

"Girl, you know I gotta be flamboyant fa da Playa's Ball!" Rose said excitedly. "I took Pam wit' me ta help me find somethin' ta wear tonight."

"You workin' that dress too, girl. Pam ain't gone never come to a Playa's Ball is she?"

"You know dat girl lame to da game, baby. She ain't never gon' come because she thank somethin' gon' happen. Like somebody gon' shoot at us in here," Rose explained.

"Shit. Ain't nobody gon' do no crazy ass shit like that in here. We all on da same team. She need ta get in da game and live life. Stop bein' so scary.

"Pam ain't gon' do nothin'," Rose said, looking across the club at Soulja and Rome engrossed in conversation. "Who is that brother over there talkin' ta Rome?"

Rachel looked briefly at Soulja and Rome, then said, "That's Soulja right there."

"Where he from?"

"He from the project Caesar used ta live in. He grew up with Caesar."

"Well, he thank he a bad muthafucka or somethin'?"

"Girl! Why you say that? What he do?" Rachel asked enthusiastically.

"Oh, he ain't do nothin'. It's just da way he was acting. Like he some killa muthafucka or somethin'," Rose said with hostility.

"Oh, a lot of people say he dangerous now. You know, they say he knocked off some people and shit."

"Who said that?"

"You know how niggas be running they mouth."

"Caesar grew up wit' 'em. You ain't never asked Caesar?"

"Girl, nall! You know I don't be studin' that shit."

"I wanna know if it's true girl. Go ask Caesar."

"What?!"

"Go ask 'em. You know he'll tell you," Rose convinced Rachel. "Go on. I ain't goin' nowhere."

"Ah'ight. I'll be back."

Rachel walked to the bar where Caesar sat facing the dance floor. Rome and Soulja were still talking at the small table.

"It's like this. What you got from Caesar earlier today will always be available even if you change your mind about being in my click. But if you know you don't wanna be a part of my click you need to let me know now. Because …after tonight …you'll be an official member and you

don't get out easy. You get out …complicated,"
Rome explained.

"Yeah. I get it. I know what you talkin'
about. But I told you at the junkyard that I'm in."

"I just wanna be sure," Rome noted.
"Come with me. I want you to meet some
people."

Soulja followed Rome through the club,
toward the rear of the building. Caesar watched
them as he sat on the stool at the bar. Rachel stood
between his legs with her arms hanging around
his neck

"So, you gon' tell me or not?" Rachel
asked sweetly, gazing into Caesar's eyes.

"Why you so interested in Soulja all of a
sudden?" Caesar asked suspiciously, shifting his
attention to Rachel's gaze.

"Now, I just told you that he know
somethin' about me. Now I wanna know
somethin' about him," Rachel stated saucily.

"You didn't ask me about 'em then. You
didn't ask me about 'em at first, so, why you
askin' now?"

"I just thought about it now. Now, you
gon' tell me or not baby because I thought you
was on my side. If it make me feel good to know
somethin' about him you should be willin' to tell
me, Rachel spoke convincingly.

Caesar observed the seriousness of Rachel's expression, then informed, "He shot a lot people. Beat up a lot of people."

"He ever killed anybody?"

"Yeah. He knocked off a few people,' Caesar replied simply.

"How many?"

"I'm not sure. We ain't gon' get into dat."

"Well, who then? Who was the people?"

"We ain't gon' get into dat eitha. Come on. We gotta go," Caesar said.

Chapter 14

Caesar and Rachel walked to the rear of the club together. They entered a door labeled 'Staff Only," then walked to the left of the room down a long hallway. Once they reached the end of the hallway, they turned right and walked to the door at the end. The door was being guarded by two medium sized men holding AK-47s. The bodyguards stepped aside, allowing Caesar and Rachel to open the door. On the other side of the door was a staircase, which turned to the left half way up. Two more bodyguards stood at the door on the immediate right side of the top of the staircase. They stepped aside and allowed Caesar and Rachel to enter the room beyond the door, pointing their AKs upward as one closed the door behind Caesar and Rachel.

Nineteen people occupied the room before Caesar and Rachel entered. Tables and chairs were set in the room like a small diner. Soulja sat alone at an octagonal shaped table. Caesar and Rachel walked to the table and accompanied him.

"You ready fa this?" Caesar asked Soulja as he took a seat opposite Caesar.

"I'm ready fa anything. You know me," Soulja responded.

Rachel peered at Soulja with new curiosity in her eyes and said, "What you do to Rose earlier?"

"Who is Rose? That woman that tried to snatch me out of my seat?" Soulja asked.

Suddenly, Rome raised from his seat at a table in the center of the room and announced, "Everyone is here, so we can start this thing." Searching the faces of several woman and men in the room, he said, "First, I wanna introduce someone some of you know personally and some of you have only heard of. Street Soulja! Stand up for a minute, man." As Soulja raised from his seat, looking at familiar and unfamiliar faces, Rome said, "This is Street Soulja!"

Some of the men and women in the room chattered saying, "We know Soulja. He cool. He real."

Rome acknowledge Soulja further saying, "Anyone and everyone that works in your territory needs to know that if they fuck with Soulja, they fuckin' with the click."

"Ain't nobody gon' fuck wit' that killa! That nigga don't get it!" a man in the room loudly commented with playfulness.

"That's good," Rome verbalized. "Because if they get Soulja's trouble, they get the click's trouble too, because Soulja is a part of the click now."

Rose sat at a table close to the corner of the room. She peered at Soulja as the comments were being made about him. Soulja sat down again as Rome continued to talk. He tranquilly evaluated the people in the room.

As months passed by, the days of winter had faded into the hot temperatures of summer's oppressive heat. In the past months, Rome had engulfed Soulja intensely into the routes of his daily life. They visited associates of Rome's, attended parties together, and now finally, Soulja was about to convene with one of Rome's largest buyers.

Rome drove a four-door white luxury sports coupe down the dark highway with Soulja on the passenger's side. It was Soulja's first time traveling to another state with Rome. The mild paced rhythm of the blues playing at minimum volume seemed to provide an atmosphere of explicit serenity.

"You ever thought about buying yourself a car like this?" Rome asked.

"I like the car I have," Soulja answered.

"Your car is tight. But you've had that car for a long time. You haven't even changed the color. Then, you know, when you have a car like yours …you know with the flashy rim and paint job and system and all, the police think you a dope boy off the muscle," Rome explained.

"Yeah. But you see …they just think I'm working a few ounces or something. Then …like you said …I been having the same ride for a long time so when the police see my car they probably think I ain't doing nothin'. They probably say, 'All he ain't doing nothin'. I been seein' that same car for a long time. If he was makin' some money he would be drivin' a new car.' They might just think I got a job and keep getting' my paint job renewed on my car. But I know if they see me switching cars they gon' probably wanna know what tha fuck I'm doin'."

"That's a good point. I've never really looked at it that way," Rome admitted. "So, you'll be graduating from high school next summer?" Rome asked.

"Yeah."

"Congratulations."

"Yeah. I appreciate it."

"Listen. When we get to Chicago I want you to just be yourself. I usually have to tell people how to act, but you're always yourself and I like that. So, just be you."

Soulja nodded his head in acknowledgement. Rome turned on an exit from the highway. He drove around the streets of Chicago, by-passing prostitutes, corners crowded with all kinds of people. Homeless people crouched down leaning against walls of convenience stores.

Rome suddenly drove onto a lot of a huge warehouse building. He parked backwards on the left side of the building, next to a flank of sports utility vehicles and other sport coupes.

Rome and Soulja walked into the building, grateful to be relieved from the harsh winds of Chicago by the comforting warmth of the inside of the building. Rome's attention was drawn to a thin looking man standing in the distance waving one hand in the air with an inviting gesture.

"Walk beside me," Rome said to Soulja. "It means you get the same respect I do."

They walked to the thin looking man, whose arm carried the strap of the machine gun which his hand gripped. Rome and Soulja both looked to their right, seeing a light-tan skinned man sitting at a rectangular wood table alone. The man's curly hair shone by the light above his head.

"What's goin' on, Slim?" Rome asked the thin, brown complexion man holding the machine gun. "This is Street Soulja," he introduced, pointing at Soulja with one finger as he kept walking to the table occupied by the man with curly hair. "Abdul. It's been a while, baby. You losing clout or something?"

"Everything is going well with us," Abdul answered.

"This is Street Soulja," Rome introduced looking at Soulja momentarily before shifting his focus again on Abdul. "What happened Abdul? You haven't been in contact with me in a while."

"That's why I asked you to pay me a visit. We have things to discuss that are best done in person," Abdul expressed as he noticed Slim approach the area from behind Rome and Soulja.

"Did you lock all the bolts on the door and activate the security system?" Abdul asked Slim.

"It's all good. The place is on lock, bra," Slim answered.

"Why don't everyone sit down," Abdul suggested.

Three of the seven available seats became occupied by Rome, Soulja, and Slim.

"This is the business," Abdul said, leaning his elbows on the table. "Just straight up. Somebody gave me a better purchase deal, Rome. I get a hundred ki's for the price I paid you for seventy-five.

"You could've negotiated with me. I could've done that for you. We've done business together for a long time. You know I can handle a deal like that."

"Oh, I know. But see that's not the total deal. I buy a hundred ki's, I get a hundred on front. Then I get to use this place for meetings and stuff as long as I protect the property.

"Ok Who is he? Who's making you these deals?" Rome asked with curiosity.

"Oh, don't worry about who he is. It's like this, I've been loyal to our purchase deal for a long time. I'm still loyal. Now I wanna make an offer to you. This cat that I deal with now has millions, man. I believe we can shut 'em down. But I need to know if you willing to roll with it."

"What do you wanna do?"

"I'm telling you. I wanna take this dude for everything he got. Dope. Money. Whatever."

"Ok. What you talking about doing?"

"He comes through sometimes to check on the warehouse."

"This is his building?" Rome questioned.

"Yeah. He does international shipments. But see, all we gotta do is kidnap this nigga when he comes to check on the place. This joe ain't ready to die for any of this shit. We make this nigga give us a few million and all the cocaine he has. I know this nigga gotta be sitting on a thousand ki's or better, man. The way this nigga throw deals at me," Abdul reflected on his last sentence. "If we pull this off, we can spread the hustle a little further than we already do," Abdul said.

"That's a good plan. But how will I know when you gonna do it and how will I know that you ain't trying to play me?" Rome asked with suspicion.

"I wouldn't try to play you like that. All you gotta do is get one or two of your people to come when I call. If you and your people pull the job off with some of my people, nobody loses, nobody is blind, and nobody gets played."

"Sounds good. I just gotta choose someone when I get back."

"I'll do it," Soulja burst out quickly.

Rome peered at Soulja in consideration of his prompt volunteer of himself for the job. "You wanna be in on this?" he asked Soulja.

"Yeah. Just let me do it."

"Ok when you contact me …this will be the man that comes to assist.

On their way back to Mississippi, Rome and Soulja listened to hip-hop. The fast paced rhythm thumped from the speakers. Soulja drove cautiously, glancing at the bright summer sky as they entered Mississippi.

"Man, I could've lived in that hotel room, man! That muthafucka look like a house on the inside!" Soulja yelled over the music.

Rome reduced the volume on the car stereo and said, "You'll have more chances to spend nights or days or whatever in hotels just like the one we were in last night, Street Soulja," Rome intensively contemplated as he said, "I know Abdul said it'll probably be six months to a year until he calls about the job, but I want you to know something."

"What?"

"Abdul thinks he can repay me by making this deal with me, but he can't. I don't need to kidnap anyone. I went along with this for one reason, I want that punk muthafucka dead. So, whenever Abdul calls for you ...the first chance you get you blast 'em. You know, after the job is done. You can keep whatever it is you get from the job. I don't want it."

"I can handle it," Soulja stated simply.

After arriving at Rome's house, Soulja walked to his glossy green vehicle parked in Rome's driveway, then suddenly stopped as he stared as his pager.

"Rome," Soulja said, stopping Rome in his steps to the front door of his home. "Can I use your phone?"

Rome turned to Soulja and asked, "Where is your cell phone?"

"I left it at home. I knew it wouldn't work in Chicago."

Rome pulled out a pair of car keys as he paced toward Soulja then said, "I keep a charged cell in this car," referring to another sports coupe parked in front of Soulja's car. "You can use the phone in there," he said as he opened the driver's side door on the sports coupe. "Just close the door when you're done. I'm going in the house. I'll see you tomorrow probably."

"Ah'ight. I appreciate it," Soulja said gratefully as he dialed numbers on the cellular phone in the car.

"Hello," Breanna answered.

"What's up, baby? You missed me?" Soulja asked flirtatiously.

"You know I do. I've been trying to get in touch with you."

"Well, you in touch wit' me now. You gon' meet me at my apartment? We can do a little more in-touching, you know."

Breanna giggled girlishly, then said, "Boy, you crazy. Where are you? How long will it take you to get home?

"By the time you get there, I'll already be there."

"Ok I'm about to walk of the house now then."

"Ah'ight. I'm on my way."

Soulja disconnected with Breanna and got out of Rome's car, then entered his own. He drove directly to his apartment. Arriving to his apartment before Breanna pleased him because he wanted to brush his teeth before she got there.

After brushing his teeth, Soulja went to the kitchen to get a glass of cold water. As he poured the water into a glass, there was a knock at the door. He knew it was Breanna. He took a swallow of the cold water as he walked to the door. As a precautious thought, Soulja still peeked through the peek-hole before opening the door.

"Hi," Breanna said cheerfully as Soulja held the door open for her to walk in.

Soulja put his glass down on one of the shelves in the entertainment center, closed the door, and walked close to Breanna. He hugged her tightly, but gently, then kissed her as he rubbed on her back and caressed her butt through her loose fitting pants.

"Stop!" Breanna said aggressively. Don't do that. Why are you trying to have sex with me every time I come over here?" she asked caustically. "I told you when we got together that I wasn't going to break my virginity until I was ready, so stop trying so much. This isn't why I came over here. I'm going back home," Breanna asserted as she commenced to walk toward the door, but Soulja grabbed her hand to stop her.

"Wait a minute. I wasn't trying to have sex with you," Soulja explained. "Yeah. I wanna have sex with you," Soulja admitted, staring into her hazel brown eyes, then scanning her body from the size thirty-six breasts that bulged against her tight shirt to her sandal dressed feet and to her eyes again. "But I was just kissing you and touching you. If that makes you feel uncomfortable or if that's too much for you, just tell me. You don't have to throw your virginity in my face like that because I told you I respect that."

Breanna sighed softly and said, "It's not too much for me. I like the way you kiss me and …the way you touch me. It makes me feel good. It feels very good and it makes me think about sex, but I know I'm not ready for sex," Breanna explained. "So, I guess I just feel pressured, but I don't want you to stop. I'm sorry. I apologize, baby," Breanna said as she stepped closer to Soulja. "I just have to learn how to deal with my tension," she stated just before she started kissing Soulja.

Soulja kissed her back, but he didn't put his hands on her. He was disappointed with her accusations against him. Someone knocked on his door, so they stopped kissing.

"Who is that?" Breanna asked.

"Probably my partner. I don't know why she didn't call me," Soulja said as he walked to the door.

"She?" Breanna stated with suspicion.

Soulja looked through his peek-hole and said, "Yeah, that's her," before opening the door. "What's up, Tia?" Soulja asked as he stood in the door in front of her.

Breanna jumped at the sound of the name Tia. She looked over Soulja's shoulder from where she stood. "What?!" Breanna quietly but surprisingly said.

"You must have company or something?" Tia asked, peeking over Soulja's shoulder at Breanna. "Breanna?! Breanna is that you?!" Tia asked, pushing pass Soulja. "Girl, what are you doing here?!" Tia asked excitedly.

"You know her?" Soulja asked Tia as he closed the door alternatively looking at her and Breanna.

"This is my cousin! I haven't seen her in years!" Tia announced.

"Yeah! It has been a long time!" Breanna agreed, still in surprise.

"Uncle Mike is downstairs!" Tia informed Breanna.

"You can't let him come up here! You have to go stop him!" Breanna warned.

"Well, why?" Tia asked in obvious confusion.

"You just can't!"

"Well, he's already on his way up. That's why I came by."

Mike began to knock on Soulja's door.

"That's Mike. He told me that you wanted me to show him where your apartment was."

"He's gonna tell my dad," Breanna pouted.

Soulja walked to the door, looked through the peek-hole, and opened the door for Mike to walk in. Upon entering the apartment, Mike froze still in place at the sight of Breanna standing in Soulja's apartment. His facial expression was blank. Soulja closed the door, wondering what Mike would think about Breanna being in his apartment.

"Breanna? What are you doing here?" Mike asked.

"Please, don't tell my dad," Breanna pleaded.

"Well, I don't have to tell him as long as you introduce Soulja to him. Obviously, you're dating him."

"Soulja?" Breanna stated.

"Yeah. Is Soulja your boyfriend?" Tia asked.

"He's my boyfriend, but I didn't know people called him Soulja," Breanna admitted.

"Well, what do you call him?" Tia asked.

"By his name. Geronimo," Breanna answered.

"No one calls him Geronimo," Tia informed Breanna.

"So, why don't we all just sit down and chit-chat for a while?" Mike suggested.

Chapter 15

Rome, Caesar, and Rachel sat at one of the beach tables surrounding the pool behind the house. Rachel wore a two-piece burgundy bikini and shades. She cuddled to Caesar's bare chest as Rome, fully clothed, sat across from them. They were discussing the trip he and Soulja took to Chicago. Rome was communicating the events that had transpired during the trip.

"So, Soulja gon' knock Abdul off after everything is finished. After that --," Caesar said.

"Wait," Rome said, interrupting Caesar's sentence. "When Soulja handles Abdul there's only one play to the plot that completes all," he stated sneakily. "You see, after Soulja kills Abdul everybody is gonna be looking at our click. Abdul's people will blame us for Abdul's death. So, we knock Soulja off and say we did it to show that no-one goes against the click. We say that Soulja went rebel and killed Abdul on his own. So, we handled Soulja because he went against what we wanted. Then we'll have Abdul's territory back for ourselves," Rome explained. "The only question is which one of you is going to handle Soulja?"

"Rachel looked at Caesar's unwilling facial expression, then said, "I'll do it. I can handle Soulja."

"I thought about you myself," Rome said. "I know Caesar is …or at least was close to Soulja at one time. So, it would probably be hard for him to do."

"Baby, you don't have a problem with me handling Soulja do you?" Rachel asked.

"Soulja doesn't know you very well. He's not gonna trust you easy," Caesar warned.

"Rome said this might not go down until six months to a year from now. I have time to make him trust me," Rachel stated confidently.

"I'm just saying … Soulja ain't like everybody else. I've known him since we were kids and I still don't know how he responds to certain things," Caesar emphasized.

"Don't fa'get, now. Yo baby got smooth game," Rachel breathed. "Then he young. I'll infatuate him."

"You can help Rachel learn what she needs to do. The thing is whether you can deal with it. Do you have a problem with it?" Rome asked.

"Tis," Caesar sighed. "Don't trip on me. I ain't got no problem wit' it."

"Well, you can start telling Rachel what she'll need to do in order to slide under Soulja. I gotta go. See y'all later," Rome said as he raised from his seat, then walked toward the rear entrance of the house to leave.

"Baby, what's up?" Rachel asked. "I know when somethin' botherin' you."

"I'm ah'ight. I just want you to know that you need to be at the top of yo' game fuckin' wit' Soulja.

"I will, baby. I can handle him." Rachel assured Caesar. "Tell me what I need to do first."

"You need to get Soulja to trust you enough to come see you when you call."

Breanna drove her car into her driveway, followed by Mike and Tia in Mike's car, and Soulja in his own car. Breanna got out of her car and waited for everyone else to exit their car. As Mike and Tia walked past her, she said to Mike, "I hope you're right about my dad liking Geronimo since you already know him." After Breanna spoke, Mike and Tia continued to walk to the front door while Breanna waited on Soulja.

"Are you nervous?" Breanna asked Soulja.

"No. Should I be?" he asked.

"Just try to ignore him if he starts to act crazy," Breanna suggested as they began to walk to the front door.

Breanna opened the front door of her home and allowed Mike, Tia, and Soulja to walk inside. Soulja had been there a few times without Breanna's father knowing. When they walked through the entrance of the home, they immediately saw the medium size Charles sitting on a chair in the living room.

"Uncle Charles!" Tia burst aloud, walking quickly toward him with her arms open in invitation of a hug.

Charles stood from his seat and hugged Tia saying "What are you doing here? Where did you come from?"

"Well I was with Mike and --," Tia commenced to explain, but was interrupted by Charles when he noticed Soulja standing in his living room.

"Who is this boy?" Charles asked.

"He came with me and Breanna," Mike stated.

"What did he come with Breanna for?"

"Dad, this is Soulja, I mean, Geronimo," Breanna clumsily spoke.

"Soulja?!" Charles repeated sarcastically.

"His name is Geronimo, Dad. Some people just call him Soulja. He's my boyfriend," Breanna clarified.

"They met at martial arts class. Clarence made her his sparring partner," Mike offered.

"Well, you all have a seat," Charles said. "Oh, not you Mike. If you don't mind, I need to talk to you for a moment. Let's go to the kitchen."

Charles and Mike walked to the kitchen. Breanna and Soulja set side by side on the sofa.

"I think he likes you," Breanna said excitedly.

"We just got here," Soulja responded.

"Yeah, but he usually tells my boyfriends to get the hell out of his house."

Charles leaned against the island in the kitchen as he said, "Tell me that's not the same boy you're chiseling to take your job."

"He is the perfect match for her. He'll respect her, he'll be loyal to her, and he'll protect her at any cost. I've been spending a lot of time with him over the past couple of years. He's the one for her," Mike assured Charles.

"What the hell is wrong with you?!" Charles chided. "You think I want my daughter with someone that's gonna have your job in a few years!"

"What the hell is wrong with you?!" Mike scolded. "You don't think someone with my job is good enough for your daughter?"

Charles briefly contemplated, then said, "I see what this is about. You did this on purpose.

230

You made sure that the same person you chose to mold for your job was the same person you chose for Breanna's companionship."

"You never thought I was able to protect the woman in my life from my job. So, you made it your duty to run off almost every woman I ever met until you finally married one. So, yeah. This was my duty. Now you'll see that people that do the kind of work I do can have a life with someone they love. Now Breanna loves Soulja and there's nothing you can do to break them up."

You're wrong. I'll find a way. I can go in there right now and tell Breanna about this whole set up," Charles remarked angrily.

"No. You can't," Mike calmly noted. "Because if you do, she'll hate you, she'll hate me ...she'll hate Tia and Amanda too for going along with this. But she won't hate Soulja because he doesn't know."

"Tia and Amanda only had small parts in this. All they had to do is live in the projects for a little while and find some normal, appreciative companions for themselves and Breanna and make sure they didn't run into Breanna."

"Breanna won't be very understanding of over two years of secrets."

"I'll find a way," Charles said, then walked back to the living room.

Mike followed Charles shortly. He sat on the couch with Tia. Charles sat in the chair again.

"So, Soulja. What do you intend to do for my daughter?" Charles asked.

"I don't understand what you mean?" Soulja said.

"Well, it a simple question. What do you intend to do for my daughter?"

Breanna gazed at the side of Soulja's face and placed her hand over his.

"What does she want? What does she need?"

"You asking me? You should already know. What kind of boyfriend are you?" Charles asked mockingly.

"Dad, please," Breanna whined. "Don't do this to me. Geronimo is good to me."

"I'm just asking a few questions. How long have you been his girlfriend?"

"Over a year," Breanna softly replied.

"Over a year. Why haven't you told me about him, Breanna?" Charles asked hotly.

"Because I knew you would act like this," Breanna continued to whine.

"Do you love my daughter, Soulja?"

"I love him!" Breanna yelled.

Charles momentarily stared at his daughter. Her outburst took him by surprise. She had never raised her voice at him that way. He knew that breaking her up with Soulja would be hard. He could see the sincerity of Breanna's love for Soulja all over her face and in the way her voice begged to protect him.

"I'm talking to Soulja," Charles finally said. "Do you love my daughter, Soulja?"

Soulja glanced at Breanna, then back at Charles, then answered, "Yes."

"You love my daughter?"

"Yes."

Tia's face revealed awe and amazement of Soulja's admittance of loving Breanna.

"Ok Dad, that's enough," Breanna said with irritation. "Can we talk about something else? We haven't seen Tia in a long time. Why can't we just talk to Tia?"

"Alright, baby. We can change the subject," Charles agreed. "For now," he said. Slowly shifting his focus to Tia, he asked, "So, how have you been Tia? How did all of you come together like this?"

"Oh, well. I live in the same apartment complex that Soulja lives in. There's a pool there and I was on my way to the pool when I saw Mike driving by. At first, I thought my eyes were going bad, then I just yelled and Mike stopped. When I walked up to the car, we started talking and he told me he was trying to find Soulja's apartment.

So, I took him to the apartment and Breanna was there with Soulja. It was all like magic," Tia explained.

Soulja frowned at the inconsistency of Tia's explanation. Suddenly, Asia opened the front door and walked into the living room.

"Well, I see we have company. Hello everyone," Asia greeted.

Chatters of hello responded to her salutation.

"Charles, I have groceries in the trunk. Why don't you go get them?" Asia suggested.

"Soulja and I will get them," Mike volunteered.

"Well, who is Soulja?" Asia asked.

"Breanna's boyfriend for over a year," Charles stated mockingly as Soulja raised from the sofa.

Seeing Soulja stand from the sofa, Breanna remained seated and, Asia said, "Well, she probably was too scared to tell you. You're too protective of Breanna. The girl is almost grown," then walked closer to Soulja. "Hi, baby," she said, extending a hand to shake Soulja's hand. "Don't you worry about Charles. He's just an overprotective father."

"Come on, Soulja. Let's go get the groceries from the trunk," Mike said, leading

Soulja out of the house to the trunk of a small sports car.

"What the hell is wrong with Breanna's dad? He acts like I'm some sort of dummy," Soulja voiced.

"Don't worry about Charles. Like Asia said …Charles is very overprotective of Breanna."

"I don't think we're gonna get along very well," Soulja commented as he grabbed two bags from the trunk.

Chapter 16

The arid cool days of winter were less severe than the preceding year. No frost covered the windows of homes, apartments, and cars. No shapes lacking geometric identification have been formed on the ground by frozen water. The clear sky promised cold weather, but less than frigid temperatures. Soulja sat on a couch in the family room of a moderate sized house nicely spaced from the other similar houses in the neighborhood. The land guaranteed beautiful green grass in the on-coming summer season. Soulja stared out of the glass sliding double-doors on his left that led to the back yard of the house. Rachel sat cross-legged on the lime colored carpet wearing only a large and lengthy yellow T-shirt in front of Soulja. She reached for a remote control on the table separating her and Soulja, then pointed it behind her back, pushing the power button to turn on the stereo system accommodating the entertainment center behind her. The mild paced beats of hip-hop played at low volume through the surround sound speakers. Rachel fiddled with her unpolished nails as Caesar walked into the room. The thick, timber brown, hooded sports sweatshirt, knit cap, and corduroy pants conspicuously provided Caesar's intent to leave the house as he propped his arms against the brim of the backrest of the chair in the room.

"You need to put some clothes on Rachel. What the hell wrong wit' you?" Caesar emphasized with his eyes strongly focused on Rachel.

Caesar's words alerted Soulja to his presence. Soulja turned his attention to Caesar, then Rachel as she nonchalantly said, "Boy, stop trippin'. Ain't nobody here but Soulja." The gesture of Rachel's hands denoted innocence and her facial expression indicated nuisance, accommodating her feeling of Caesar's concern being of null nature as she continued to sit on the floor. "Where you goin' anyway?" she asked, further degrading Caesar's request for her to fully clothe herself.

"I'm goin' where I wanna go. Don't worry about that," Caesar snapped back, slightly raising his voice. "I'll be back. You need to have some clothes on when I get back," he said as he commenced to walk out of the room.

"You want me to roll wit' you, bra?" Soulja asked.

"Nall. I'll be back," Caesar answered. "I'ma slap Rachel on her ass though if she ain't got no clothes on when I get back," he mocked playfully.

"Boy, get cho ass outta here and go handle whatever business you finna go handle," Rachel urged.

"I ain't playin' wit' cho ass," Caesar yelled as he walked down the hallway to exit the house.

"How he gone tell me what to do in my house?" Rachel asked Soulja with hypothetical verbalization and an open mouth smile.

"You know, I didn't even know you had your own house. I thought you lived with Rome and Caesar," Soulja said, evading her question.

"Yeah. You know, I just like to be over there because I can use they swimming pool in the summer and I can use they Jacuzzi in the winter," Rachel stressed. "I remember one day I was walking to tha pool and Caesar gone tell me I need ta gain some weight," Rachel said with discontent as she stood to her feet. "Now look," Rachel said as she raised her shirt above her stomach. "Do I look like I need to be thicker?" she asked as she looked down at her own flat, aerobicized abdomen, ignoring that her white mesh-seamed lingerie panties gave a print form to her vagina. "Look," she insisted further as she turned her back to Soulja, shifting her weight from one side of her body to the other, causing her butt checks to jiggle. Rachel bent over to pick up the remote control that laid on the carpet beside her feet, her vagina bulging a print from the back this time as she picked it up. She place the remote control on the table as she turned around and asked, "What do you think."

Soulja stared at Rachel's smiling face, then responded, "I think you better go put on some clothes like Caesar said."

"What?! Unh-unh! Don't you start trippin' wit' me like Caesar do!" Rachel said with saucy disappointment. "You niggas gon' learn that y'all don't control me! I do what I wanna do, baby!" she declared. "Like if I wanted to walk out on the patio right now …I'll walk out there, ok?" she said, pointing at the glass sliding double doors.

"It's cold out there. You don't even have any clothes on," Soulja rationalized.

"So, I guess that mean you'll try to stop me from goin' out there because you don't want me to get sick or nothin'?"

"Yeah. Why would I want you to be sick?"

"But see, that's just tha point," Rachel replied with a smile as she pulled the shirt from her body, standing in front of Soulja wearing only a lingerie bra and panties. Slowly walking to the glass sliding double doors, she looked back at Soulja and said, "If I wanna go out here and take a chance of getting' sick that's my choice."

Rachel slid one of the glass doors back and stepped outside on the patio bare feet. She threw her hands in the air and screamed, "Aaaaaaaaaha! Wooooooo! Y'all niggas got me fucked up!" Soulja was enjoying Rachel's appearance of complacency. Her actions, to him, didn't seem to typify asininity at any angle. Her independence, courage, and strong will was discernible to him.

Rachel ran back into the house and quickly slid the glass door closed. "Oooh, shit. It's cold out there!" she admitted as she bounced and rubbed her arms in an attempt to warm herself. "I told you I would do it. Y'all nigga's gon' learn one day that y'all don't control women," Rachel declared. "I'm going to put some clothes on now."

"Aye!" Soulja uttered for Rachel's attention. "I wasn't trying to control you. I didn't mean to make you feel that way."

"Don't worry about it," Rachel smiled. She picked up her shirt from the floor and said, "I'll be back."

Caesar and Tate sat at a table in a casual style restaurant. Plates, glasses, forks, and spoons made noises in the background as waiters and waitresses traveled the restaurant with their dish tubs. Tate spread a few bills of money on the table and stuffed the remaining bills in his hand back into his pocket.

"Listen, man. I got everything on lock, right. But, I need a little time to collect the rest of the money," Tate communed.

"How much you lackin', baby boy?" Caesar asked.

"It ain't nothin', you know. Bout twenty g's."

"Twenty g's?"

"Yeah. Don't even trip on dat tho 'cause I got you bra," Tate assured.

"Oh, I ain't gone trip. You say you got me, then you got me."

"When Amanda comes back from the restroom we can gon' out to tha car so I can give you what I got now."

"Oh. Nall. You gon' pay me all of mine at once. I don't want some now and some later. You gon' give me all my money," Caesar said with rising hostility.

"Damn, bra. I tol' you I got you," Tate vocalized in an attempt to appease Caesar.

"Man, fuck that shit. You told me ta meet you in here this mornin' fa my money and you ain't even got it all. Fuck that," Caesar said bitingly. "You just need to get my muthafuckin' money man befo' I cut cho ass off," Caesar said as he raised from his seat, then walked out of the restaurant.

Amanda saw Caesar exiting the restaurant as she primly walked to the table Tate was walking away from to meet her.

"Why did he leave?" Amanda asked.

"He need ta go handle somethin'," Tate lied. "Let's go. I already paid for the food."

"Whatever he's going to handle must be pretty intense," Amanda said as they walked out of the door of the restaurant. "He looked upset when he was walking out of the door."

"Yeah, he was mad," Tate confirmed as they walked through the parking lot of the restaurant.

"Did you have the chance to pay him?" Amanda asked, opening the passenger's door on the dark orange painted short-frame, four-door sports car.

Tate and Amanda entered the car and Tate answered, "Nall. He gon' pick up his money another time."

"Baby, I told you that these people I know won't deal with you if you're still selling dope for someone else. You have to pay him and tell him that you don't want to work for him anymore," Amanda urged.

"I'm gon' pay 'em, Amanda. He'll probably holla at me tonight or somethin'," Tate replied, igniting the engine.

Rachel emerged from the hallway, entering the family room where Soulja remained seated on the couch. Rachel flipped the hood of her zip-up sweater over her head and walked to the couch, then took a seat on the end away from Soulja.

"Tell Caesar, I went over Rose house," Rachel instructed.

"You just gon' leave me in the house?" Soulja questioned.

"What? Ch'you scared to be in my house by yo'self or something'? Caesar gon' be back in a little while."

"I'm not scared to be here alone. I just didn't plan to be sitting around all day," Soulja explained.

"Let me call Caesar and see what he gon' do," Rachel suggested, pulling her cell phone from her purse.

Rachel dialed Caesar's cell phone number and he quickly answered as he drove the highway. "What's up," he answered.

"What you gon' do 'cause I'm finna go and Soulja ready to go too."

"I gotta handle a few thangs, man. I'm comin' back in a little while."

"Boy, you know you slow," Rachel said playfully. "I'm just gon' take Soulja where he wanna go, then I'm goin' over Rose house for a while."

"Ah'ight. Tell Soulja I'll holla at 'em later."

"Ok," Rachel said before disconnecting with Caesar. "He said he gon' holla at'cha later. Where you want me to take you?"

"I left my car in the projects," Soulja said, raising from the couch, grabbing his black leather jacket.

"So, you want me to take you to da projects?" Rachel asked, leading Soulja out of the house.

"Yeah," he responded, waiting for her to walk out of the front door.

"You ain't gon' be ashamed to ride wit' me are you? Caesar don't like to ride wit' me because of tha color," Rachel noted, referring to the darkened pink paint detail on the sports utility vehicle she and Soulja entered.

"It's nothing to be ashamed of, but it's not a color I would want on my car," Soulja replied. "What's that smell?"

"What kind of smell?"

"Like perfume or something. I didn't really smell it until I got in."

"Oh, that's my perfume. You like it?"

"Yeah. It smells good."

"It's a foreign perfume. They have some for men too. You want some?"

"It depends on how the men's kind smell."

"Well, I believe you'll like it if you like what I got on now. I'ma get you some ok."

"Yeah. Whatever."

"Tis," Rachel sighed as she ignited the vehicle.

Clarence sat behind an office desk with Mike sitting on the opposite side. Martial arts trophies and awards decorated the room with various martial arts weapons. The two casually dressed men slouched in their seats.

"It's amazing how Geronimo has excelled in the arts," Clarence noted with reverence. "I've never had one of my students learn the application of the arts and innovate their own techniques as fast as he has done so," he continued. "When you told me to pair him with Breanna I thought that she might be too much for him to deal with, but he puts her on her back almost at will and she's about to graduate to fifth degree black belt. Geronimo has only graduated to third degree black belt, but I have to admit that if not for wanting to spare the feelings of Breanna and the rest of the students, I would give him fifth degree.

"Tell me about the tests," Mike requested.

"Yeah, well …I keep him paired with Breanna like you asked. I asked them to come to the class together while no-one else is here. And I give them both the same advanced technique to practice. Breanna learns the techniques as fast as Geronimo, but she doesn't learn how to apply the techniques as fast. There was this one time when Geronimo and Breanna came to class alone and they were ready to demonstrate the techniques I showed them. So, after they did their demonstration, I told them to try to use it on each other. Well, Breanna was in a position to use the technique on Geronimo so she went for it. Now she actually applied the technique on Geronimo, but he reversed the technique on her and added to it, knocking Breanna on her butt. But here's the point to that, I hadn't taught either of them the counter-technique. What that shows me is --,"

"Soulja's fore-thought in practicing the technique is exceeding Breanna's?" Mike questioned.

"Exactly. He's just naturally inclined to the arts or something. He's really impressed me because at first I didn't think he was going to stay here past three weeks," Clarence said. "So, how's he doing at the gun range?"

Mike's physiognomy revealed cogitation as he responded, "He's doing very good. It's almost like he was born for this job."

"So, when will you ask him about the job?"

"He'll be graduating this summer. I'll ask him soon, but that depends on how you answer my next question. Is he ready?" Mike asked.

"Yes."

"Tia, I can tell you like Geronimo a lot," Breanna said, lying flat on the couch in Tia's living room. "Did you two ever have a serious relationship?"

"No!" Tia answered, sitting erect on the sofa. "Soulja's my friend. I mean, he's attractive and stuff, but I wouldn't want to lose the friendship I have with him."

"So, you're saying you've never thought about being with him," Breanna teased.

"No. I'm not – Well …you know, there was this one time I was really, really drunk at a hotel party. And Soulja was in a room by himself and I stumbled into the room. Oh, my goodness," Tia reflected. "I tried to take his liquor from him," she laughed. "But I was totally drunk. Then I threw myself on top of him and started kissing him. And he pushed me off of him and said, 'Tia! You're drunk! You need to lay down!'" she laughed again as she mimicked Soulja. I was so embarrassed the next morning, but he didn't give me a hard time about it. He just told me to stop getting so drunk that I don't know what I'm doing and I swear I haven't been that drunk since," Tia emphasized.

"But wasn't he drunk too? I'm surprised he didn't try to have sex with you."

"But see, that's just it. He isn't like that. Even though he had been drinking he wasn't drunk because he doesn't get drunk, but he felt the same way I felt. He didn't want to ruin our friendship for some drunken one-night stand. He really values our friendship."

"That is impressive. Most guys would've taken advantage of you. But I get confused with him sometimes. I don't know what to think about him sometimes."

"Confused? Confused how?" Tia asked.

"Well, sometimes it seems like all he wants to do is try to have sex with me and sometimes it seems like he doesn't care about me at all."

"You haven't had sex with him?" Tia questioned with wide-eyed surprise.

"No. I'm still a virgin," Breanna said sadly. "But he never tells me he loves me when I tell him I love him. That's why it seems like he doesn't care about me sometimes. He only answered to my father that he loves me. Never just to me."

"First of all, if he hasn't had sex with you and he's still with you he must love you or something. I would've broken up with you a long time ago. And if you want him to tell you that he loves you, why won't you just ask him.

"I don't want him to tell me he loves me because I'm telling him to tell me. I want him to tell me because he wants to."

"No, I mean you should ask him why he never tells you that he loves you. That way you're not telling him to tell you, you're just asking him a question and waiting for an answer. He'll have to decide for himself," Tia explained.

"Yeah. Maybe I'll do that someday," Breanna considered.

Chapter 17

Soulja walked through the solid wood carved detail front door of his mother's home. He walked through the vent designed double-doors that separated the living room from the family room and found his mother, Ms. Walsh, and his two siblings, Angel and Chris.

"What are you watching?" Soulja asked his mother.

"Oh, I'm just watching the adventure channel with your brother and sister," Ms. Walsh responded.

"Do you want me to wait until it goes off or can I just go ahead and take them to the mall?" Soulja asked.

"Let us go to the mall mama. Let us go," Angel and Chris chattered.

"Yeah. You can go," Ms. Walsh said to Angel and Chris. You can take them with you, baby," she told Soulja. "Go get your coats Angel and Chris."

"Ok," Chris said as he ran to the rear of the home with Angel.

"You need me to get you something?" Soulja asked his mother.

His mother smiled at him, then asked, "What else can you give me, baby? You've given me more than I've ever asked for. You got me part ownership of a club, a house, furniture, a car, and I may never spend all the money you've given me."

"Mama, if I could give you the world and everything in it, I would. And if you ask me for it, I'd do everything I know how to get it for you."

Angel and Chris ran through the hallway into the family room yelling, "We ready to go!"

"You just take them to the mall and let them have some fun. Why don't you call Tia or Breanna and ask one of them to help you find me some things for Angel," Soulja's mother suggested.

"I know what I want mama," Angel said.

"You come tell me what you're going to get then," Ms. Walsh said to Angel as she glanced at Soulja using his cellular phone.

"Hello," Breanna answered her cell phone.

"Breanna, what's up?" Soulja asked. "You feel like going to the mall with me and my little brother and sister?"

"Yeah. I don't mind going. When are you leaving?"

"I'm about to leave now, but listen, you don't have to come if you don't want to."

"No. I wanna go. I'm at Tia's apartment," Breanna said. "Hold on for a minute," Breanna told Soulja. She looked at Tia and asked, "Do you want to go to the mall with me and Geronimo and his little brother and sister?" Noticing Tia's affirmative nod, she said, "Geronimo, can Tia come along with us?"

"Yeah. She can come. Listen, I'm walking out of the door in one minute."

"Ok. We'll be ready," Breanna assured before disconnecting the phone.

"Mama, I'm going to pick up Breanna and Tia. Both of them are coming with me. You sure you don't want anything?"

"No. I'm fine. You go ahead."

"Alright," he replied. "Come on. Let's go," he said to Angel and Chris.

Mike sat in the living room of Charles' house, on the sofa, while Charles sat on the chair.

"I've talked to Clarence and he's certain that Soulja is prepared to perform the job. I've decided to ask him if he wants the job the next time I see him," Mike said calmly.

"Oh, I don't know," Charles said, referring to Mike's deputation. "I'm not sure I still want him to have your job."

"Don't turn this into a conversation about Breanna and Soulja," Mike said corrosively.

"You made this about Breanna and Soulja!" Charles yelled angrily. "You did this! You had to prove a point!"

Mike examined Charles' emotional state, then said, "If you hadn't married the woman that was supposed to be my wife maybe we wouldn't be in this situation where I have to show you that--,"

"You don't have to prove anything!" Charles yelled with more anger. "What the fuck makes you believe… that this will prove anything to me!"

Mike abruptly said, "Ok. It isn't your job to choose someone for my job. It's my decision. It's my choice. This is my job. I'm not leaving the organization. I'm just giving up my responsibilities to someone I know is capable of performing them. So, deal with it. Soulja's my choice.

Nikki laid on top of Caesar under the quilted bedspread in a bedroom of a hotel.

"You still ain't ready to go again," Nikki asked Caesar, extending her upper body over Caesar with her arms. Her breasts dangled over his face as she said, "You need to hurry up. You know I gotta go back home befo' Fat make it back."

"Don't sweat that. I told you Fat is out of state. He won't be back until tonight," Caesar assured her.

Nikki began to rotate her pelvis against Caesar's limp penis as she said, "Maybe I can help you get hard again." She laid her upper body on Caesar again and began to kiss him, then whispered softly, "Get this pussy, baby. Get this pussy." She commenced to kiss him passionately again, then with frustration, "What's wrong with it, baby. Damn."

"I told you to give me some time."

Nikki rolled off of Caesar and sat erect against the bed rest. She reached to the nightstand on her left and picked up the half smoked blunt and lighter, then lit the blunt. She took a long puff and blew the smoke down toward her uncovered hard nipple breasts.

"Did you have sex with Rachel earlier today, like early this morning or something?" Nikki asked.

"Man, what the hell you askin' me somethin' like that fa?" Caesar asked.

"Oh, I'm just askin' 'cause it ain't never took you this long to get hard again unless you been fuckin' that bitch," Nikki said, then puffed the blunt again.

"Man, you trippin."

"Nall, I ain't trippin'. That bitch sneaky. She thank she slick. You gon' marry that girl?"

"We don't need ta get married. We straight."

"She ain't never asked you about it?"

"Nope," Caesar answered. He began to think about Rachel's sexual prowess and began to get aroused. "Put that down," Caesar instructed as he climbed on top of Nikki.

Nikki placed the blunt in the ash tray on the nightstand and Caesar began to kiss her.

"Now tell me, why would you run yo' butt outside like that just to prove a point?" Rose demanded of Rachel as they sat on the couch in Rose's living room.

"Girl, you know I let them niggas know I run it. My life is Rachel's show."

"Girl, you crazy as hell," Rose laughed. "I'm surprised that nigga didn't try to get wit' that while you was runnin' around in yo' panties and bra."

"Oh, it's no doubt he noticed me. But Soulja ain't like I thought he was gon' be. I thought since he already had a reputation fa being ruthless he was gon' be all hot-headed and... you know... just crazy. But he smart and real.

"I thought you already knew him before he joined the click?" Rose asked.

"Oh, yeah, but that was just through being wit' Caesar when Caesar have Soulja wit' him. But, you know, since he been spending a lot of time wit' Rome he been around a lot more so I be kickin' it wit' 'em and we cool. I think me and Soulja gon' be real tight wit' each other. I like him."

Soulja and Breanna held hands as they walked through the mall with Tia, Angel, and Chris walking ahead of them. Evidence of the Christmas holiday's gradual approach decorated the aisles, railings, and sections of the mall, advertising individual discounts on clothes, shoes, televisions, and other products of merchandise.

"Have you bought me anything for Christmas yet?" Breanna asked Soulja as she gazed around the mall, admiring the decorations.

"If I did, you think I would tell you?" Soulja replied. "Is there something in particular that you want?"

"No. I think its electrifying to be surprised. I'll be satisfied if you didn't buy me anything and just tried to stop arguing with my father," Breanna offered. "I love you a lot Geronimo. That's why it hurts me so much when you two start arguing. You make me feel like I have to choose and it doesn't feel fair."

They all walked into a children's department store. Tia, Angel, and Chris walked to the shoes section and Breanna and Soulja flipped through a clothing rack. Angel immediately commenced to pick up shoes saying, "I like these. I like these too."

"Geronimo, why haven't you ever told me that you love me?" Breanna asked, focusing on Soulja's eyes.

Soulja stood, silently cogitating. He actually couldn't think of a reason why he hasn't told her that he loves her.

"Tis," Breanna sighed with disappointment. "Forget it. I'm going to help Tia," she said, then turned to walk away.

Soulja grabbed her wrist stopping her and said, "Don't do that. You don't have to go anywhere." Soulja stepped closer to Breanna and said, "I've never told a girl that I was in love with her."

Angel insisted on getting a white and red pair of shoes she held in her hands. Tia told her, "If you're sure those are the shoes you want you should go tell your brother."

Angel walked to Breanna and Soulja. She could see them only a few steps away.

"But... I love you, Breanna," Soulja said, unaware that Angel was standing behind him. "I'm in love with you. I guess I--,"

"Soulja, I want these shoes," Angel declared, holding up the red and white pair of sports sneakers.

"Oh…, ok, Angel," Soulja said, reaching into his pockets for money.

"Geronimo," Breanna said as Soulja sifted through a fold of hundred dollar bills. "Let me pay for the shoes. As a gift," Breanna smiled.

"Ok, but she's gonna see something else she wants so I was just gonna give her some money to put in her pocket."

"Let me do it," Breanna insisted, reaching into the purse strapped over her shoulder. She pulled out two hundred dollar bills and passed them to Angel saying, "Merry Christmas, Angel."

"Thank you, Breanna. Merry Christmas," Angel replied as she accepted the money, then ran back to Tia.

"You know, Chris is gonna be over here soon with a pair of shoes in his hands. What're you gonna do, give him two hundred dollars too?"

Breanna giggled and responded, "Yeah."

The group proceeded to shop in various departments of the mall. They left with about four bags each. Some bags were smaller than others.

As they entered Ms. Walsh's house, Angel and Chris ran directly to her as she sat on the couch reading a book.

"Mama! Mama, look what I got!" Chris demanded excitedly as he threw a bag on her lap.

"Put it down on the floor. I'll look at it, baby," Ms. Walsh promised as she turned her head to Soulja, Tia, and Breanna walking into the room. "Did they give you a headache Breanna and Tia, because for some reason they just don't get on Soulja's nerves?" she asked.

"No. They didn't bother us at all," Breanna answered.

"Breanna bought us a Christmas present!" Angel yelled as she pulled out the red and white sneakers from their box.

"I just gave them some money to buy whatever they wanted," Breanna clarified bashfully. "Oh, I bought you something though," Breanna announce passing Ms. Walsh one of her bags.

"You didn't have to do this, baby," Ms. Walsh said as she reached into the bag. "Well, what is this? A map? What am I gon' do with a map, child."

It goes with the gift Geronimo has for you," Breanna informed excitedly.

"I told you I didn't want anything, Soulja," Ms. Walsh reiterated.

"Yeah, but I'd already did this before I talked to you earlier. I told Breanna and Tia about it a few weeks ago. Then I told them today that I would go ahead and tell you what I have for you."

"Ok. Where's the present then so I can open it for everyone to see."

"You can't exactly do that. You'll have to bring it back to us. You remember the passports I asked you to get, because one day we might all want to travel together a few places, right. Well, that's what you and Angel and Chris are gonna do this summer because I got a world trip for you and them."

"Soulja! You can't be surprising me like this son. You'll make me faint," his mother said as she stepped toward him to hug him. "You always find a way to surprise me don't you," Ms. Walsh said as she embraced her son tightly.

"You deserve it, mama," Soulja replied. Tia and Breanna said they would help you shop for the things you'll need to take with you. A travel agent had made arrangements for flights and hotels in the countries you'll be visiting and made sure that daycare services would be available. You're scheduled to leave the day after my graduation. You'll be gone all summer. So, you have a lot of shopping to do. I might not be able to give you the world, but I can send you to see it."

"You're my little Soulja," Ms. Walsh smiled. "So, what did you get Breanna? Where are her gifts and your friend Tia's gifts?"

"He bought her something special, mama! Soulja loves Breanna!" Angel yelled.

"Angel don't put words in Soulja's mouth. Now you know he doesn't like people lying on him," Ms. Walsh scolded.

"Uhn–uhn, mama. I heard him. He said he love Breanna," Angel said with a whine.

Ms. Walsh realized that Angel had obviously overheard something and looked at Breanna and Soulja with evaluating eyes. Tia helped Angel and Chris sort their bags, trying to gain Angel's concentration by asking, "What will you wear with this shirt, Angel?"

"She heard me tell Breanna that I love her at the mall," Soulja informed his mother.

"Soulja, is this mine?" Angel yelled holding a red and white sports shirt in the air.

"I'll be right back," Soulja said before walking to Angel and Tia sitting on the floor. "This shirt is yours. It goes with your red and white shoes," Soulja told Angel.

"I told you it was yours," Tia said.

"You know, Soulja is very protective of his feelings. He doesn't open up to people on many levels. Especially love. So, if he told you he loves you, his feelings for you are a lot deeper than that," Ms. Walsh told Breanna.

"Mama, I'm gonna go ahead and take Tia and Breanna home. I have some things to take care of," Soulja said with Tia standing behind him.

Soulja kissed his mother on the cheek of her face, then turned to his siblings and said, "I'll call both of you to see how you're doing later. Take care of your mama or when I come back I'm bringing water balloons." Tia said, "I have a Christmas gift for you, but I'll give it to you later," then hugged Ms. Walsh. Ms. Walsh looked at Breanna and said, "Come here, baby," then hugged her also.

Soulja drove Tia to Breanna's house. When they arrived into the driveway, Soulja noticed an unfamiliar luxury sports coupe.

"Whose car is that?" he asked Breanna as they walked to the front door of the house.

"That's Mike's car. You've never seen that car?" Breanna asked plainly.

"No. I'm used to--,"

"You're probably used to seeing him in one of his other cars," Breanna said.

Tia searched Soulja's face for evidence of suspicion, but couldn't immediately discern.

Soulja, in fact, was accreting suspicion about bits and pieces of unfitting information he had been gaining pertaining to Mike. They entered the house in the presence of Charles and Mike.

"Hi, dad. Hi Uncle Mike," Breanna smiled. Her hazel brown eyes seemed to glitter as she said, "I had the greatest time today."

"What happened?" Charles asked. "Did Soulja ruin it for you? I know he's mentally impaired so maybe he's retarded.

"What's wrong with you, dad? Geronimo didn't do anything wrong. He's the reason why I'm so happy.

"Tia, what did you do today?" Mike asked, trying to change the subject.

"Breanna and I went shopping with Soulja and his little brother and sister, Tia answered as she walked to the sofa and sat down. It was a lot of fun."

"You think you can keep my daughter's heart by taking her to the mall, Soulja?" Charles asked sarcastically.

"I think I better leave. I'll call you or something, Breanna," Soulja said as he walked away.

"Boy, don't you turn your back on me when I'm talking to you!" Charles yelled aggressively.

"You ain't my daddy, nigga!" Soulja bit back.

"Geronimo!" Breanna screamed with a whine as she rushed behind him before he walked out of the door. "Wait a minute," she said as she opened the front door and stepped outside with Soulja. "I'm sorry."

"It's not your fault, Breanna. It's your dad. It's not me. I hadn't been in your house five minutes before he jumped down my throat."

"I'm still sorry though. I know it's gonna be hard, but just keep trying. I'm not gonna let him make me choose," Breanna said, then kissed Soulja as she leaned herself against him.

Mike opened the front door, alarming Soulja and Breanna. They stopped kissing.

"I'll call you," Breanna said before she walked into the house.

"Soulja, I need to talk to you," Mike said.

"About what?" Soulja asked as he walked to his car, followed closely by Mike.

They entered Soulja's car and Soulja asked, "Who's car is that?" pointing to the unfamiliar luxury sports coupe.

"That's my car."

"I thought you told me you only had one car. Tell me what's going on. Why you lie?"

"Listen to me. I wanna explain something to you. I've noticed that you detect a certain weirdness when Tia, Breanna, and I are together.

I'm a part of an organization that does underground bargains."

"What?! You--,"

"The reason everything seems weird is because Amanda, Tia, and I try to hide it from Breanna."

"You serious too, ain't it," Soulja realized.

"I'm gonna make this simple. I have a job for you that can keep you out of sight of law enforcement and give you all the money you'll ever need in life."

"What kind of job?"

"The thing you're better at than anything else in the world. Out of all the things you can do, you can use a gun, and use martial arts better than anything else. You have the courage, the discipline, and the mental strength it takes to pull the trigger and leave someone dead."

"Oh, you want me to kill somebody for you?" Soulja asked.

"No. Not just kill somebody. Not just for me. I'm offering you a permanent job. I'm asking you to do this for the organization. You would have the opportunity to invest in drug profits, arms profits, and legitimate company profits, but your job will be to kill."

"So, what you're saying is, I can still sell dope for myself, but my job would be to kill people."

"Yeah. That's what I'm saying."

"Ok."

"Breanna can never know about this."

"I won't tell."

"I'll be in touch with you."

Chapter 18

Soulja drove down the highway after his conversation with Mike. The order of killing was simple and seemed almost natural to him. Killing was as simple to him as walking on two legs. Soulja's cellular phone rang.

"Hello," Soulja answered.

"What's up, nigga?" Rachel greeted cheerfully.

"Oh, what's happening?"

"How long would it take you to come over here?"

"Where?"

"To my house."

"Not long I'm kinda close to your house now. Why?"

"I want you ta come over here right fast."

"For what?"

"You coming or not? I wouldn't ask you come over here for nothing."

"Yeah. I'm on my way," Soulja said, then disconnected with Rachel.

When Soulja arrived at Rachel's house, he saw only her SUV. As he walked to her front door, he wondered where Caesar was and what was so important for Rachel to summon him to her house. Soulja knocked on the door.

"Who is it?!" Rachel yelled.

"Soulja!"

Rachel opened the door allowing Soulja to enter.

"What's up? Where Caesar?," Soulja asked.

"He'll be over later. Come to the living room with me," Rachel requested.

Soulja followed Rachel to the living room. He sat on a chair and she sat on the couch beside him, parting her legs, showing that she wore no panties beneath the short silky robe wrapped around her body.

"Open that box," Rachel said, pointing to a rectangular box on top of the table in front of them.

"What's in there?"

"Something that belongs to you. Just open it."

Soulja opened the box, lifting the top off. Several large bottles of cologne neatly filled the box.

"You bought this stuff for me?" Soulja questioned.

"Yeah. You said you liked the perfume I was wearing earlier so I bought you the same kind of cologne and a few other kinds I thought you might like."

"I didn't mean for you to buy me any."

"I bought it for you because I wanted to. If you don't want it, just say so. It ain't no thang."

"No. I want it. I just didn't expect you to buy it."

Rachel raised from her seat and grabbed one of the bottles of cologne, then said, "This is the cologne for men that's the same as the perfume I was wearing earlier. Let's see how it smells on you."

Rachel took the cap off of the bottle, then dabbed a little of the cologne on her fingertip and slowly rubbed it on Soulja's neck.

"Let me see how it smells on you," Rachel said as she leaned over Soulja, putting her nose on his neck and sniffing softly. "Ummm. That smells real good on you," Rachel whispered, then sniffed a little while longer.

Soulja could see Rachel's breast as she leaned over him. Her breasts hung down as she leaned over him.

"Smell my finger," Rachel offered, sitting on the table in front of Soulja, extending the finger she had used to spread cologne on his neck.

"Smells good. I like it," Soulja admitted.

"What do you think of my Christmas decorations?" Rachel asked.

Soulja actually hadn't noticed the minor decorations until she mentioned it but remarked,

"It looks nice. Look, I gotta go. I need to get ready for tonight."

"Yeah. I need to finish getting dressed myself," Rachel said, standing almost simultaneously with Soulja. Rachel put the cologne back in the box and placed the top back on the box, then passed it to Soulja saying, "Why don't you wear some... either one of the colognes tonight."

"Yeah. I'll probably do that."

"Come on. Let me walk you to the door so I can lock it behind you," Rachel suggested, following Soulja to the front door.

"Aye!" Rachel said alarmingly as Soulja stepped out of the door.

"What? What's wrong?" Soulja asked with concern.

"Got'cha," Rachel smiled.

"What?"

"We're standing under a mistletoe," she said, referring to the mistletoe penned above her door.

"Man, you believe in that mis--,"

Rachel began to kiss him. Her tongue worked his mouth as if in competition.

"I'll see you tonight," Rachel said, promptly closing the door in Soulja's face, all in one motion.

Precious walked through the dimly lighted strip club, passing a stage occupied by three women exotically dancing. One of the women on stage squatted her butt, spread her legs, and pumped her hips against the stage. Guys surrounding the huge semi-circle shape stage yelled in applause as they slapped her butt cheeks with fists full of money. Others stuck money into the seam of her thong panties. Precious stood against the wall close to the stage, watching the men that surrounded it. Some of the men eye-balled her legs and the way her miniskirt fit her waist and cuffed her hips.

Nikki and Fat sat at a table remote to the stage, evading the bedlam of individuals that occupied the stage's ambiance. As Nikki glanced around the strip club, her attention was grasped by a man and woman sitting three tables away. The woman was leaning against the table with her elbows, slowly lowering herself onto the man's penis. Nikki looked at Fat to see if he noticed. Fat's attention was focused on the stage in front of them. Nikki began to look at the man and woman again, glancing around to see if anyone else was aware of the sexual activity. She was amazed that no one else seemed to notice, but thought to herself that the dark corner of the club in which the section of tables were arranged around her was the perfect place to try what the man and woman were doing. Nikki knew that Fat wouldn't agree with anything so audacious. She began to think about Caesar. Her vagina tingled mildly. She could almost feel the rush that the man and woman must feel right now. Nikki thought about the way she sexually aroused Caesar in the hotel room today. It was obvious when the man and woman were done. The man pulled the woman's pants up to her waist, and then zipped his pants, covering his limp penis. "They got away wit' it," Nikki thought to herself. She was disappointed they were done because she enjoyed the stimulation she was getting from watching them, but she was also gratified because her vagina was beginning to lubricate and she didn't want to have to go wash herself in the restroom. Nikki turned her attention back to Fat. He was still focused on the stage of strippers. Suddenly, Nikki saw Caesar and Rachel walking in her direction. As they approached the table, Nikki glanced slyly at Caesar with an accommodating sly smile. Caesar returned the gaze, alternating his eyes for a glimpse of Rachel's face to determine if she had noticed the glance of attraction between him and Nikki. Rachel's eyes searched the club before she sat down.

"What's the word bruh?" Caesar greeted Fat as he shook hands with him.

"It's gravy, baby. These bitches on stage finesse with that ass," Fat remarked.

"Who you lookin' fa, Rachel?" Nikki asked with a smirk and smile.

"She tryin' to find one of her potnas. You don't know her," Caesar answered.

"Yeah. I'm tryin' ta find my girl Rose. You wanna go over here to the bar wit' me?" Rachel asked.

"Yeah, girl," Nikki smiled, gratefully, stealing another gaze at Caesar before raising from her seat, following Rachel.

Caesar watched Rachel and Nikki walk to the bar and take seats on a couple of available bar stools, then turned to Fat and asked, "So, you ready for another package?"

"Yeah. You know I'm on top of mine like clockwork, nigga," Fat boasted. "What you gon' do about Tate?"

"That nigga there just need to pay me befo' I fuck 'em off."

"Man, Soulja ain't gon' roll wit' you on dat."

Caesar didn't want to discuss Soulja's disagreement, so he changed the subject saying, "I'm gon' page you and let you know where to go ta get cho package."

"Ah'ight."

Fat and Caesar began to watch the women on stage. A different group of three women were now on stage. Rachel and Nikki sat on stools at the bar sipping glasses of liquor. Nikki saw Tate, Soulja, and Rose approaching the bar from the opposite side of the strip club.

"Ooh. There go Tate and Soulja," Nikki announced unaware that the woman with them is Rose.

"Girl, that's my girl, Rose wit' them," Rachel said excitedly.

Rose walked in front of Tate and Soulja, smiling at Rachel with flamboyance as she paced toward her. Rachel raised from her seat and stood beside her stool.

"What's up, girl?" Rachel blithely said with her arms outstretched to hug Rose.

Rose hugged Rachel and said, "Look who I ran into on the other side of the club girl," looking Soulja up and down.

"What's up nigga?" Rachel said happily, then she hugged Soulja tightly. She whispered in his ear as she hugged him, "You wearing the cologne I bought you ain't it? Smells sexy."

"What's up, Soulja?" Nikki said as she walked to Soulja and hugged him also. "Tate, where yo' wife at, boy? She know you in dis club wit' all these women and strippers and shit?" She asked playfully.

"Man, fuck you," Tate remarked also playful.

Precious saw Soulja standing at the bar. She brashly walked pass the stage and approached the bar. She tapped Soulja on his shoulder. He turned around, surprised to see Precious.

"What are you doing in this club? How did you get in here? How old are you?" Precious drilled with a serious expression.

Soulja just stared at her in calm composure.

"He always come to dis club. He old enough to be in here," Rachel said.

"I'm talking to him," Precious said banally. "You need to come with me," she told Soulja with a firm voice. "Walk that way," Precious directed Soulja, pointing toward the stage of strippers.

Soulja walked in front of Precious. They walked past the stage, still surrounded by yelling men. They walked through a door behind the side of the stage. Lisa sat behind a desk on the phone when they walked in.

"I'll call you back," Lisa said into the phone, and then hung it up." "Soulja, hi," Lisa said, raising from the seat behind the desk. "We've missed you the past couple of weeks. Why haven't you stopped by?"

"I've been handling some things. That's all," he answered. "I didn't know either one of you were working tonight or I would've called to let you know I had a meeting here tonight.

"Well, come here. I want a hug or something," Lisa requested.

Soulja walked to Lisa, hugged her, then Lisa pecked his lips with her own.

"Oh, it's like that now, huh?" Precious said saucily. "You didn't hug and kiss me."

Soulja walked to Precious, hugged her and pecked her lips as Lisa had did his.

"You crazy as hell," Soulja said to Precious. "You made them think you were gonna call tha police on me or something?" Soulja laughed mildly.

"Oh, I just wanted to bring you back here... Give you a dick tease or somethin'," Precious laughed and Lisa joined with a giggle.

"You know Soulja can't stand that kind of torture. He got a virgin girlfriend too," Lisa emphasized.

"Why that girl won't have sex wit' you? You tell her what she missin'?" Precious asked as she sat on a sofa in the office, almost simultaneously with Soulja.

"She say she ain't ready so if she can wait I can wait too."

"Don't worry, baby. I know how you feel. Remember, I told you I didn't have sex for years after me and Lisa broke up," Precious said. "If I could go as long as I did without fuckin' I know you can too."

The phone rang in the office and Lisa answered immediately, "Hello." She held the phone to her ear briefly, then said, "Ok, tell her we said thanks," then hung up the phone. "She here," Lisa said to Precious.

"Who?" Soulja asked curiously.

"Oh, we finna go do somethin' just fa us," Precious said flirtatiously. "We were just waiting on the manager we put on staff to come. She here now, so we finna go. You wanna come wit' us?"

"Yeah. We miss the way we use to have fun together," Lisa added. "Or, maybe you're afraid you can't handle us anymore," Lisa said playfully, as she walked toward Soulja.

"Oh, I can still handle both of y'all. You better be glad I'm--,"

"Whatever, Soulja," Lisa said as she leaned over him, them kissed him on the cheek of his face. "We'll be waiting on you though. Whenever you get ready for us," Lisa smiled and winked one eye. She opened the door and said, "I'm going to the car, Precious," then walked out of the office, closing the door behind her.

Precious stared into Soulja's eyes and said sincerely, "I really have missed you. Both of us miss you. Sometimes when we're together we talk about how good it would be to have you there with us." Precious leaned closer to Soulja and smiled saying, "I think you spoiled us. You know we picky about our sex partners. We don't think we'll ever feel as comfortable with another person joining us."

"The last time I talked to you, you told me you and Lisa were happy," Soulja voiced.

"Oh, we happy. We satisfy each other. We appreciate you getting us back together too. I don't think we would've ever gotten back together if not for you," Precious said plainly. "You remember when we first fucked? How tight I was?"

"Yeah. You guided me through it though. I thought you enjoyed it," Soulja smiled.

"Oh, I did, baby," Precious said sexily. "When you have sex with your girlfriend for the first time… think about how patient and caring and slow and careful and everything you had to be with me. Because her pussy gon' be as tight as mine was." Precious kissed Soulja on his neck, gently sticking her tongue through her lips, licking his neck softly, then said, "You know I wanted to kiss your lips like that and uh– Look, I'm finna go. Give me a hug before I leave."

Soulja and Precious stood from the sofa. They hugged each other, then walked out of the office, Precious grabbing her purse before exiting. Precious took a key from her purse, then locked the door with it then walked a few steps behind Soulja as they walked pass the stage. Soulja noticed Tate, Caesar, Fat, Rachel, Nikki, and Rose as Precious walked passed them on her way to exit the club. He watched for a second, standing close to the bar, but then primly walked to the table were they sat.

"What that woman say to you, Soulja?" Rachel asked.

"Oh, we got an understanding. You see I'm still here. Why y'all leave the bar?" Soulja asked changing the subject.

"Tate and Caesar was over here about ta fight," Nikki answered. "That woman would've seen it, she probably woulda kicked they ass out."

"What's up, man? What y'all 'bout ta fight about?" Soulja asked, shifting his eyes from Tate and Caesar.

"Aye. Check this out. Let's walk to tha restroom right fast, man," Fat suggested.

Soulja, Tate, Fat, and Caesar walked to the restroom.

"What's up?" Soulja asked. "We came here tonight for a meeting, not to fight in front of everyone."

"I'm tired of this chump," Caesar said, with hostility as he punched Tate in the face.

Soulja grabbed Caesar and Fat grabbed Tate.

"Man, what the fuck wrong wit' you, nigga?" Tate yelled.

"Say, man… What the fuck going on, bruh?" Soulja asked, releasing Caesar.

"This nigga need ta pay me, man! He thank he gon' play me because we potnas, man, but every time I front this nigga he come up short! He gon' pay me tonight, tho! I don't give a fuck how he do it!" Caesar yelled.

"I told you I'ma pay you, man. I just need a lil' time," Tate pleaded.

"Man, fuck that --,"

"Hold up! Bruh, listen. What Tate owe you?" Soulja interrupted.

"He owe me thirty g's."

"Thirty g's?" Soulja questioned "I'll give you thirty thousand dollars tonight."

"Nall, 'cause then he gon' owe you, bruh," Caesar rationalized.

"Oh, don't worry about that. He gon' owe me, that mean he gon' have ta sell dope fa me and you ain't gotta worry about him no mo'."

Caesar thought about the torture Soulja inflicts on his dope boys that don't pay him all of his money. He figured to let Tate work for Soulja would be a perfect way to make sure Tate gets critically injured, because he was certain Tate would be incompetent in selling drugs for Soulja also.

"Ah'ight, yeah. You right, bruh," Caesar agreed. "You deal wit' 'em 'cause I'm sick of fuckin' wit' 'em."

"I'll give you your money tonight after the meeting is finished," Soulja assured Caesar. "Now let me talk to Tate one on one," Soulja requested.

"Ah'ight, bruh. We gon' go out here and watch these bitches do they thang on stage," Fat said.

Soulja watched Fat and Caesar walk out of the restroom.

"Man, I told you to stop letting Caesar front you dope. You need to buy yo' own dope. Sell for yourself, bruh. Then you ain't gotta worry about nobody sweatin' you about no money," Soulja explained.

"Don't… I appreciate you helpin' me out, man. I'ma pay you back," Tate assured.

"Nall, I don't want you to pay me shit, bruh!" Soulja said, raising his voice. "You don't owe me. We slick, nigga, you just need to buy yo' own dope from now on."

Chapter 19

The next day, Soulja side-kicked the practice dummy in the second bedroom of his apartment. He stopped, stood in a martial arts stance, and commenced to practice spin-kicks, followed by a back-fist punch with one hand and a ridge-strike with the other hand. He heard the phone ring and walked to it.

"Hello."

"What's up, potna? What you doing?" Rachel asked.

"I'm gonna take a bath in a little while. What's up with you?" Soulja asked.

"I wanted to know if you were gon' stop by and kick it wit' me for a lil' while today."

"Caesar over there?"

"Damn. You think you gotta be wit' Caesar every time you talk ta me? You can't just come kick it wit'cha girl fa a while?"

"It ain't like that, Rachel. I'll stop by there for a little while later on," Soulja said. His telephone beeped at the call of someone else so he said, "Hold on. Let me see who this is on the other line," then pushed the dial-tone button. "Hello," Soulja said into the telephone.

"What are you doing right now, Soulja?" Ms. Walsh asked her son.

"Uh. Nothing really mama. What's up?"

"Can you come stay here with Angel and Chris until the babysitter gets here?"

"Yeah. I'll come right now. Let me get off the phone with someone right quick. Hold on." Soulja pushed the dial-tone button again to switch the line back to Rachel and said, "Aye. I'ma holla at'cha later. I have to talk to somebody about something."

"Ok. I'll see ya, then," Rachel said.

Then, Soulja pushed the dial-tone button to switch the lines again, but obviously failed because he heard Rachel talking.

"Oh, I got that nigga, baby. I told you I was gon' fade Soulja," he could hear her say boastfully.

"Yeah. I gotta give you yo' props. You smooth," Caesar replied to Rachel.

Soulja listened, thinking to himself, "They must be on three-way calling. Caesar's on the telephone."

"You thank you gon' be ready ta handle business when Rome give word about that Chi thang?" Caesar asked.

"Man. When Rome give word I'ma be ready to take Soulja out the game like… like… shit, you just wait."

"Ah'ight. Well, I need ta handle somethin'. I'ma holla later," Caesar said.

"Ah'ight, boo. I love you."

"I love you too. Don't give that nigga my pussy."

"You know dis pussy on lock fa you, baby."

"Ah'ight. Bye," Caesar said, then disconnected with Rachel.

Soulja was calmly enraged by the sheer dimension of betrayal involved in the scheme to kill him. He wondered why, but he knew that was irrelevant to the fact that he had to improvise a plan to kill all involved first. He understood the implication of the conversation that denoted Rachel would try to kill him after the kidnapping in Chicago was committed. Soulja didn't just want to kill Rachel. He wanted to kill Caesar and Rome too. He knew they were all involved in the plot to kill him and that was enough to settle his mind.

Charles' living room was filled with the babble of Mike, Soulja, Breanna, Asia, Amanda, and Tia as he silently glanced alternately at each of them. He didn't feel the excitement everyone else in the room felt. The obvious contentment that everyone else felt was of no consequence to him, because he still hadn't separated his daughter and Soulja. Amanda and Tia were talking with

Mike and Asia about the way the couple felt when they had graduated from high school years ago. The day before, they had all enjoyed sharing in Breanna's happiness of graduating from private school and Soulja's contentment with graduating from a local public high school. Now, Breanna sat close to Soulja on the sofa. She held his hand and stared at him with an open mouth smile.

"So, have you thought about everything your mom is going to experience on her trip?" she asked.

"She just got on the plane this morning. She hasn't even arrived at her first destination yet," Soulja rationalized.

"I know, but can't you imagine how much fun she's gonna have? And your little brother and sister… they have to be really happy. I mean… to be so young going on a trip around the world," Breanna emphasized. "So, have you made up your mind about college?"

"Yeah, I'm going. But I don't know which one I'm going to or what I'ma major in or anything. I really don't care. I'm just doin' it for my mom."

"You hear that, Breanna?" Charles said.

"Daddy, don't start this," Breanna warned.

"No. No. Just listen to him. That boy doesn't have any goals. He doesn't have ambition. He's going to college for his momma," Charles voiced sarcastically. "I bet your mother doesn't know that she really raised a retard. Because you're too slow to make your own decisions."

"Leave my mama outta this. You leave my mama outta yo' mouth," Soulja warned.

Mike, Asia, Amanda, and Tia ceased their conversation. Their attention was drawn to the growing hostility detected in the exchanges between Charles and Soulja.

"Boy, you don't tell me what to say or do in my house. I'll knock your young ass out!" Charles stated angrily.

"Daddy, leave him alone. Why are you doing this?" Breanna whined.

"Man, you ain't gon' touch me without getting touched back. Bet you that," Soulja calmly remarked.

"You threatening me in my own house? Get out! Get your ass out of my house now!" Charles said aggressively.

"Geronimo, don't leave. Just wait," Breanna begged. "Daddy, you can't just throw him out every time you get upset about something," she tried to reason.

"This is my house! I'll throw whoever I wanna throw out!"

"Mom," Breanna continued to whine.

"Charles, cut them some slack. You did threaten him first," Asia said.

Charles rose from his seat and walked to the media cabinet beneath the tall built-in bookshelves in the room. He opened a cabinet door next to the television, pulled out a drawer, opened a black box within, and grabbed the chrome .45 automatic.

"Daddy, what are you doing?" Breanna shrieked.

"Charles," Mike said with alarm and almost simultaneously with Breanna.

"Charles, put that gun down. Now you don--," Asia was interrupted.

"This little punk is leaving my house now!" Charles said loudly and angrily as he walked toward Soulja.

Breanna rose from her seat and ran to her father, saying, "You don't have to do that! He'll leave, daddy! Just put the gun back!" Breanna's watery eyes threaten to drip tears at any moment.

"I know he's leaving! Nobody threatens me in my own house!" he said as he stepped around Breanna, then pointed the gun in Soulja's face.

"Get outta my house boy!"

Soulja stared at the barrel of the gun, then shifted his focus on Charles' eyes and said, "You ready to shoot me? You gon' shoot me or what Charles."

"You get your ass outta my house!"

"Fuck you! Shoot me you coward muthafucka!" Soulja exploded. "Shoot me, you coward ass bitch!" Soulja continued, clamping his hands in tight fists and pressing his forehead against the barrel of the gun Charles was holding to his face.

Everyone in the room was silent. It seemed no one moved or even breathed hard. They all waited, staring at Charles and Soulja as if the occurrence had hypnotized them. Soulja's eyes were fixed on Charles. Charles felt that the flames of hell were being poured into his body through Soulja's eyes. He had never experienced anything like it. He realized that he'd gone too far, but he couldn't just put the gun down. Suddenly, Soulja turned from Charles and walked toward the front door.

"Damn. Soulja might be going to get a weapon," Mike thought to himself. "Hey man, let me talk to you for a second, Mike requested, hoping to make sure Soulja didn't go to his car for a gun. But Soulja kept walking and exited the house.

Mike quickly raised himself from his seat, saying, "Ok, everyone needs to stay inside the house."

"I'm not staying in here. Why I wanna make sure Geronimo's alright," Breanna whined.

"Just stay inside," Mike said, walking to the door.

"He's not gonna do anything. He loves me too much to do anything to my daddy," Breanna voiced, following Mike out of the door. Charles walked behind Breanna out the door, still holding the gun in his hand. Mike, Charles, and Breanna stood on the porch of the front yard, watching Soulja walk to his car with a pace that almost appeared to be jogging. As Soulja walked to his car, he felt the car was farther and farther away. He also felt as if he was walking in slow motion. Breanna and Mike yelled his name, but he didn't hear them. All he heard was his footsteps. His fast steps seemed to sound like loud thumps. When he finally reached his car, he promptly opened the driver's side door and got inside, leaving the door opened. He immediately reached under the seat and retrieved a nine millimeter, then laid it on his lap. He reached under the seat again and pulled another nine millimeter, cocked it and laid it on his lap also, picked up the other nine millimeter and cocked it. He held one of the guns in his left hand and the other in his right as he commenced to step out of the car with his left leg. But he stopped his motion suddenly when his eyes locked on Breanna. Although she stood on the porch with Mike and Charles, she seemed to be the only person Soulja could see. He sat in the car with one leg still outside the vehicle as he stared at Breanna. Although she stood at a distance, her face seemed to be directly in front of his face. Her half-wavy and half-straight textured hair mixed of copper, gold, auburn, and medium brown; her hazel brown eyes; her gorgeous skin complexion only slightly lighter than her eyes, the very essence of Breanna's presence was extremely intense and intimate to Soulja. Breanna's present state of distraught encompassed him, but his present desire to kill Charles battled against it. Ambivalence pertaining to a need to elude causing Breanna more pain and a desire to kill Charles apprehended Soulja. Mike stood on the front porch beside Breanna, thinking to himself, "Soulja, don't do it." Soulja continued to stare at Breanna. He knew what to do now. He placed his left leg inside the car, then laid the gun in his left hand on his lap. Soulja closed the driver's side door and leaned against the backrest of the seat. He reached in his pocket for his car keys, laid the gun in his right hand on his lap also, then he ignited the engine of his car. As he reversed his car out of Breanna's driveway, he looked at her as if it was the last time he would ever see her again. Turning into the street to drive away from Breanna's house, Soulja took another glance at Breanna, then slowly drove away. Breanna watched Soulja drive away. She was relieved that he was leaving, but pained by the fact that her father pulling a weapon on him caused him to leave. Breanna burst into tears and ran into the house straight to her room. Asia, Amanda, and Tia saw her run pass them and immediately walked to the staircase to follow Breanna. Mike and Charles remained outside. Mike peered at Charles dyspeptically.

"You took it too far, Charles. You may not be able to come back from this," Mike evinced, then walked into the house, leaving Charles on the porch alone.

Tia sat close to Breanna on her bed. She eagerly desired to comfort Breanna. Her arms were wrapped around Breanna. Amanda and Asia stood in Breanna's room, listening to her weep.

"Breanna, please. Talk to us. Soulja wouldn't want you to sit in your room crying," Tia said.

Breanna cried with laughter as if Tia's words were consoling her or serving as an emotional analgesic.

Breanna sobbed, saying, "I know what Geronimo would say. He'd tell me that I shouldn't even be crying. That crying isn't gonna make it better or solve anything. That… that I should be trying to find a solution to the problem instead of crying."

"Yeah. That's right," Tia softly whispered to Breanna. "That's what he would say."

"I still don't see how he does it," Breanna sobbed. "I need his strength because... because I just can't stop crying."

"It'll be fine, honey," Asia said to Breanna. "Geronimo's a strong young man."

"No. I won't be fine because I can't stay in this house. I can't be around Dad anymore. I have to leave."

When Soulja made it to his apartment, he strapped on a pair of sparring gloves, knee pads, elbow pads, and foot pads as he stood in front of his sparring dummy. He slightly bounced from the floor for a few seconds, then dynamically attacked the dummy. Soulja kicked the dummy's face with a right round house, then without hesitation he swiveled his body to impose a half-spin back kick to the dummy's face. In one motion, he followed the half-spin back-kick with a right elbow to the dummy's jaw, followed by a right back fist, a left knee to the abdomen, a left ridge hand to the temple, a left elbow, a right upper cut to the chin, a left hook to the jaw, a right hook to the jaw, a left punch between the eyes, a right side-kick to the nose, a right roundhouse-kick, a left roundhouse-kick, a spinning heel-kick with the right heel, a right hand back fist, a left forward thrust-kick, a combined jumping right knee and upper cut, a jumping right side-kick, a jumping left roundhouse-kick, a jumping spinning right heel-kick, a jumping double-crescent-kick with a right outside crescent and a left inside crescent, and a crouching palm strike to the solar plexus. Soulja perpetually attacked the dummy for about an hour.

Once Soulja was finished attacking the sparring dummy, he took a bath. He stretched his body out in the steamy, bubbly water. He laid his head against the end of the tub as he flicked ashes off of the blunt in his hand onto an ash tray that sat on the lid of a brown laundry basket next to his cell phone, then took a long puff of the blunt, holding the smoke in his lungs momentarily before exhaling. Soulja's body was relaxed by the steaming hot bath water, but the relaxation and natural calm state of Soulja was further induced by the psychoactive results of marijuana. He took another puff of the blunt, enjoying the floating relaxation. Soulja cogitated of Breanna. He thought to himself that it would probably be best if he never went to see her again. Suddenly, Soulja's cell phone rang.

"Hello," Soulja answered.

"I'm blowing snowballs, baby. Come chill with me," Rome requested with excitement in his voice.

"Alright, I'll be right over."

Chapter 20

Soulja disconnected with Rome, thinking to himself, "It's time, I know what I gotta do." Soulja placed the phone on the lid of the laundry basket, then took another puff of the blunt. He stared at the ceiling in meditative thought as he exhaled smoke.

After Soulja finished his bath, he groomed himself and clothed himself in charcoal color distressed pants and a stone color shirt. He drove directly to Rome's house. Soulja stuffed both of his nine-millimeter weapons in his pants, barrels touching each other, then walked to Rome's front door and rang the doorbell. He ignored the elaborately trimmed short bushes lined on each side of the doorway.

"Let's go to the back," Rome suggested to Soulja as he held the door open invitingly.

Soulja walked into the house, waited for Rome to close the door, then allowed Rome to walk ahead of him to the glass doors that gave an immediate view of the pool in the back yard.

"It's beautiful outside today," Rome said as he stepped onto the patio.

"Yeah. It's not too hot. Sun feels just right," Soulja remarked as he stepped onto the patio, observing Caesar and Rachel play in the pool as he waited for Rome to close the glass doors.

Soulja allowed Rome to walk ahead of him again. Rome walked to the beach tables situated around the pool, then took a seat. Soulja sat across from him, keeping Caesar and Rachel in his view.

"So, you remembered the codes," Rome asked Soulja.

"Yeah. Blowing snowballs– cold winds. Chilling- another sign of cold. All signs of Chicago. Not hard to remember, "Soulja rationalized. "So, Abdul called?"

"He says everything is ready. He's just waiting on you now. You wanna take anybody with you?"

"No, I'll go alone. Less complication."

"Ok, then. Just come see me when you get back," Rome suggested. "Someone important to me wants to meet you."

"Who is it?" Soulja asked.

"You'll see when you get back," Rome said before he walked away from the table.

Soulja watched attentively as Caesar exited the pool saying, "Rome, let me holla at'cha for a minute." Rome stood in front of the glass doors as Rachel got out the pool and walked to the beach table, then sat beside Soulja.

"You gon' swim wit' me and Caesar for a lil while, while you over here?" Rachel asked, leaning her back against the chair very slouchy.

"I'm about to leave."

"Why you leaving so fast? Where you goin'?"

"I need to go visit someone."

"Oh, Ok," Rachel accepted. She gapped her legs open and said, "Just come visit me when you get back," then raised from her seat and walked to the pool.

Soulja watched Rachel dive into the pool, immediately followed by Caesar running from where he stood conversing with Rome. Soulja immediately raised from his seat and quickly walked in the house behind Rome. When Rachel and Caesar's head emerged, they didn't see Soulja. They wondered how he left so hastily. Soulja walked through the living room pass Rome saying, "See you when I get back." Without pause or hesitation, he primly walked out of the house, got in his car and left Rome's house.

Traveling to Chicago, Soulja thought hard in regard to the assassinating intentions of Rachel and her co-conspirators. His thoughts provided animated elaboration to the devise of destroying their plans. He evoked a content and acute realization of definite necessity to kill them immediately after overhearing Rachel and Caesar's conversation on the phone. Now he knew exactly how he would achieve that necessity. He was completely prepared to activate his plan, but first he would kill Abdul as Rome expected. Soulja was confident his plan would work. He carefully militarized.

After entering Chicago, Soulja drove directly to the warehouse he met Abdul and Slim in. He parked the white luxury sports car in the parking lot of the warehouse. Soulja sat in the car dialing on his cell phone. The darkness of night accompanied him in the parking lot along with a black, short frame, chrome-trimmed sports coupe.

"Hello," Abdul answered his cell phone.

"I'm outside. Where ya boys?" Soulja communed.

"We coming out now," Abdul said, then disconnected with Soulja.

Soulja's vehicle was parked in the center of the parking lot. Abdul, Slim, and two more men stepped out of the warehouse. They all walked to Soulja as she stepped out of the white sports coupe. Soulja's metallic bomber jacket was open, displaying his two nine millimeters, one in each of the holsters strapped on his shoulders. The silver baseball cap on his head didn't hide his face, it only seemed to be enhanced in the reflection of the parking lot lights. The silver color sparkled.

"Tight ride, Soulja," Abdul said, approaching Soulja.

"It's a rental car," Soulja replied.

"What's poppin, Soulja?" Slim greeted.

"I'm ready for the business."

"This is Magic," Slim introduced the brown skin man with a medium build standing beside him. "And this is Kent," Slim also introduced with a point of a finger at the man with a similar complexion and build as Magic. "This the crew, bruh. Me, you, Magic, and Kent."

"Tomorrow morning, maybe around five or six a.m., the dude gon' come," Abdul informed. "Y'all will already be waiting on him to come to the warehouse. Y'all will be in that car," Abdul pointed to the black sports coupe parked beside the building. "When he comes you'll be able to see him because there's a hole drilled into the door for you to peep through. All y'all gotta do is lay the seats back, look through the holes, and wait for Slim to tell you the dude's here. Before he can get out the car I want y'all to get' 'em," Abdul explained. "I know you had a long ride, Soulja. So, we brooming so you can get some rest. Follow up on calling me around four in the morning so I can tell Slim where to come pick you up from."

"Ah'ight, bruh," Soulja said as Abdul and his minions walked to the black vehicle, got in, and drove away.

Soulja watched them drive out of the parking lot, then he entered his vehicle and drove out of the parking lot himself.

The next morning, at 4:21 a.m., Slim sat on the driver's seat of the black sports coupe while Magic sat on the front passenger's seat, Kent sat on the rear passenger's seat, and Soulja sat on the rear passenger's seat behind Slim. The commodious vehicle allowed them to comfortably slouch so that their heads were below the windows of the car. Each door on the car had a small hole drilled through the key panel, next to the handle of the door. They all peeked through the hole in their doors.

"Police car pulling into the parking lot," Slim announced.

"Yeah, they're driving towards the car," Soulja confirmed.

"Shit. Man, we need to uh," Kent eagerly uttered.

"Just wait, nigga," Slim demanded. "They'll probably drive by us."

The two officers in the police squad cars peered at the black vehicle parked on the side of the enormous rectangular shaped building. The Caucasian officer driving said to the African American officer on the passenger's side, "What the hell is this car still doing here? You don't think this place is open do you?" The officer stopped the squad car, staring at the license plate of the black vehicle. "I'm gonna run the license plate by dispatcher," the Caucasian officer said.

"It's probably just a company car, man," the African American officer offered. "Don't even bother. Let's just go patrol the other side of the neighborhood," he urged.

The driving officer glanced at his colleague, then said, "Yeah. You're right. It's probably just a company car," rationalizing the situation.

"He's on your side Magic and Kent," Slim informed as he observed the police car drive away.

"I see 'em," Kent said, "He's going all the way around the warehouse."

"He was just patrolling," Slim said. "Yo' panicky ass."

"There they are. They leaving," Soulja informed, watching the police car leave the parking lot.

Thirty minutes later, Slim saw a gold colored Jaguar drive onto the lot of the warehouse.

"Ole boy here!" Slim excitedly voiced. "As soon as I say so we finna get this nigga," Slim said. Slim watched the gold colored vehicle pull into a parking space close to the front end of the parking lot and firmly said, "Get paid!" as he promptly opened his door, pulling his ski mask over his face as his accomplices did also.

As Soulja exited the black vehicle, he watched Slim run to the gold vehicle, saying, "Don't flinch, don't breathe nigga or I'm a blast," pointing a .45 automatic weapon at the driver of the Jaguar. Soulja allowed Kent and Magic to run ahead of him to the aid of Slim, then he ran to their aid. Soulja held both of his nine-millimeter weapons, pointing them at the driver of the Jaguar as he got closer to the gold vehicle. He focused his eyes on the driver sitting behind the steering wheel of the Jaguar with his hands up and the driver's side door open as if he was attempting to exit the vehicle when Slim approached. Soulja couldn't believe his eyes. Everything began to be in slow motion to him. The man sitting behind the steering wheel of the Jaguar was Charles. Soulja stood directly in front of the car staring at Charles.

Charles couldn't tell it was Soulja because he and his accomplices wore a mask over their face. This was the perfect opportunity for Soulja. He could kill Charles now and Breanna wouldn't know he did it. The realization struck Soulja hard as he gripped his weapons tighter. Magic and Kent stood on the right side of the car and Slim stood on the left side of the car, pointing his weapon at Charles. "Bitch get in the back seat!" Slim yelled at Charles, moving closer to the car almost simultaneously as Magic and Kent did.

Charles quickly complied with Slim's request, commencing to climb to the back seat. Suddenly, Charles heard three shots. He ducked his head, catching a glance of Magic and Kent as they fell to the pavement. Charles raised his head only to find Soulja standing were Slim previously stood, pointing his weapons at Charles. Soulja shot Slim in the head once with the weapon in his right hand and shot Magic and Kent each once in the head with the weapon in his left hand. He stood at the driver's side door of the vehicle watching Charles stare in a frozen posture.

"Get in the front seat!" Soulja yelled.
Charles quickly complied, too frightened to recognize Soulja's voice. Soulja waited until Charles was situated in the front seat, then entered

the Jaguar, pointing the weapon in his left hand at Charles as he stuffed the weapon in his right hand into his pants. Soulja reversed the Jaguar out of the lot of the warehouse, keeping the weapon in his lap with his finger on the trigger. Charles gazed at the unfamiliar weapon, and gave cognizance to the gloved finger on the trigger. Soulja drove away from the warehouse with the mask still on his face. The traffic was moderate and he didn't have to stop.

"Listen. Whoever you are, I'll give you two-hundred and fifty thousand dollars if you just tell me who put you up to this. You don't have to tell me who you are or even let me see your face, but I'll pay you. Just tell me who put you up to this," Charles pleaded.

Soulja pulled the mask off of his face and said, "I don't want shit from you! Fuck you!"

"Soulja!" Charles said with surprise, "How did you know I was coming here? Did you follow me all the way to Chicago? Do you wanna kill me that bad?"

"Nigga, shut the fuck up!" Soulja demanded aggressively." I don't wanna hear shit you got to say! Just shut tha fuck up!"

Charles remained quiet, alternately looking at the weapon and Soulja. Charles knew he was about to die soon. He knew Soulja was taking him somewhere to kill him during the waking light of morning. Suddenly, Soulja parked the Jaguar next to the white luxury sports coupe he drove to Chicago Charles scrutinized the expensive hotel on the lot Soulja parked on.

"Get out of Chicago right now. Don't go back to the warehouse; don't go anywhere but home," Soulja instructed Charles, then exited the Jaguar.

Charles attentively observed Soulja as he walked to the white vehicle, entered, then reversed the vehicle out of the parking lot and drove away. Charles remained on the passenger's side in shock, momentarily apprehended by the sequence of events that occurred. He quickly hopped to the driver's side of the gold vehicle, then reversed the car to leave the parking lot of the hotel as Soulja did.

Chapter 21

In sunny Mississippi, Rome sat in his living room with Rachel and Caesar. Rome sat on the chair with a large brown paper bag of hundred dollar bills in front of him, reaching his hand into the bag. Caesar sat on the couch with a large brown paper bag full of twenty-dollar bills. He counted them as he stacked them on the table in front of him as did Rome with the hundred dollar bills, and Rachel with a large brown paper bag full of ten-dollar bills in front of her while she sat on the sofa.

Rome's cellular phone rang. He picked it up from beside him.

"Hello," Rome answered.

"Nigga, yo' boy fucked up," Abdul said with anger.

"What do you mean?"

"Nigga, I got three funerals to go to soon. But you going to at least one real soon. So, when you see yo' boy...tell 'em everybody gets their day of judgment."

Abdul disconnected with Rome. Rome looked at Caesar then Rachel.

"Something went wrong," Rome said.

Caesar and Rachel stopped counting the money in their hands and looked at Rome with confusing expressions on their faces.

"Something went wrong wit' what?" Caesar asked.

"That was Abdul. From what he's saying… Soulja knocked off three of Abdul's boys that was supposed to be handling that business. I guess Soulja decided to cross them out. He talking about knocking Soulja off."

"That ain't shit," Caesar nonchalantly replied. "Long as Soulja find Abdul and gone blast Abdul ass," Caesar rationalized.

"Yeah. That's all we wanted him to do anyway, right," Rachel offered.

"Yeah, but the way… I don't know," Rome said, expressing uncertainty. "I guess if Soulja finds Abdul and handle 'em that'll put everything on track, but if he doesn't we'll still get rid of Soulja and find another way to get rid of Abdul."

"Man, don't sweat it," Rachel communed. "If Soulja don't kill Abdul, then after I get through wit' Soulja, I'll handle Abdul. You know I'm a winner."

Charles paced the hardwood, dark stained floor of the game room in Mike's house. Mike sat on the edge of the pool table positioned in the corner of the room. Charles paced back and forth, holding his head down. His face still sustained evidence of emotional confusion. The agitation he felt was conspicuously visible on his face.

"Charles, I know you went through a lot in Chicago. From the way you described everything that happened… It even confuses me a little. But pacing this floor isn't gonna get Soulja over here any faster," Mike said.

"Are you sure he'll come and he'll do what you say?" Charles asked as he stopped pacing the floor, searching Mike's eyes.

"He's on his way now," Mike assured. "I told you I'll handle this." Mike's doorbell rang and he said, "That's probably him, don't worry. You know I always do my job," then began to walk out of the room.

"Mike," Charles said to get Mike's attention.

"Yeah."

"Tell Soulja that I'm sorry and I wish…"

"I'll tell 'em you're sorry," Mike said, interrupting Charles' sentence. "But you'll have to tell 'em everything else on your own."

"Ok," Charles agreed. He felt regret for the extent of harsh behavior he treated Soulja with, but grateful for the mercy Soulja bestowed on him and said, "Ask him if he wants the house."

"I'll ask. I gotta go to the door," Mike urged, hearing the doorbell ring again.

Mike walked to the door. He could see Soulja's green vehicle outside in the driveway through the mesh draperies on the windows beside the front door. He opened the door invitingly for Soulja to enter the house.

"You got here pretty fast," Mike said as he closed the door.

"Yeah. I think I already know what this is about," Soulja admitted as he sat on the slipcover denim chair.

"Alright," Mike said, approaching the sofa positioned diagonal to the chair. "No small talk or anything," he said as he sat on the couch. "I think I know why you didn't try to kill Charles when he pulled his gun on you... but from what he tells me about what happened in Chicago you had a chance to kill him without anyone knowing. So, why didn't you?"

Soulja looked at Mike intensely and said, "I wanted to. I still want to, but Breanna... Breanna. I know Breanna wouldn't know I did it, but she would probably go crazy. She needs her dad."

"So, you didn't kill him because of Breanna?" Mike questioned.

"You know… you know, Breanna told me one time that it hurts her to see me and Charles argue. She asked me to try to stop arguing with him. So, I ignored a lot of things Charles said. You know, just for her. Because I told her I would. Even if I kill Charles and Breanna never knows I did it, I would know. And I would know that because of me she doesn't have her dad anymore. She wouldn't know about my betrayal to her, but I would know and I'm not gonna betray Breanna," Soulja rationalized.

"Ok," Mike said with an expression of understanding. "How did you know Charles would be in Chicago? How did you know where he would be? Did you follow him?"

"That's what he asked me," Soulja smirked." He offered me two-hundred and fifty thousand dollars to tell him. But it was a deal with this cat Abdul."

"Abdul?" Mike questioned, jumping to surprise. "Does he have a partner named Slim?"

"Yeah. You know 'em?"

"Yeah. How did you get connected to them? Were you buying from them or something?" Mike asked in an investigative manner.

"Nah! I buy from a partner of mine named Caesar and another one named Rome, but mostly now I been buying from Rome. Rome introduced me to Abdul. Abdul had this lick. Said he wanted to let Rome in on it, all Rome had to do was find someone to come to Chicago when he call. So, I told 'em I'll do it. Slim was there when I met Abdul. Abdul told us that the lick was kidnapping the owner of the warehouse because he supposed to have over a thousand ki's and shit. I didn't know Charles fuck wit' dope."

"He doesn't. I never told you, but Charles is a big part of the organization. He sends people to certain regions to claim territories or establish territories with all kinds of drugs. Charles was introduced to Abdul and Slim as the owner of the warehouse, but one of our associates initially delivered cocaine to Abdul and Slim in exchange for their protection of the warehouse. Then the deliveries continued with a low-cost purchase as long as they continued to protect the warehouse. Abdul must've just assumed the large quantities of cocaine were being supplied by Charles and decided he wanted more," Mike explained. "I'll kill Abdul for this."

"He's probably ready to kill me," Soulja said. "I'd planned to kill him. But fuck him right now. This cat Rome is planning my funeral with the help of Caesar and this bitch Rachel. Rachel thinks she's gonna do me like she did this nigga name Legend a while back," Soulja smiled.

"What did she do to Legend?" Mike asked with curiosity.

"Oh, Rachel is a real sexy ass girl. She thinks her looks, her weak ass game, and her pussy will get'er anything she wants. This nigga Legend had just come to Mississippi. He was selling a lot of dope. So, Rachel slid under the nigga and set 'em up. Now, my boy Caesar wanted me to kill the nigga. So, he took me to the nigga apartment, but when we got there Rachel had already killed 'em," Soulja explained. "They think I'm just this ignorant muthafucka or something. But Caesar been getting me to knock other dope boys off for him for years so that he can get more territory and sell more dope. He didn't think I knew. But I didn't care because I just wanted the dope and money from when I knock 'em off. Now I guess I'm getting a little too powerful in their territories, because they wanna kill me now," he continued nonchalantly.

"This Rachel chick. She kill Legend by stabbing him in the throat with something, right?" Mike questioned.

"Yeah. How did you know that?" Soulja asked.

"I've got your first job for you. This Rachel chick… she killed a member of the organization."

"Legend was a part of it?"

"Yeah. He was a loyal member," Mike reflected.

"She needs to die for what she did."

"I was gonna kill that bitch anyway."

"You focus on Rachel, I'll handle Abdul. I have somewhere I wanna take you though, because Abdul will probably use some of his resources to find you."

"Fuck Abdul. I was supposed to kill him too. Why can't I just go find Abdul and kill him myself?"

"Just concentrate on Rachel. If you try to go after Abdul you'll be searching for him, but all I'm gonna do is make a call before I go to Chicago and Abdul's gonna be waiting for me," Mike assured.

Soulja sat contemplatively, then asked, "Where do you wanna take me?"

"You'll see it when we get there. No one will be able to find you though. You'll need to leave your car here. I'll park it in my garage or something later," Mike explained. "This place I'm taking you to will be perfect for you to get some rest and think about what you're gonna tell your partner Rome."

"Fuck Rome. Fuck Caesar too. Them niggas gon' die too. They down wit' the idea of killing me, they just lettin' that bitch do it for 'em."

"You still need to be able to explain why the lick didn't happen."

"You said you gon' take care of Abdul. So, I'll just tell them that Abdul's boys tried to flip the game on me so I had to blast first."

"What about when they ask you what took you so long to check in?"

"I had to find Abdul, so I could get him too. I was hiding out and waiting until I see him."

"Ok. That's believable. That'll work," Mike said. "Come on. Let me take you to the place."

Mike and Soulja raised from their seats and exited the house. They entered Mike's BMW and left the house. Charles stood in the window of the game room, observing through the mesh draperies covering the window as Mike and Soulja left the house.

As Mike drove on the highway, he asked Soulja, "Are you gonna call Breanna? She says she hasn't talked to you."

Soulja glanced at Mike then out of the window and said, "I'm thinking about doing Breanna a favor and just stay away from her. She lives more on emotion. Her feelings mean a lot to her. It's hard for her to deal with the way things are between me and Charles."

"I think things will get better between you and Charles. He told me to tell you that he's sorry."

"He's just happy that I didn't let those cats kill 'em and I didn't kill 'em, but when he gets over it he'll be ready to treat me the way he did before it all happened."

"I don't think so. How do you get over the fact that someone saved your life?"

Soulja remained silent, staring out of the window.

"I'll get you some food, clothes, and whatever else you want from this store on the way."

Mike pulled into the parking lot of a small store. He exited the BMW, leaving Soulja inside alone. Soulja attentively analyzed the surroundings of the store and the few cars in the parking lot. The few night-light poles provide great illumination for the parking lot. As Mike walked back to the car holding four bags in one hand and his cell phone to his ear with the other hand, he talked to someone, saying, "Just meet me at the house on the water," then disconnected with a push of a button on the phone as he slipped it into his pocket. Mike entered the car, placing all the bags on Soulja's lap.

"Everything you need is in those bags. The house isn't very far away from here," Mike said as he ignited the vehicle.

When they reached the house, Soulja's attention was first drawn to the lamp posts leading to the front door of the house, and the other lamp posts around the house and the pool. Mike pulled into the driveway. After they exited the car, Soulja stared at the tall windows on the house.

"Whose boat is that over there on the water?" Soulja asked, turning his attention to the lake not far from the house.

"You can go check it out later if you want to. Let's get you settled into the house first," Mike responded.

They walked to the large front door of the house and Mike opened it with a key, then passed the key to Soulja. Soulja followed Mike through the dining room, looking out of the tall high-arch windows as he passed by them. He could see the moon glittering on the dark waters of the lake. Soulja noticed the entertainment center in the dining room was different from the entertainment center he now saw in the family room as he paced toward the kitchen. "You can drink as much of the wine as you want," Mike said as he opened the doors of a built-in wet bar close to the kitchen.

Soulja immediately noticed the sink, glass shelves and wine rack. "You can go ahead and put that food in the refrigerator," Mike said as he walked toward the kitchen.

Soulja walked into the kitchen, followed by Mike. The stained concrete floors in the kitchen didn't compare to the cream marble floors in the foyer of the home. Soulja placed all the bags on the wide, long, and fabulous cooking island in the kitchen.

"There's a sunroom on the other side of that door," Mike said, pointing to a door at one end of the kitchen. "What do you think about this place?"

"I like it. I like it a lot. I could live in a house like this," Soulja said, glancing at the buffet-style cabinets, pantry, and ceiling fan in the kitchen.

"Would you like to live here, I mean you know, own this house?" Mike sincerely asked.

"Man, shit. How much does this house cost?" Soulja stressed.

"It's worth more than half a million dollars."

"Man, I can't buy this house. I'd almost have to start all over again in the game if I bought this house."

"No. You wouldn't have to pay for it. If you want it you can have it."

"Man, you crazy as hell," Soulja said, not realizing that Mike spoke genuinely. He looked at Mike, realizing Mike was definitely serious and said, "You're serious. How the hell could you afford to give me this house?"

"Is that really important? Because I would have to describe all the jobs I've done to tell you how I could afford it. But just look at it as a gift. Besides by the time you get tired of living here, you'll be able to buy yourself two or three more of these."

"Get tired of it. Are you crazy?" Soulja energetically said.

"So, do you want it?"

"Yeah. What do I have to do?"

"Just sign the papers when I come back. I'll be gone for a couple of days. But I'll be back with the papers after I finish the business we discussed."

"Alright."

"Go ahead and look around your new home," Mike said, then walked out of the kitchen toward the front door of the house.

Soulja took all the food out of the bags and put them in their appropriate places. He took the remaining bags with him as he checked the rooms of the house, searching for the master bedroom. Finally, he walked into a bedroom that was clearly larger than the rest. His attention was drawn to the full-length bay window with blinds and slanting draperies. He placed the two bags in his hand on the bed that was positioned in front of a huge built-in entertainment center, then walked to the windows, enjoying the view of the lake. Soulja walked back to the enormously wide and lengthy bed and sat beside the bags he placed there. He looked around the room for a moment. The ceiling fan was motionless and the double-door closets were wide. Soulja grabbed the two bags and raised from the bed, walking to the open bathroom. He saw a panel of light-switchers and flicked the bathroom lights on, then flicked a couple other switches, searching for the switch to turn on the ceiling fan. The ceiling fan began to turn and Soulja walked into the bathroom. He immediately noticed a Jacuzzi close to another fireplace in the bathroom. He glanced at the glass double-door shower and water closet. He saw a walk-in closet and placed his bags inside the walk-in closet. Soulja kneeled down and pulled out soap, a bathing treatment, a face towel, and a dry off towel out of the bag. He walked to a huge bathtub separate from the shower, then adjusted the cold and hot water. Soulja poured the bathing treatment into the water as it filled the tub. The bathing treatment created bubbles in the steaming water. Soulja stripped himself of his clothes and stepped into the bathtub. He felt relaxed by the steaming water. Soulja reached for the soap and face towel he put in the tub. Once he found the soap and towel, he began to rub the soap all over his body. Soulja bathed in the bubbly water, then remained inside, enjoying the still, steamy water. Suddenly, Soulja heard a door close in the house. He immediately assumed it was Mike.

"I'm in here Mike!" Soulja yelled very loudly. The house was huge, so he knew he had to yell loudly as he said," I'm in here!"

About one minute after Soulja yelled, Breanna walked into the bathroom with an illuminating smile on her face. "My name isn't Mike," she smiled.

Soulja seemed to be surprised but pleased as he asked, "How did you know I was here?"

"I didn't," Breanna said as she walked closer to the bathtub. "I was supposed to be meeting my Uncle Mike here. He told me to pack some clothes and stuff and meet him here."

"Mike is gone."

"Yeah. Obviously," Breanna smiled. "I think he did this on purpose. When I asked him why I had to come meet him tonight he wouldn't even tell me. I just thought that maybe he was gonna take me out on the boat for a while and let me stay out here for a while to get my mind off of a few things." Breanna sat on the edge of the bathtub and ran her fingers through the bubbles close to the wall of the bathtub, then asked, "So, what are you doing here?"

"I'm supposed to start living here soon."

"You're supposed to start living in this house?" Breanna questioned with minimal giggles.

"Yeah. You don't think I could pay for a house like this? What's funny?"

"No. That's not it," Breanna continued girlishly giggling. "This house belongs to my father and Mike. The only way you could live here is if my father agreed. They bought this house a long time ago. They would tell me all the time that I could have it when I get married, but from time to time either Mike or my dad would bring me out here to stay for a little while."

"This house belongs to your pops and he's gonna give it to you when you get married… I won't stay. I'll leave when Mike comes back."

"No. That's not what I 'm saying. I want you to stay. My father wants you to be with me or else he wouldn't have agreed to let you live here," Breanna emphasized. "Don't leave. Stay for me," Breanna said as she leaned toward Soulja and kissed him on the tip of his lips. "For whatever reason, my father finally accepts you," Breanna said as she raised from the edge of the tub, then walked out of the bathroom.

Soulja watched Breanna walk out of the bathroom, thinking, "Maybe Charles is finally convinced that he doesn't have to protect his daughter from me." Soulja stepped out of the bathtub, pulled the drain cork, and walked to the walk-in closet.

When Soulja came out of the bathroom, Breanna stared at his bare chest and glanced at the shorts he wore. She was listening to the stereo at a low volume.

"Come sit with me, Geronimo," Breanna invited, sitting on the center of the bed.

Soulja complied, rolling onto the bed, positioning himself beside her flat on his back.

"How did you get the lights so dim?" Soulja asked.

"There's an adjusting knob beside the closets right there."

"Oh, I didn't see it."

"I bet you didn't see this either," Breanna said, then straddled herself on top of Soulja and started kissing him slowly. Breanna started kissing on Soulja's neck, then whispered in his ear, "I'm ready for you, Geronimo."

Breanna began to kiss Soulja on his neck again. She kissed his neck with such intimate, slow, and strong passion. Soulja knew what she meant, but it was so sudden. He didn't expect anything like this.

"Breanna, I don't have any condoms," Soulja informed.

Breanna raised her upper body and smiled at Soulja. She pulled her tight t-shirt off. "Geronimo, I love you. I don't want to feel some lubricated rubber going inside me for my first time. I want to feel you going inside me."

Breanna got off of Soulja. She pulled the elastic waist shorts and boxers off of his body as she got off of the bed. Soulja laid in the bed naked, watching Breanna take her pants off. They didn't take their eyes off of each other. Breanna's size thirty-six breast, firmly round and full, stared at Soulja. As she removed the panties from her size twenty-four waist, her size thirty-six hips curved perfectly from side to side.

Breanna smiled at Soulja for a moment as she stood in front of the bed naked. She walked to the side of the bed and sat down. Soulja crawled to her and kissed her on the back of her neck as he rubbed her arms and ran his hands over her breast caressingly. He gently tugged at Breanna's nipples as she softly moaned. She laid her back on the bed and looked up at Soulja. He laid his body on top of hers and began to kiss her. He rubbed the lips of her vagina with one hand then slowly pressed the tip of one finger inside. He felt the wetness of her vagina, then pressed the tip of two fingers inside of her, slowly working the two fingers deeper inside of her tight, gripping hotness as he ran his thumb over her clitoris. Breanna moaned into Soulja's mouth. He began to kiss her on the neck as he ran his other hand down the bottom lower part of her thigh and squeezed her butt cheeks, "Ahh," Breanna moaned. Her breathing was steady, but heavy. Soulja began to kiss Breanna's breast, teasing her nipples as he continued to thrust his two fingers in her slowly and occasionally use his vagina juice covered thumb to stroke her clitoris and gently massage and squeeze her butt cheeks with the other hand. It was causing burning arousal for her. Breanna's vagina was oozing wet and hot. She had begun to rotate her hips a little. Soulja took his two fingers out of her and rubbed the juices of her vagina on his penis, then inserted the head in. "Ahhh," Breanna exhaled at the feel of Soulja's throbbing penis entering her. Soulja felt her body brace. "Breanna, relax. I'm not gonna hurt you. I promise. You're going to enjoy this," Soulja whispered. Breanna began to relax. Soulja's words comforted her. He began to kiss Breanna's breast again, noticing that she enjoyed it. Soulja slowly eased himself into her until half of his penis length was inside of her. He made an effort to be sure that he rubbed his body against hers in a way that caused her clitoris to be rubbed on by his body. Breanna's breathing got faster and heavier. She felt her stomach spasmodically contracting; her thigh muscles began to shake like electricity was running through them. She clasped her arms around Soulja tightly as she applied her soft lips to Soulja's neck and delicately used her mouth for suction, her sexual desire intensely stimulated by this unfamiliar pleasure deriving Soulja's slow and steady strokes and his attentive hands and mouth. Breanna thrust her hips against Soulja as she wrapped her legs around his back releasing a deep and rich sound, "Ahhh." She thrust her hips again, sinking Soulja's penis deeper inside of her. "Ohhh," she voiced. In comparison to the pain of thrusting, the pleasure she felt exceeded. Her concentration was locked on the pleasure of feeling his skin slide in and out of her; the way he gently but firmly worked his mouth on her breast and nipples. The quivering in her stomach increased with the electric feeling in her thighs. She had never felt this way before. Soulja could feel her vagina contracting. Breanna muffled her moans, but suddenly she burst with moans. "Ahhh. Ahhh. Ahhooh. Umm. Uhh," she moaned, her vocals finding relaxation, carrying her moans with a soft tone. Soulja continued to kiss on her breast, gradually tracing his lips and tongue to her neck, then kissing Breanna's lips.

'I've never felt anything like that," Breanna said,

"You liked that feeling, huh?"

"Yes," Breanna purred, then kissed Soulja.

"I have another feeling for you," Soulja confessed with a grin.

"Oh, you do? What kind of feeling?" Breanna smiled.

"If you come to the shower with me, I'll show you when we get back."

"Then why are you still in the bed?" Breanna giggled as she got off of the bed.

Chapter 22

Mike walked through his front door. Charles was sitting on the couch watching television and eating popcorn.

"I got hungry," Charles admitted. "So what did Soulja say? Were we right?"

"Yeah," Mike answered as he walked to the chair, sat down, and placed his keys on the table in front of him. "But there are some things that we didn't know."

"Like what?"

"Soulja wasn't buying anything from Abdul. He was buying from someone named Rome, and Rome connected Abdul and Soulja."

"Ok, so, Soulja's connection to Abdul is through Rome, but not because of buying from him?" Charles questioned.

"Right. Now you remember how hard it was to find out who killed Legend. Apparently, Rome is connected to a man named Caesar and a woman named Rachel. Alright, Caesar asked Soulja to kill Legend. Rachel was setting Legend up for it. When Caesar took Soulja to Legend's apartment to kill him, Rachel had already killed Legend," Mike explained.

"It sounds like a territorial defense method. What are you gonna do about Rachel? You know this girl… whoever she is… she has to pay for what she did. We have to honor Legend's death," Charles emphasized.

"It's all in progress. Soulja's going to handle Rachel. He has personal issues with all three of these people, I'm gonna go to Chicago tonight by flight. I called some of our associates. They have people on Abdul as I speak. By the time I get there he'll probably be beaten and battered pretty good. I'll take care of him though."

Charles leaned back on the couch, then asked, "Is Soulja receptive to everything?"

"Oh, yeah. We came up with the plan together."

"No, that's not what I mean. I mean is he willing to accept my apology? The house?

"He thinks you're just going through a phase of grace. Is that what's going on?"

"No. Listen, I knew you wouldn't kill me when you found out that I was seeing Asia at the same time you were because you're my brother," Charles reflected with humbleness. "But... it's different between Soulja and I. I'm not related to him. He only knows me as Breanna's father. He doesn't really know anything else about me. So... he had every reason in the world to kill me and he didn't. And... the only reason I can think of is he really loves Breanna, he really thinks in her best interest even over his own feelings," Charles expressed passionately. "I hate that it took a near death experience like this one to make me realize that I was wrong to think that people that do the jobs you and Soulja do… can't have feelings or don't have feelings about anything." Charles briefly paused as if searching for words to express more, then he said, "I'm not only sorry for what has happened between me and Soulja. I never said this because I never saw a reason to, but… Mike, I promise… I promise with everything I am that I'm sorry for what has happened between me and you too. And… these words aren't just evoked from a grace period. These words come from my reasoning and my rationale about the life that I know Soulja can give my daughter and the life I know you could have given Asia."

Mike could see the sincerity of Charles' commiseration. He knew Charles finally realized the unnecessary trouble he'd caused for Mike in their archrival relationship over Mike and Asia, including the preceding complications he caused for Soulja and Breanna.

"I don't doubt that your words are true," Mike admitted. "But you know that your words alone won't prove themselves to be true… and… the notion of us giving Soulja that house and sending Breanna over there in hope of sending a message of approval isn't going to erase the bad history."

"I know. I know it'll take a lot for Soulja to trust my actions. But this isn't a temporary thought, it's a permanent intention. I want them to be together," Charles said. "Do you think she went over there?"

"Yeah," Mike breathed. "She's very intelligent. She probably knows she was set up to spend time with Soulja alone."

"I think I'll stop by there tomorrow. Just to talk to him face to face."

"Yeah, well. That's probably a good idea. I told him that you are a big part of the organization tonight. So, you can talk to him about that a little too. Look, I better go. I'll be back by tomorrow evening. Make sure you let the garage door down after you leave. Soulja's car is in there.

"No problem. Tell Abdul to enjoy his promotion."

Breanna's naked body laid on the bed. Soulja enjoyed looking at her attractive, athletic body as he kneeled over her. Breanna smiled at him as he bent down to kiss on her stomach. She closed her eyes to the sensational feeling of his lips and tongue caressing her stomach. Soulja slowly worked his massaging kisses around the area of her navel. He stroked the small bush of hair just above Breanna's vagina with the spread fingers of his hand, and used the other hand to fiddle with Breanna's nipples. The kisses traveled to the inner thigh. Soulja softly planted his lips and tongue on Breanna's inner thigh with the application of gentle suction. Breanna felt a bolt of passion rush through her body, exhaling intensely through her nose as if releasing some of the overwhelming energy. The osculation on her thigh began on the outer skin of her vagina. Soulja kissed the lips of her vagina as if tongue kissing. He pressed the oval of his finger against the upper wall of Breanna's warm wetness as he began to work his skillful tongue on her clitoris. Breanna's hips swayed with the motion of Soulja's tongue and head. She gasped moans to the spine-tingling pleasure of the oral experience. She teased her upper body with her hands as they rubbed across her body searching for somewhere to settle. Breanna licked her lips and arched her back. Her energy releasing moans motivated Soulja. Her pulsating vagina seemed to vibrate his flicking tongue as he distorted it inside of her. Breanna's moans went from gasps to ragged. Her breathing was uncontrolled as she allowed a high-pitch whimper to escape her throat. Soulja's coddling hand squeezed her butt cheek as the other caressed the outer part of her vagina while his tongue and lips continued to perform on, in, and around her vagina. Breanna moaned loudly as her vagina tightened with contractions. Her ragged gasps continued as she reached climax, rhythmically rotating her hips in circular motion. Soulja pushed himself on top of her and eased his steel hard penis inside of her drooling wet vagina. Breanna quickly pulled his head to her and kissed him with her eager lips and strong, passionate slurps.

Mike stepped outside of a cream colored car. His thick black coat protected him from the cold night weather. He walked to the door of a poorly conditioned house the vehicle he drove was parked in front of. Mike knocked on the door.

"Who is it?" a male voice yelled.

"The gates are open!" Mike yelled.

A man about Mike's height opened the door. The African-American man held a machine gun in one hand and held the door open with the other as Mike walked into the house.

"He's in the back," the man said to Mike.

The man closed the door and led Mike to a room in the rear of the house. The room smelled like mildew and whisky. The trash covered floor of the room that had one chair. Two men, also holding machine guns, stood next to Abdul as he sat on the chair tied up. His mouth was muzzled with a bloody white towel and a rope. His hands were bound to the armrest of the chair with rope and chains as where his legs to the legs of the chair. He peered through the puffy tissue surrounding his eyes, swollen from conspicuous assault. Dried blood covered Abdul's bruised face and parts of his chin. Mike stood in front of Abdul. He looked at the two men, one on each side of Abdul, then focused on Abdul. He examined Abdul's wounds with his eyes.

"You knew, I could've just ordered either one of these guys to get rid of you for me," Mike said confidently. "But you... you came so-." Mike stopped mid-sentence and pulled a lighter out of his pocket and said, "Fuck this. Where's the chemical?" looking at the two guys alternatively.

The two guys looked at one another, then one walked into the adjoining room and came back with a large container. The container had a long nozzle with a spray end and a pump on the top of the container. The man passed the container to Mike. Mike placed the container on the floor and the other man standing beside Abdul moved aside. Mike held the nozzle in one hand, pointing it at Abdul and pumped the container with the other hand. A clear chemical began to spray out of the nozzle. Mike started covering Abdul's feet and gradually covered his body.

"What's that? What?" Mike mocked at Abdul's muffled vocals sounding resistance.

Abdul began to wail because of the sting of the chemical on his wounds. Mike picked up a piece of paper amongst the trash and lit it with his lighter, then threw the burning paper on Abdul. Abdul immediately burst into flames. His muffled screams and persistent shaking was vain. His flaming body burned as Mike turned away and walked out of the room.

Mike walked to the cream colored vehicle as the three men walked to a dark colored mini-van. As Mike drove away, he pressed a speed-dial button on his cellular phone and waited for someone to answer. The phone rang four times.

"Hello," the sleepy voice of Charles answered.

"Hey, I'm on my way back. Our business is fine. Tell our associate at the house," Mike said.

"Ok," said Charles.

The morning sun shined beautifully through the windows of Soulja's new house. The grandiose exhibition of the sun flashed the brightness of Breanna's eyes from a peripheral view. Soulja held Breanna in his arms as they comfortably laid on the hammock in the sunroom. They both relaxed in silence until the doorbell rang.

"I'll go answer the door." Soulja lethargically said.

"I'll go. It's probably Mike," Breanna insisted, simultaneously rolling off of Soulja's body and releasing herself from his arms. "I'll be back," she said with gaiety and a smile, then leaned to Soulja and kissed him on his lips with a peck of her own.

Breanna walked to the front door of the house and opened the door with a smile that slowly formed into a straight face and said, "Hi, Daddy."

"Hi, baby," Charles fatherly greeted. "Is Soulja still here?" he humbly asked.

"Daddy, I really thought all of this was over. I'm not gonna let you-"

"No. No," Charles interrupted. "I just want to talk. No confrontation. Just talk. I swear, baby," he sincerely assured.

Breanna held the door open for her father to enter the house. Charles followed Breanna to the sunroom. As Breanna opened the door to the sunroom, followed by Charles, Soulja turned his head to the door. He immediately began to feel defensive, but remained open-minded. He held a stare on Charles as Breanna paced to the hammock and Charles sat on one of the chairs in the sunroom. Soulja sat up in the hammock and Breanna placed one of her hands over his.

"How are you this morning, Soulja?" Charles asked with awkwardness.

"I feel pretty good," Soulja replied calmly.

"Ok, well… listen… I know this is ah…ok," Charles stumbled for words, "I came over here this morning because I believe… well, I know I owe both of you an apology. So… I just want to say that I'm sorry for the turbulence I've caused your relationship with each other," Charles noticed Soulja and Breanna's attentiveness. "My stereotypical behavior, my over-protectiveness… my foolish determination to prove that you are unworthy of my daughter's love, all stared me in my face like the barrel of a gun," Charles voiced gracefully as he glanced at Breanna then briefly focused on Soulja. "Sometimes certain things happen in life, you know, you see things or hear things, but things happen in life that cause an instant realization for you," Charles said with lecture. "I've given a lot of thought to my mistakes… the facts of life I've neglected and regardless of what happened to spark these realizations, they're there now and I'm not going to overlook them." Charles tersely paused, then focused on Soulja and said, "Soulja, there isn't a fiber of skepticism in me concerning whether or not you can give my daughter everything she deserves in any angle of a relationship because I know you can. I know you're capable of returning all the virtue my daughter gives and I know you will. I realize your dedication and loyalty to Breanna. I realize your fidelity." Charles peered at his daughter and said, "Breanna, I don't know if you know about this or not, but Mike and I decided to sign this house over to Soulja. We kind of set things up for you two to be alone together. Now, I know we said that we would give you this house when you get married, but honestly… I'm hoping Soulja's the man you decide to marry."

Breanna smiled and looked at Soulja eye to eye then Charles said, "I know that what I'm saying isn't going to automatically make everything alright." Charles alternatively looked at Breanna and Soulja as he said, "This is just a start. I hope both of you can forgive me and accept my apology."

Breanna and Soulja looked at each other, then at Charles and almost simultaneously said, "Yeah."

"Thank you," Charles said with a relieving expression. Charles raised from his seat and walked to Soulja and shook his hand, then he hugged his daughter as she raised from the hammock, and asked, "Soulja, there's something I want to show you. Would you mind walking outside with me?"

"No, I don't mind," Soulja calmly answered, raising from the hammock.

"Guess what I have in my pocket," Charles said with a smile to his daughter as he reached in his pocket and pulled out a pair of keys.

"Those are the keys to the boat," Breanna replied with recognition.

"Well, the boat is yours, you should have the keys," Charles said, dangling the keys in Breanna's face.

"Are you serious?! You're giving it to me!" she said, grabbing the keys with excitement covering her face. "Thank you, Daddy!" she said, embracing her father again.

"It's not a problem, Breanna. Why don't you go prep and take Soulja for a tour when he gets back," Charles suggested.

"Yeah. That is a good idea," Breanna agreed, then kissed Soulja on his jaw-line." Everything should be ready by the time you get back," Breanna said to Soulja, then walked out of the sunroom through a side door.

Charles and Soulja walked out of the sunroom, entering the house, then exited the house through the front door. Soulja followed

Charles to the driveway. Charles had a BMW parked beside Breanna's BMW. He reached in his other pants pocket and pulled out a pair of keys on a key ring with a garage door opener. Charles opened the double garage doors with the push of a button on the garage door opener. He walked to the black Jaguar in the garage, followed by Soulja.

"I used this car to pick up supplies from the store a few times," Charles said, staring at the vehicle. "It only has a few hundred miles on it. I just bought it a few months ago." Charles looked at Soulja and said, "I want you to have it."

"Man, you don't have to give me this and you didn't have to give me this house," Soulja said.

"Oh, I know. But I'm pleased that you accepted the house. But you can think of the car as a gift from me to you for your membership to the organization. Mike says he's on his way back. He's done with what he went to do, so, I guess that means you can do what you need to do now. I know that you know I'm a part of the organization, but what you don't know is essentially the organization is ran by me and Mike. The business of our organization stretches nationwide. We even dabble in a few things in other countries. I'm not going to tell you that you can't sell drugs anymore. I just want you to know that your options are varied and greater. If you want to continue investing in the drug trade, then I want you to know that you don't have to put your hands on street drugs anymore. I can connect you to who you need to be connected to so that you can get the amount of supply you need in any quantity. Any time you want to you can begin to invest in arms trade, legitimate business investments, various product smuggling, anything."

Soulja contemplatively looked at Charles and said, "I think for now I'll want to take you up on the drug connection and the business investments."

"Ok. We can get together and discuss both. Give me a call later or something and we'll schedule a meeting."

"Alright."

"So, what do you say about the car?" Charles asked, extending his hand with the keys in them.

"Thanks," Soulja simply replied as he accepted the keys.

"Just give me a call on those investments," Charles said as he walked to his vehicle.

Soulja watched Charles reverse out of the driveway, then walked inside the house. He picked up his cell phone from the island on the kitchen and walked into the sunroom. He looked outside at the yacht and dialed a number on the cell phone.

"Hello," Rome answered his cell phone as he stroked his fingers through Rachel's hair while she laid her head on his stomach.

"Yeah, what's up, man?" Soulja greeted.

"Soulja," Rome said, causing Rachel to look up at him. "Where are you, man?"

"I'm handling a lil business. Check this out. Things went sour when I went ridin' snowball. It took me a while to get to you because I was looking for someone to ride with me, but I found 'em and I did what I was supposed to do. That's what really mattered, right?"

"Yeah. That's good. Well, I'm glad to know you back from ridin' snowball. Don't forget to holla at me when you get through doin' what you doin'. I told you I got someone important I want you to meet."

"Ok. I'm gon' holla."

"Yeah," Rome said, then disconnected with Soulja.

Rome placed the cell phone on the nightstand next to the bed.

"I told Soulja I got someone I want him to meet so we'll have a back-up plan. You know, just in case he doesn't come running when you call," Rome said to Rachel. "Oh, he coming. He know why I want him to come see me," Rachel said. "That nigga want this good pussy," she boasted. Rachel ran her hands across his bare chest and said, "You startin' to doubt me?" in a questioning tone.

"You know I don't doubt you. I never have," Rome sincerely replied.

"You betta not," Rachel smiled, then kissed Rome.

Rachel strongly kissed Rome, then begun to trace her hand down the lining of his abdomen. Beneath the sheets they were under, her hand found his penis and began to pamper and fiddle with it in its limp state. She stopped kissing Rome and put her head under the sheets. Rachel gobbled Rome's penis into her mouth greedily. She wrapped her soft lips around the head of his penis. "Mmm," she hummed. Rome closed his eyes to the vibrating sensation of the droning sound Rachel produced. She molded her tongue around the head of his penis, then slid her mouth down the length of his penis. She could feel the hardness accreting as she slowly came up to the head again, then quickly slid her lips and tongue down to the base and engulfed his testicle sac. The sensation engendered strong arousal in Rome. He clenched the bed sheets and muffled a grunt.

Rachel held the base of his penis with one hand and caressingly rolled his testicles in their sack with the other hand as she sucked and licked his penis. She slowly and gently formed her lips over his penis, bobbing her head up and down. The feeling of rushing pleasure was beginning to be too much for Rome. He found himself pumping his hips. He felt that he would climax soon, but he wasn't ready for this amazing feeling to end. Rachel took Rome's full length into her mouth and throat. She felt Rome's penis jerking and she gave suction to each jerk she felt. Suddenly, Rome pulled her off of him and quickly mounted himself on top of her and inserted his penis into her vagina. He started pumping himself inside of her slowly. Rachel's hips thrust against Rome fast and strong. "Just fuck me, baby," Rachel softly breathed with her eyes closed. Rome began to speed his movements. He grabbed her legs and pushed her knees to her shoulders as he pumped harder and faster into her. Rachel began to make guttural moans. "Hmm. Hmm. Hmm. Hmm," she sounded from her throat. Rome rested the back of her knees on his shoulders and curled his arms around her shoulders. He strongly pumped into her. Each stroke inside of her made a slushing sound. Rachel groaned with rattling sounds. Her breast bounced against her chest as Rome slammed his body against hers with each thrust into her hot vagina. "Ahhah. Ahhah. Uhmahhah," her vocals loudly released. Their bodies were sweaty. Rachel humped him off of her and quickly straddled herself on top of him. Her vagina quickly swallowed his penis. She arched her back as she began to sit erect on top of him. Rachel rotated her hips with a swing forward with rhythmical speed. She elongated her body with an arch, then laid her belly against Rome's. She curled her arms under his shoulders and began to hump her hips strong and fast against Rome. She could hear him grunting as she released soft, gasp-like groans of her own. Her breast were pressed against Rome as she held him tightly, simultaneously tightening the muscles of her vagina around the base of Rome's penis. She snatched with her vagina and burst with furiously fast humps against Rome. Rome's grunts strongly released as he held her butt cheeks. He squeezed them as he climaxed. Rachel thrust down hard as he climaxed. She gripped his penis at the base with her vagina and slowly came up to the head, then quickly and powerfully thrust down hard again. "Ahh. Shh. Ahh.," Rome grunted and slurped loudly as Rachel continued to thrust down hard and slowly come up. "Nigga you can't handle me," she smiled as she continued her movements, then kissed Rome forcefully.

Chapter 23

Caesar stood in Fat's living room in front of Nikki. She walked closer to him with her eyes focused on him.

"So, you gon' give me a kiss before you leave?" Nikki softly asked. She pulled up the front of her short flannel skirt, then said, "You haven't touched me since you been here. You scared or somethin'?" She grabbed Caesar's hand and placed it on her vagina as she kissed him, then asked, "Why you actin' so paranoid, baby?"

"Man, you crazy. If Fat come from back there he gon' beat cho ass," Caesar warned.

"Oh, he slow. You see you already been waitin' bout ten minutes," Nikki said as Fat walked into the living room.

"Waitin' ten minutes fa what?" Fat asked.

"Waitin' on you," Nikki mockingly said, "Yo slow ass always have people waitin'."

"Man, fuck you," Fat simply said. "Don't nobody take as long as you do to go somewhere," he turned his attention to Caesar and asked, "You ready to go, dogg?"

"Yeah. Let's bounce, my nigga."

Fat opened the door and began to walk out of the house, followed by Caesar.

"Bye, Caesar," Nikki flirted. "Take Fat somewhere and drop 'em off. Come back so we can have a smoke-out," she laughed.

"Fuck you, nigga," Fat remarked as he closed the door. "That bitch crazy," he said to Caesar as they walked to a cherry-red glossy finished suburban parked in his driveway. "Aye, I like this one fa real," Fat complimented as he observed the interior, while he commenced to step into the passenger's side of the vehicle.

"Yeah, I just decided to bring it out today. I'ma put this bitch on full and we gon' break this muthafucka in, bruh," Caesar said excitingly, then ignited the vehicle.

Caesar drove to the local gas station with the stereo system in his vehicle thumping like a concert. As he pulled into the gas station, he noticed Becky pumping gas into a navy-blue long-frame four-door car. She watched the glossy cherry-red suburban park beside the gas tank next to her, finally noticing it was Caesar. Becky finished pumping gas into the four door vehicle and walked to the driver's side door of the suburban.

"What's up, nigga?" Becky asked Caesar as he stepped out of his vehicle.

"They tell me you da lady wit' the answers Becky. You tell me what's up. Who car you in? Where yo' car at?"

"I'm drivin' a front car. I just didn't feel like drivin' my car," Becky said as a man in his car behind the navy-blue vehicle stuck his head out of his window, looking at her and Caesar.

"If that's yo' car you need to move it! I need gas just like you!" the man yelled.

"Playa talking ta you, man," Caesar alarmed Becky.

"Hey!" the man yelled.

Becky turned to the man and said, "It's four mo' gas tanks down there. Why you can't go down there?" referring to the four tanks behind her.

"Bitch, I want this! You don't tell me where ta get no muthafuckin' gas!" the man yelled with hostility, watching Becky walk to his car.

"Who da fuck you thank you talkin' to, nigga?!" Becky angrily asked as she stood beside the driver's side door of the man's car. "You got me fucked up!"

"Bitch! Get cho ass in that car and move out my muthafuckin' way!"

"Nigga, fuck you!" Becky yelled as she pulled a nine millimeter from the clasp of the front of her pants and began to shoot the door of the man's car.

The man stepped on the accelerator of his vehicle and sped out of the gas station. Becky jumped in the long-frame vehicle and sped after the man. Caesar stood there watching them speed down the highway.

"What the hell wrong wit' Becky, man?" Caesar asked Fat."

"Man, Soulja got that lil bitch like that."

Soulja looked out of the window of the yacht, concentrating on the water. Breanna walked behind him and wrapped her arms around him.

"So, what do you think?" Breanna asked.

"I didn't realize this boat was so big" Soulja responded as he turned to face her.

"It's a yacht. These kind of boats are generally bigger, but I like this one. It's just the legal size to drive around the river, but I have fun just floating on the lake," Breanna replied. "I wasn't talking about the boat though."

"Oh, my fault. What were you talking about then?"

"You remember what my dad said earlier today?"

"He said a lot."

"Yeah, but... before he left he mentioned that he wanted you to marry me."

"Oh, yeah," Soulja reflected. "You think he means it or you think-"

"I just wanna know what you think," Breanna interrupted.

"What? About marrying you?" Soulja questioned. "If you were ready for it, yeah."

"Is there something that makes you think I'm not ready?"

"No. We just never talked about it."

"So, if I said I was ready you would marry me?"

"Yep," Soulja calmly answered.

"Ok then, I'm ready," Breanna smiled.

"You're ready?" Soulja asked with slight surprise.

"Yeah."

"You're ready?"

"Yeah," Breanna smiled.

"Then, we'll get married."

"When?" Breanna excitedly asked.

"Now if you want to."

"No! No! We can't get married now! I have to make plans!" Breanna said with more excitement. "Are you serious? Are you really gonna marry me?"

"Yeah, as soon as you make up your mind when."

Breanna grabbed Soulja and tackled him onto the bed in the yacht. She mounted herself on top of him.

"Man, you wild as hell. What did you throw me on the bed like that for?" Soulja smiled.

"I'm crazy about you. Do you know that?" Breanna sincerely asked. "I love you."

Breanna kissed Soulja with slow attentive fervency.

The nightfall maintained an accommodation of cool breezes that made the summer night comfortable. Caesar watched a dark brown vehicle drive through the park. As the two-door vehicle parked beside him, he noticed it was Soulja. "Who car Soulja drivin?" Caesar asked Rome. "He probably rented a car," Rome rationalized. "You know Rachel said he was coming to her house tonight. Look at 'em," Rome said as Soulja got out of the brown vehicle. "He about to give an excuse for not coming wit' me tonight so he can go to Rachel's house."

Soulja walked to Caesar's cherry-red suburban as he looked at the three guys on the basketball court of the park. The playground close to the parking lot had monkey bars that slightly obstructed the view from the distance of Caesar's vehicle, but the sliding-board in the playground completely obstructed the view from the distance of Soulja's vehicle. He entered the suburban and sat on the rear passenger's seat.

"Ain't no way I could miss you in this muthafucka right here. You ridin' clean, bruh. When you get this one?" Soulja asked.

"I just started ridin' it today," Caesar responded without noticing Soulja slide his two nine millimeters from his pants as he reclined and slouched on the back seat.

Soulja placed one gun under each leg, then leaned forward and asked, "So, who you want me to meet?"

Caesar and Rome looked at each other, perplexed by Soulja's question. They were expecting him to give them some sort of excuse for not being able to go meet the person Rome speciously mentioned to Soulja as a significant individual.

"You'll see when we get there. You ready to go?" Rome asked.

"Yeah," Soulja replied. "I'm ready to go," he said as he pulled the guns from beneath his legs, then shot Rome and Caesar in the head simultaneously.

The three mean on the basketball court heard one shot. They looked around them, searching the surrounding area with their eyes.

Soulja just sat in the suburban for a while, then pulled a face towel out of his front pocket and began to wipe the seat. He used the towel to wipe the door, open the door then close the door. He wiped the handle of the door, then walked to the brown vehicle. He glanced at the basketball court as he entered his vehicle. The three men on the basketball court were playing basketball. Soulja reversed the brown vehicle out of the parking space, then slowly drove out of the park.

Soulja drove the highway listening to instrumental blues music. He appeared calm and mentally clarified. No psychological stressors displayed in his character.

As Soulja drove into the driveway of Rachel's house, Rachel was peeking through the curtains of her window. She quickly opened the front door, wearing pink lingerie. She watched Soulja walk to her.

"Why don't you have on any clothes?" Soulja asked as he walked into the house.

"How long you gon' play crazy wit' me? You act like you don't even know what's up," Rachel said as she closed the door and followed Soulja to the living room.

"Oh, I know what's up," Soulja replied.

"Well, why you keep acting like you don't care?" Rachel softly asked. "You act like it don't even matter," she said, walking closer to Soulja. She held his hand gently and said, "you know I been wantin' to get wit' you for a long time. That don't matter to you?"

"Yeah, it matter," Soulja calmly said.

Rachel kissed Soulja's ear, then whispered, "What's up, then?" She kissed on Soulja's neck, then said, "I wanna see if the king of the bed really tha king."

"What did you say?"

"King of the bed... You don't know do you?" Rachel smiled as she studied Soulja's facial expression of incomprehension. "Nikki told me and Rose that a lot of other women call you king of the bed. They say you da king of all in the bed," Rachel laughed. "You know I want some of that," she said as she pushed Soulja on the couch and got on her knees in front of him.

Rachel reached for the zipper on Soulja's pants. She felt Soulja's gun and reached for the handle of it. Her perfect opportunity to kill Soulja if he allows her to move it. But she wanted sex first.

"I'll move it," Soulja said, then pulled the gun from the grip of his belt and pants before her hands settled on the handle.

"When did you get a silencer?" Rachel asked, noticing the weapon silencer on the muzzle of Soulja's nine millimeter.

"It doesn't matter, baby. You know what I want you to do?" Soulja seduced.

"What?" Rachel smiled.

"I wanna see your sexy ass body. I want you to stand in front of me and take off your clothes so I can look at your body. Can you do that for me?"

"Yeah," Rachel responded as she stood erect, taking off her bra with felicity.

Rachel turned her back to Soulja and slowly took off her panties bending over as she stepped out of them. Her round butt cheeks switched from side to side as she turned to face Soulja. Her cute face had a wide smile as she rubbed one hand between her legs. "Yeah. That's what I wanna see," Soulja said as he raised his weapon and shot Rachel in the head. Rachel's body fell to the floor and Soulja stood to his feet, looking at her. He stared at her for a moment then shot her two more times in the face. Rachel's dead body laid on the floor exuding blood from the three bullet wounds on her face. Soulja shot her six more times in her upper body and stood over her watching blood ooze from her stomach and chest.

Later that night, Soulja drove into the parking lot of a hotel. He parked the brown two-door vehicle next to a motorcycle with 3D artwork of exotic red, orange, black, and gold. He grabbed a bag from the back seat and pulled out a flaming colored yellow, black, and red knit cap and similar color biker jacket. He put the knit cap and biker jacket on, then reached in the inside pocket of the biker jacket and pulled out a pair of shades. Soulja extracted his cell phone from his pants pocket and dialed a telephone number.

"Yeah," the masculine voice answered the phone.

"Hey. Listen, man. I'm going for a ride on my bike," Soulja said to the man.

"I'll be on my way to get the car."

"Alright," Soulja said as he disconnected with the man.

Soulja placed his cell phone in the inside pocket of the biker jacket and leaned over to the glove compartment for the gloves inside. He put on the gloves and used the towel in his pocket to wipe the cars' interior. Soulja got out of the car and hopped on the motorcycle as he glanced around the parking lot. The motorcycle growled and barked after Soulja ignited it and drove out of the parking lot.

When Soulja arrived home, he parked the motorcycle in the driveway. As he walked through the front door, Breanna was approaching.

"I heard you pulling into the driveway," Breanna smiled.

"Did you enjoy your ride?" she asked as she embraced him.

"Yeah. You wanna come with me next time?"

"I'm not afraid," Breanna teased as they walked to the living room.

"I want you to have something," Soulja smiled as he reached into the inside pocket of his biker jacket and pulled out a ring box. "This is for you," he said, extending the ring box to Breanna.

Breanna's felicity was obvious as she opened the box, smiling widely. The enormous diamond ring came unexpected to Breanna.

"This is my engagement ring?" Breanna questioned with watery eyes and a smile.

"Well, you're gonna be my wife," Soulja said, taking the ring out of the box. "You have to have an engagement ring," he said as he slid it on her finger.

"How did you even know my ring size?" Breanna asked as she admired the ring.

"I just remembered one of the rings you wear on that finger sometimes and took it with me," Soulja said, extending a gold ring from his pocket, holding it in her face.

"You're so slick," Breanna laughed, then embraced him.

"Breanna. You're my love. I love you," Soulja sincerely said.

"I love you too," Breanna said, then kissed Soulja.

Soulja sat in the living room of Mike's house on the couch. Charles sat next to him. Soulja stared at the first page of the thin stack of documents in his hands. "Hey," Charles said as he tugged slightly on the short-sleeve of Soulja's crimson colored shirt to get his attention. "Are you understanding how it works now?" he chuckled.

"Yeah," Soulja responded without shifting his eyes. "I think you explained it well enough," he continued as he placed the documents on the table in front of them, turning his attention to Charles. "You're right, though. I'll take a minor in some sort of investment management course when I start college. That way I'll be able to follow the investment process better like you said," he admitted. "I ah... I appreciate you taking the time to explain to me the way my business investment will work," he gratefully expressed.

"It's no problem. Now all we have to do is convene with my lawyer so he can do the paper work process."

"Yeah. You said he'd be my lawyer too for this?" Soulja expressed with a questioning gesture.

"That's right. Come on. We don't wanna be late," Charles urged as he began to raise from his seat.

"Wait… Wait a minute," Soulja rushed. "I wanna ask you something before we leave," he said as Charles lowered himself back onto the couch. "I wanted to tell you that I'm gonna need that connection you were tellin' me about as soon as possible."

"You mean the cocaine?" Charles questioned.

"Yeah. I'm gonna be supplying a large territory. I need to be prepared as soon as possible," Soulja seriously replied.

"Well, it usually takes a little while for shipments to land where they do, but if you need some now, I still have about seven-hundred ki's in powder. How many do you need?"

"Right now, I believe about sixty will be enough. You sellin' 'em to me for the same price you told me your connection wants?"

"No," Charles simply said.

"Well, how much?" Soulja quickly asked.

"I'm … I'm not gonna sell you any," Charles said with a strict look. "I'm gonna give you three-hundred ki's.

"Tis," Soulja breathed. "You don't have to keep givin' me anything man. I-"

"You… ok…," Charles stammered. "Just do me a favor and take what I'm offering," he pleaded. "When people buy from my connection, they normally buy in the number of thousands of ki's. You can use what you make from the three hundred and add it to what you were gonna spend. Get one big shipment and you won't have to constantly go back and forth buying," he expressed with gesticulation. Charles turned his body to face Soulja and leaned forward, then humbly said, "I know it's probably hard for you to accept people giving you things, especially me. It's probably very awkward, but you –for whatever reason– you allowed me to keep my life after everything I put you through. That's a reward I can never forget and you deserve to be honored and… the gifts that I give and will continue to give you are just tokens of my honor and loyalty to you. The gifts won't prove it, but time will show it. Just, please, allow me to extend these small tokens."

Soulja's facial expression revealed cogitation as he lowly said, "This is what you want. I'll accept your offer."

Fat and Nikki sat in their living room sharing a laugh with Becky when they heard a knock on the door. "Girl, you crazy as hell," Nikki giggled as she walked to the front door. She opened the door and Rose was standing there in almost a hypnotic daze as she asked, "Rose, what's wrong wit' you, girl?"

Rose appeared not to hear Nikki then she asked, "Can I come in?" with a low tone, holding her head to the ground.

"Come on in," Nikki invited as Rose stepped into the house.

"What's up, Rose?" Fat asked. "You look like you been in funky-town all night," he mocked, then fulminated to laughter.

Becky and Nikki seemed to be immune to Fat's humor due to their recognition of the distraught plastered on Rose's face.

"Girl, what's up? Why you lookin' so depressed and shit?" Nikki asked with strong concern as she walked closer to Rose.

Rose glanced at all of them then with perturbation evoking in her voice she said, "Rome... Caesar and Rachel... they got killed." She wasn't focusing her attention on anyone as she continued, saying, "They were like family to me. Somebody killed them."

"Who... Who did it, Rose?" Nikki asked on the verge of tears exuding her eyes.

Fat and Becky peered at Rose with blank thought. They couldn't fathom who would be idiotic enough to kill Rome, Caesar, and Rachel. It was unbelievable and impossible that someone could accomplish a thing of that nature in their minds. "Who could perform with the faculty necessary to accomplish this?" they both essentially thought.

"Whoever did it is crazy, because if Soulja find out who did it, he gon' retaliate," Fat assured as Becky's head gestured in affirmation of Fat's statement.

"I don't know who did it... but I know he'll find out," Rose said. Rose's cell phone rang and she reached into her pocket to answer, "Hello."

"Rose?" Soulja questioned.

"Yeah," her cracked voice murmured.

"I guess you heard about Rome, Caesar, and Rachel?" Soulja empathetically asked.

"Yeah."

"Check this out. I'm getting everybody to meet me at Rome's club, but I need you to meet me there first so that you can open the door. You're gonna open the club tonight, right?"

"Ah. I didn't think about it, but I can if you need everyone there."

"Yeah. Open it in their memory, but I need everyone in the click in the V.I.P. room right now, though. That gives everyone about two hours to get ready for later tonight.

"O…ok, I'll be there."

"Alright. Everything will be alright," Soulja assured as he disconnected with Rose.

He dialed a number on his cell phone as he sat in his glossy green vehicle. Soulja waited for an answer as he leaned against the backrest of his driver's seat.

"Hello," Becky answered as she peered at Rose and Nikki while they conversed.

"I want you to meet me at Rome's club."

"Right now?"

"Yeah. You can come, right?"

"Yeah, I'll come right now, man."

"Alright."

"I'm on my way," Becky assured, then disconnected with Soulja. She raised herself from her seat as she said, "I have to go y'all, I'll see y'all later."

"Yeah. I'll see y'all later too," Rose said as she followed Becky out of the front door. "Becky," Rose said, getting her attention. "Was that Soulja calling you?" she asked as Becky opened the door to her car.

Becky seemed to be contemplating an answer, then asked, "Why? Did he call you?"

"Yeah. He asked me to meet him at the club. Is that where you're going?

"Yep."

"He probably wants to talk about the retaliation for what happened."

"Well, let's just go. I'll follow you," Becky suggested.

Rose got in her car almost simultaneous to when Becky got in her car.

As Rose drove onto the parking lot of the club, followed by Becky, it appeared to her that everyone made it there before she did. She looked at all the cars, lacking their ultimate shine as the sky's fixated colors threatened to darken by the second. Becky parked in the space beside Rose's car as Rose got out of her car. Rose walked toward Soulja trying to determine the nature of the conversation he was having with the two men standing in front of him. She glanced at the complacency of Soulja's posture as he leaned against his car, then altered her focus to the agitated gesticulated expressions of the two dark skin men standing in front of him. She tried to motivate her psychological functions to apply perspicacity to her visual analysis. Her attempts were a fiasco and they ended the conversation as she approached.

"I didn't expect everyone to get here so fast," Rose said to Soulja. "Hi, Allan," she said.

"What's up, Rose?" the man on Soulja's right, wearing a black and white baseball cap to the back responded.

"Hi, Chip," Rose said to the other man on Soulja's left, wearing a white and green pinstripe baseball cap to the back.

"Aye, what's up?" Chip responded.

"So, y'all ready to go in?" Rose asked.

"Yeah, let's go in. I wanna get this over before the club-jumpers get here," Soulja said. "Aye, come on! Let's go inside!" Soulja loudly said to everyone in the parking lot.

Rose walked to the door of the club with a pair of keys in her hand. She opened the door and walked inside followed by Soulja and the approximate sixteen people that were in the parking lot. Rose and Soulja stood at the door until everyone walked inside. Some of the men and few women greeted Soulja verbally as they passed by him.

"Becky, come' ere for a minute," Soulja requested as the last man walked through the door and Rose locked it from the inside.

"What's up?" Becky asked.

Soulja put his arm around Becky and guided her to Rose, then said, "Y'all know the click is mine now, right?"

"Yeah. You gon' have some problems though," Rose voiced. "People like Allan and Chip gon' think they should be helpin' you run the click."

"Yeah. That's what they were asking me about outside, but I already know who I want to help me."

"Ok, who?" Rose asked.

"I want you and Becky."

"I ain't gon' doubt that you can get the dope to supply everybody, but you sure you want us to do this with you?"

"I can do it," Becky said with a certainty of being useful.

"Rose, if you don't think you can do it. I'll find another person," Soulja simply said.

"I can do it. I just wanna be sure you want me to."

"Yeah. I want you and Becky. Let's go upstairs."

They walked upstairs and entered the V.I.P. room. Everyone was already situated at one of the many tables in the commodious room. Soulja walked to the front of the room. He stood in front of everyone, staring at some of the faces in the room before he glanced at Allan and Chip. Everyone was silent.

"I think everybody know what happened yesterday," Soulja said.

"Yeah, we know," Chip said, adding to the chatter in the room after Soulja's statement. "What you gon' do about it?"

"What I'm gonna do, when I'm gonna do it… all that's in my mind. Just know something's gonna happen," Soulja responded.

"Who did it, man?" Allan asked. "Was it them boys from the Chi?"

"I'm gonna handle this hit on my own. Don't sweat it. All I want you and everybody here to know is the click ain't gon' die. We still gon' control tha city same way we did before today."

"So, you sayin' you gon' make sure you supply us wit' the dope we need to keep our profits rollin'?" a bright skin woman at the back table asked.

"As much as you can handle on front or buy, Rose and Becky gon' have it for you."

"Becky and Rose?!" Chip frowned with loud disagreement.

"They gon' give us the same price deals Rome gave us or we gon' have to pay more?" the woman asked.

"They'll give you tha same price deals."

Controversial chatter covered the room momentarily.

"Becky and Rose gon' get wit' everybody to see what you need. I have to meet someone, so, I'll get at y'all another time," Soulja said as he walked to the door of the babble-filled room.

Soulja drove the highway listening to fast pace beats of hip-hop music. His face covered with satisfaction, he cracked a slight smile.

When Soulja pulled into the driveway of his home, he showed no sense of surprise that a number of cars were parked in his driveway. He walked to the front door of his home and entered. He walked into the living room, immediately making eye contact with Breanna. She raised from her seat beside Tia and walked to Soulja.

"I've been waiting for you," Breanna said as she embraced Soulja.

Soulja glanced at the faces of Charles, Mike, Asia, Amanda and Tia as he wrapped his arms around Breanna, then said," I didn't mean to be late."

"It's ok," Breanna smiled, then led Soulja to the couch and sat next to Tia.

"Ok, what's this big surprise Breanna keeps talking about, Soulja?" Tia exuberantly and eagerly asked, beaming her eyes on him.

Everyone sat attentively, anticipating Soulja's response.

"Ah," Soulja glanced at Breanna searching for a glimpse of a sign of responsive direction. "I thought Breanna would tell everyone what... you know, about the surprise," he responded, alternately focusing on each face in the room.

"You can tell them. I just wanted us to be together when they found out," Breanna fervently said, clasping Soulja's hand and hers together.

"Ok. Ah. Well," Soulja hesitated. "Me and Breanna decided to get married," he said as a matter of fact.

The room became a coalescence of exultation. The common physiognomy of felicity in the room provided implication of acceptance and support of their decision. Breanna reached into the pocket of her white shorts and pulled out the engagement ring Soulja bought her, he placed it on her finger glowing a smile as bright as the enormous diamond ring.

"Here's my engagement ring," Breanna sang with her hand in the air, wiggling her fingers.

"Oh, girl, that's a pretty ring," Tia burst. "Soulja, you bought that?" Tia asked with a tone of compliment.

Soulja nodded his head affirmatively as Charles raised from his seat and walked primly toward him. Tia focused on Charles with uncertainty of his intentions. Asia seemed prepared to jump out of her seat with the alarmed composure of a bodyguard as Mike and Amanda lethargically reclined in their seats.

To the conspicuous surprise of everyone but Soulja, Breanna, and Mike, Charles extended his hand to Soulja and fervidly said, "Congratulations."

"Thank you," Soulja responded as he shook Charles' hand.

"There's not a doubt in my mind that you will make my daughter happy for the rest of her life," Charles said.

Tia, Asia, and Amanda held obfuscated facial expressions. Breanna stood to her feet and embraced her father.

"We should celebrate," Charles lively said to everyone. "Soulja, you mind? That's you and Breanna's wine over there."

"No. Come on. Let's break out the good stuff," Soulja suggested.

The lights in the club were minimal and dim. Becky sat in a security room with Rose staring at the union of monitors. They watched people dancing on a couple of monitors, others sitting at tables drinking on a few more monitors, the bar region of the club on another monitor, and the doors of the club on other monitors as well as other areas of the club.

"Hey. I need to do a few things. I'll be back. Do you need anything?" Becky asked.

"Uh, no. I'm straight," Rose answered.

"Ah'ight," Becky said as she raised from her seat. "I'll be back in a lil while," she continued as she commenced to walk toward the exit of the room.

"See you later," Rose voiced as Becky walked out of the door.

Rose watched Becky walk down the hallway, after exiting the room, on the monitor. She followed Becky on the monitor as Becky walked down the staircase, through another hallway, through a couple of doors, across the club, and out the front entrance of the club. Allan and Chip walked out of the front entrance seconds after Becky, but Rose didn't see them leave because she had begun to watch a different monitor.

Outside the club, Becky walked to her car. Allan and Chip walked in a fast pace toward her.

"Aye, Becky!" Allan yelled. "Hold up for a minute, man. Let me holla at' cha."

Becky stopped in front of her short-frame luxury vehicle and asked, "What's up?"

Her frown indicated agitation during her wait for Allan and Chip to get closer.

"We know how much we need," Allan said to Becky.

"Ah'ight, how much?"

"We gon' gone get ten ki's," Allan replied.

"Ah'ight. I'll get cho cell number. I'm a get wit' cha."

"What's wrong wit' now? Why you can't give it to us now?" Chip asked with irritation.

"Because I'm tellin' you I'm gon' holla, nigga. We gon' do this on my time. My way," Becky firmly said.

"This bitch ain't got no dope," Chip aggressively said as he promptly grabbed his .38 revolver from his pants and aimed it at Becky. "Bitch you ain't got no dope."

"Yes I do," Becky humbly said, peering at the gun in her face.

Allan punched Becky on her forehead.

"Ahh, shh," Becky breathed and slurped in agony as she placed her hand over her head. Becky submissively looked at Allan and Chip.

"Bitch get in that car," Chip ordered, referring to Becky's dark purple short-frame luxury sports car. "Get the fuck on in tha car bitch! You gon' get that muthafuckin' dope!"

Chip guided Becky to the driver's side of her car. He opened the rear passenger's side door, then opened the driver's door. Allan pushed Becky against the opened driver's door. She got inside the car on the driver's side, then Chip entered the rear passenger's side and Allan ran to the front passenger's side. "Crank this muthafucka up!" Chip yelled. "If you do anything... bitch I'm gon' leave yo' trick ass right here in this car stanky."

Soulja sat beside Breanna with a glass of wine in his hand. They amused themselves with the chatter of everyone around them. Suddenly, Soulja's cell phone rang. He reached in his pocket to answer it.

"Hello," Soulja answered.

"Check this out, nigga. We got cho bitch. You need to bring all tha dope and money you got to Parker St. right now. You know what I'll do to this bitch so don't play no games. Hear, listen,"

Chip said, then placed the phone to Becky's ear as she drove down a neighborhood street.

"They serious, Soulja. Come get me. He already hit me in-..."

"You don't need to hear no mo'. Just do right and ya pretty lil pussy gon' live, bruh," Chip said, then disconnected with Soulja.

Soulja placed his cell phone in his pocket as he raised from beside Breanna, guiding her to stand erect by holding her hand.

"I just got a very important business call," Soulja said to Breanna.

"Is everything ok?" Breanna asked with concern, noticing the expression of profound thought on Soulja's face.

"Yeah. Ah. Everything is ok. I'll be back in about an hour," Soulja assured, then hugged Breanna.

"One day you're gonna have to tell me the truth about what you do," Breanna whispered in his ear, "I love you."

"I love you, too," Soulja replied, then pecked Breanna with a kiss on her lips. "I'll be back in about an hour," Soulja announced to everyone as he walked to the door.

The heads of everyone in the room nodded with acknowledgement as Mike stood to his feet and followed Soulja. As he walked out of the house, he noticed Mike behind him, but continued to walk to his Jaguar.

"What's going on?" Mike asked as Soulja opened the trunk to his Jaguar.

"Becky got kidnapped. They wanna trade her for dope and money," Soulja said as he retrieved a black one-piece bike uniform from the trunk and began to put it on.

"Who? Do you know who it is?"

"Yeah," Soulja said, zipping the uniform to the stomach. "One of them is Chip," Soulja said reaching back into the trunk for his shoulder holster, already equipped with a gun on the right and a gun on the left. "He was one of Rome's most loyal," he continued, strapping the holster on. "But he said, 'We.' He probably has his partna, Allan wit' 'em," Soulja theorized.

Soulja zipped the uniform to his neck and walked to his motorcycle.

"What are you gonna do?" Mike asked. "You gonna give him what he wants?"

"Nope," Soulja said as he sat on the motorcycle. "This'll be easy. I'll be back in about an hour. Just wait."

Soulja put the helmet on his head then sat on the motorcycle, then ignited the bike. As he accelerated, it growled with power. He drove out of the driveway with speed. Soulja drove on the highway, speeding past the cars ahead of him. He turned off the highway, down an exit, then sped down the street. Soulja turned onto a by-street, then stopped his motorcycle in front of the fourth house on the right side of the neighborhood. He walked to the door of the house, then knocked and rang the doorbell. Seconds later, a woman opened the door.

"What's up, Soulja?" the woman greeted with a smile.

Allan and Chip were smoking a blunt. Chip passed the blunt to Allan as he peered at the back of Becky's head.

"This bitch lied too, dog. She talkin' 'bout she ain't fuckin' Soulja. I bet that nigga bring that package," Chip said.

Allan watched Becky's cautious composure as she drove, then asked, "Is he gettin' tha pussy or not bitch?"

"I tol' y'all me and Soulja just tight. We ain't never had no relationship like y'all talkin' 'bout."

"Bitch stop lyin!" Chip yelled as Allan puffed the blunt and his cell phone rang. "Hello," Chip answered.

"Chip," the nervous feminine voice of the woman that opened the door for Soulja said. "You need to let that girl go," she urged then Soulja took the phone, holding a gun to her head.

"Baby, what you talkin' 'bout?" Chip asked.

"This ain't yo' baby, chump," Soulja said.

"Soulja?!" Chip exploded with surprise. "What the fuck you thank you doin' man?"

"Nigga, shut up." This is just the beginning of my list of people to take away from yo' life if you don't let Becky go. You know, I'm just gon' start wit' cho wife. But then I'm going to the back room where yo' lil' boy is sleepin', then I'm goin' to yo' mom's house, then yo' grandma's house. And everybody that I know you close to like yo' boy Allan. And his wife and children. And every muthafucka he cared about. Now you know I don't play no games. So, what you need to do is let Becky go. Just let her go."

"O… hold up. Ok, but hold up. How I'm supposed to know you, you, you, gon'… you know… do what you sayin'," Chip erratically verbalized.

"Tell Becky to call me on my cell. When she call me and tells me she gone, I'll leave. You trust yo' wife, right?"

"Yeah."

"Ok, she'll tell whether I'm gone or not. You stay on the phone and tell Becky to call me now."

"Becky, call Soulja," Chip nervously ordered, shifting his focus to Allan.

Allan looked at Chip with a frown of confusion, Chip just stared at him.

"Hello," Soulja answered his cell phone.

"This Becky."

"Ok. Listen. Where are you?"

"I'm almost at Parker St."

Soulja held the home phone to his ear and said," Chip, tell Becky not to go on Parker St."

"Becky, don't go on Parker St."

"You driving, Becky?" Soulja asked.

"Yeah."

"Ok. Hold up."

"Get out the car, Chip. You and whoever else you got in there with you need to get out and let Becky drive away."

"How we gon' get home?"

"Fuck how you gon' get home. You just wanna make sure yo' wife alright."

"Ok. Ok," Chip emphasized. "Stop tha car and let us out."

Becky stopped the car and Chip opened the door to exit the car.

"What's up, man?" Allan asked.

"Man, just get out, man."

Allan got out of the car.

"We out, man," Chip disappointingly voiced. "Hey. Aye. Gone drive off," Chip urged Becky. "Drive off!" he yelled.

Becky drove off as Soulja asked, "Are they out of the car?"

"Yeah. I'm drivin' down the street now."

"Ah'ight. Call me when you get home."

"Ok," Becky nervously said, then disconnected with Soulja.

"Ok. I'ma give your wife the phone and leave," Soulja said to Chip.

"Aye, man. You shouldn't have fucked with my wife, man. You didn't have to do it like that," Chip said.

"Fuck you. You did this, chump," Soulja said, then gave the woman the phone.

"Chip?" the woman whined, watching Soulja walk out of the house. "He leaving. Why did you do this?"

When Soulja arrived home, he walked through the door wearing the crimson colored shirt and shorts he left wearing. He walked into the living room, noticing that everyone was still felicitously involved in conversation. Breanna still sat where she did before he left and he sat beside her, placing his arm around her shoulders.

"You miss me?" Soulja smiled.

"You know I did," Breanna returned a satisfying smile. "You haven't-"

"So, Soulja when is the wedding?" Asia asked.

"Yeah," Amanda added with enthusiasm.

"Well, if it was up to me we would've gotten married yesterday, but we decided to wait until my mom gets back," Soulja responded.

"You know it wouldn't be right to get married before your mother gets back," Breanna said.

"Yeah, and before you can decide how many cakes and decoration you want," Soulja laughed.

Everyone else in the room giggled, full of good humor as Breanna gently shoved Soulja's shoulder with a giggle of her own.

"So, how many children will you have?" Tia enthusiastically asked.

"Ah," Soulja stammered.

"We'll talk about that another time," Breanna cautioned.

"Yeah," Asia laughed. "Breanna if we talk about that now, Charles and I will have to discuss all the grandchildren we want."

Everyone chuckled benignly. The event was filled with exultation.

"How about I go get some more wine," Mike suggested.

"I'll come with you," Soulja said, grabbing an ice bucket.

They both raised from their seats and walked to the wine rack. Mike searched for an appropriate bottle of wine while Soulja filled the ice bucket with more ice.

"I assume everything is ok. I mean you came back as fast as you said you would," Mike said.

"Yeah. But I'm still gonna make them cats heart stop."

"You can't keep throwing yourself into these kind of situations. You have people that will do these things for you."

"She needs to set an example to keep the rest of 'em in line," Soulja eagerly said.

"Then let her do it. If you wanna help her, then send some people to do it. She doesn't have to know how you got 'em to do it. She doesn't have to know about the organization or your position," Mike emphasized. "You have to use your resources. Don't just jump into every situation that occurs just because you know you can handle it. Now you had to do something to get her out of trouble. Now help her by using your resources," Mike advised.

Soulja held a contemplative look on his face that Mike recognized, then said, "You're right." He held the physiognomy a moment longer, then said, "You're right."

Mike acknowledged Soulja's sincerity, then said, "Let's go back to the living room."

"I'll be in there in a minute. I just need to make a couple of calls."

Mike nodded with acknowledgement, then said, "Ok," grabbing the ice-bucket.

Soulja watched Mike walk away, then dialed on his cell phone. He held the phone to his ear waiting for an answer.

"Hello," Becky answered.

"What happened? Why didn't you call me like I told you to?"

"Because I'm not at home. I'm in a hotel room."

"You wanna make an example of those cats or what?"

"Yeah."

"Ok then. You pay attention to what I'm about to say."

Mike poured wine in everyone's glass then placed the wine in the ice bucket.

"What about Soulja's glass?" Charles asked. "You didn't pour him any wine."

"Oh, he doesn't drink very much," Mike said as he sat down. "He got a call, though. He'll be back in a minute. He'll probably pour himself a glass and sip on it the entire night," Mike laughed, being joined by everyone else's chuckles.

"Does he get drunk easily or something?" Asia asked.

"Oh, he can drink a lot," Tia volunteered. "I've seen him drink an entire bottle of whiskey by himself and still not be drunk. He just doesn't do that a lot. But I still don't understand how he does it. If I drink that much whiskey I'd fall out of my seat," she emphasized, cranking up more laughter in the room. "He's immune to being drunk or something," Tia giggled.

"What are you talkin' about, Tia? My drinking immunity again," Soulja mocked as he walked into the room smiling.

"You know you some kind of alien when it comes to drinking," Tia mocked.

Everyone laughed as Soulja sat down beside Breanna again. She tugged on the front of his shirt as she giggled. "Is everything ok," Breanna asked with a low tone.

"Yeah. Especially if you're ok," Soulja said, then kissed Breanna's neck with a peck.

"Breanna and Soulja are perfect for each other because she's a drinking alien too," Tia mocked.

The night was filled with exuberant quality. They celebrated the announcement of

Breanna and Soulja's decision to marry with frolicking, drinking, and amusement.

Becky stood between two men dressed in all black gear. Their faces were covered with masks and they held assault rifles in their hands aimed at Allan. Allan's eyes were typical of lassitude. His body was strapped to a chair in his house. His mouth was gagged and his nose was bleeding. Suddenly, one masked man walked into the room, carrying and assault rifle, followed by two men carrying Chip, and another man behind them carrying an assault rifle. Chip's face was puffy and swollen wounds on his face exuded blood while other places on the surface of his face and on his shirt had dry blood. The last masked man to walk into the room stood at the door of the room.

"This is what is going to happen to people like you," one of the men holding Chip said, then nodded his head at Becky.

Becky pulled her gun from her shorts, then aimed it at Allan. She shot him in the chest twice, then turned to Chip. She aimed the weapon at Chip's head.

"Please… Becky, please," Chip wept. "They already killed my wife. Don't kill me.

Please," he pleaded. "Who gon' take care of my son?" he whined.

"Social Services will take care of your son," one of the men holding Chip said, then looked at Becky with anticipation of her shot. "Do you want me to do it?"

"No. No. I'll do it."

"Well, come on. We have to get out of here," the man urged.

Becky aimed at the head of Chip, then pulled the trigger once, shooting Chip in the head. Her composure was uncertain, but grew confident promptly.

The next morning, Breanna and Soulja laid in bed. Soulja watched the news as the morning light of the sun shined through the windows of their bedroom. Breanna slowly opened her eyes, then looked at Soulja.

"Hey," Breanna said sleepily.

Soulja peered at Breanna and replied, "Hey."

"I feel like staying in the bed all morning and all day," Breanna admitted lethargically. "Will you stay in bed with me?" she smiled.

"What? You wanna start an early honeymoon or something?" Soulja teased.

"That wouldn't be a bad idea," Breanna teased back as she rolled herself on top of Soulja and started kissing him.

The television flashed a special report and the female newscaster announced, "There has been a streak of murders over the past few days in the Jackson area. The six murders are believed to be connected. Two men were found dead in a sports utility vehicle parked in a park, a woman found dead in her home, and just last night a woman was also found in her home dead. Her husband and his best friend were found in the best friend's house dead last night also. Though the murders are believed to be linked to organized crime, the police have no suspects. These vicious occurrences are clearly a reek of havoc of Mississippi street life.

This is Vanessa Smith concluding this morning's special report. This is Jackson News keeping you up to date and up to the minute. Thank you for watching."